This Hallow'd House

Book Six

of

The Return of the Tribes

By A. A. Taylor

First Edition

The Rum Lot Publishing
Lowestoft, Suffolk, UK
2025

ISBN- 978-1-918079-16-6
Paperback Edition

Books of this series are available for download on

Amazon Kindle
or
The Rum Lot Publishing
www.rumlot.com

And we fairies, that do run

By the triple Hecate's team

From the presence of the sun,

Following darkness like a dream,

Now are frolic; not a mouse

Shall disturb this hallow'd house.

A Midsummer Night's Dream

By William Shakespeare

Dedicated to Rebecca,
Who has edited books one through six
and despite that, is still talking to me.

Book Six

Sally

The first-class section of the Virgin Atlantic flight to London was very nice, but for ten grand, it should be. Sally walked off the jetway pulling her only piece of luggage – a battered roll-on with a broken zipper – and, for the first time in her life, turned left. With that step, she departed her old world and entered a new one.

The new world had pretty people who smiled at her, made sure she was comfortable, and gave her a glass of champagne to ease the nervousness of leaving the ground and flying into the unknown. The old world was shit, and when the steward shut the heavy door and she stopped breathing the humid Orlando air, Sally just put Florida out of her mind. Instead, she looked out the window and watched the ground crew pull the luggage trucks out of the way. She saw a bored woman wearing ear protection and shorts, which were no help at all against the searing heat, waving her slow circles (what did they call those things? batons?) as she guided the huge jet away from the sad remains of Sally's old life.

When the door slammed and she felt the huge jet shudder as it lumbered to the taxiway, she hit the send button on two emails and then switched her phone to aeroplane mode. She looked at the phone for a long time after she hit send. Was it fair? Would they cry? More importantly, was she free? They would not accept, but they needed to understand why she was leaving and why she wouldn't be coming back.

Sally sighed. She worried and shouldn't worry, but it was a habit. It didn't matter if she was fair and honest or kind. She could have been kinder, she knew that, but they would make up their own reality, and their view wouldn't be fair and honest to her; it never was.

They wouldn't cry out of sadness but out of anger. No one would think for a minute about the feelings that had driven her to this rupture or their part in creating such a miserable life. She had to escape, but they would all be angry at her for making a fuss, for being selfish, for making them look bad, for being a person who demands justice. They would be furious for leaving them to their messy, chaotic, needy lives without the safety net of good, ol' Mom to clean up after them. Lisa would be incensed that she lost her unpaid, on-demand babysitter. JJ would be irritated that he didn't have a mom-shaped ATM to bum money from. Lee wouldn't miss her until he ran out of clean underwear.

It was her own fault. The more she did for her children, the more they hated her. The more she abased herself and gave in to their demands, the more contemptuous they became of their sad, depressed doormat of a mother. They hated themselves for being dependent and needy, and they hated her for being there and providing. It was a vicious cycle, one she didn't know how to break in a kind way because kindness didn't work. It just made things worse. The more she gave, the more they took, and the more they despised her for it.

Hanukkah was the final straw. She shoved that disaster out of her mind.

The steward placed a little snack on her table, and it was delicious. Sally was hungry.

She was quite sure that the overriding emotion that Leo would feel would be irritation for making him look bad in front of the kids, anger that he'd have to explain everything to their neighbours and friends, and fury that he'd look even worse than he already did to people who suspected he wasn't a nice guy.

While Sally thought the first email was the most important, the one she sent to Leo and the kids, it was the second, the one she sent to their friends, his co-workers, their neighbours and the temple that would drive him up the wall. She wasn't worried about that one; it was her bit of revenge, although the Virgin Atlantic first-class one-way walk-up trans-Atlantic ticket to London on his super-secret credit card was sweet. She took another sip of the champagne and smiled. She leaned back and enjoyed the ride.

The second email was pretty short.

"Dear Friends,

When you get this email, I'll be long gone and on my way to a new life. It might be unusual for a woman leaving her husband of thirty years to send this sort of message out, but we've known each other for years, some of you I've known all of my life, and I think it's only fair that I say goodbye properly. I'll miss you all, but I won't miss my old life. Most of you probably don't know, or maybe you know more than I thought, but I was pretty miserable. My decades with Leo have been a mind-numbing, never-ending cascade of cheating, physical abuse, and coercive control, but I stayed with him for the sake of the kids. I felt I owed it to them. Three years ago, Leo settled on a long-term mistress, a mutual friend of all of ours that some of you might know, Serena Rodriguez, and last December I discovered she was due to have Leo's baby in June. That was the last straw, and with my youngest graduating from university and seeing no prospect of change in my horrible life, I decided to make the leap. Time to go. Best wishes to all of you, and I wish your future to be as full of hope as mine is.

Sally."

The first email was a bit different.

"Dear Leo, Lee, Lisa and JJ,

When you get this email, I'll be long gone and on my way to a new life. It's probably a shock to you that a woman would leave her husband of thirty years, but I think it's only fair that I say goodbye. It's time for me to go. Maybe you didn't know, or maybe you know more than I thought, but I was pretty miserable. My decades with your father have been a mind-numbing, never-ending cascade of cheating, physical abuse, and coercive control, but I stayed with him for the sake of you kids. I felt I owed it to you, that it would make your lives better and more stable, but I was wrong. Staying solved nothing.

Three years ago, after many, many affairs, your father settled on a long-term mistress that you know, Serena Rodriguez, and this last December, I discovered she was due to have his baby in June. I found out on Christmas Day when Serena called me up to wish me Merry Christmas with her happy news, and right before you kids gave me the 'joke' present of a gold-plated toilet brush for Chanukah. Your contempt for me, your mother, was undeniable and equalled the contempt your father had shown me during our entire marriage. That yet another mistress called me up to try to get me to leave him was the last straw, and with Lee graduating from university and seeing no prospect of change in my horrible life, I decided to make the leap.

I wish all three of you children happy lives, but without me. All three of you have made it clear what you think of me. Best wishes to my grandchildren, and I hope their futures are as full of hope as mine is. Leo can go fuck himself. He's fucked everyone else.

Sally."

When Leo heard the email ping on his phone, he was at work. The first thing he did wasn't to call the kids or even Serena, but to frantically check his bank and brokerage accounts. Every single one was accessed yesterday evening, minutes before the close of business. Every single one, even the ones he kept hidden from her, his private stashes no one knew about, were empty. The business account (he owned a small electrical supply company) was empty.

Zero, zero, zero.

Buried in his spam folder was a new email from a lawyer he had never heard of informing him that Sally had filed for divorce, and as their settlement she was going to leave him the house, cars, and business but would be taking her half in cash. Her fucking half was all the cash. As if she had earned it! She didn't know that he had second-mortgaged everything she left him to keep Serena and his fun lifestyle going. He was in hock up to his ears, and the bank owned ninety per cent of everything.

Maybe she did know.

He was broke. His wife had left him, and everyone knew why. Everyone. He was CC'd on her second email. She even sent the fucking email to Serena. Serena wasn't going to stay with an old, flat-broke man of sixty-two who had to start over. She would move on and demand child support for the baby-anchor she'd made to keep him hooked to her, and he wouldn't be free of that dead weight for another eighteen years. He'd be working the rest of his fucking life.

As he looked at his computer screen, his heart pounding so hard he was sure he was having a heart attack, a bell chimed and a little alert flashed in the corner of the screen. His secret credit card, the one he used for Serena, had a ten-grand debit posted on it, maxing it out. A Virgin Atlantic first-class ticket to somewhere. He'd added Sally to the card so that he could increase the credit limit. The stupid bitch signed anything he put in front of her.

His phone rang. It was Serena.

Back in Virgin Upper Class, Sally idly flipped through a women's magazine on the tablet the steward provided for her. She was thinking of getting a new haircut, a new look to start off her new life. Thin hair, short hair, frizzy hair – there was a style for everyone. There was even a style for women who wanted to wear the fashionable new ear cuffs like the lords and elves wore. Styles that revealed the ears and allowed the ear jewellery with their fake points to be shown off.

In the privacy of her Upper Class cubicle, Sally took off the old Priscilla Presley wig she was wearing and for the first time in her adult life allowed her hair and ears to be free. Her ears were quite tall now. Ten years ago, many years after Leo had stopped sleeping with her and never saw her without her wig, she noticed that they were changing their shape. Of course, she'd had no idea why they were doing that, but after the lords appeared she stopped worrying about cancer or other weird diseases and started wondering. It was easy for an Orthodox Jewish woman to hide her ears under her wig, and for a long time she wouldn't even acknowledge they existed, just like she refused to look at the rest of her body. The body Leo despised for smelling bad and said was lumpy and disgusting. The body she kept locked in a tight, closed container of modesty and shame. The body he beat.

Last year, she stopped shaving her head and started letting her real hair grow free, and since she always wore the tatty wigs, her kids and friends never noticed. Now her hair was past shoulder length and pure white. She still never looked in a mirror for more than anything hygienic or medical as that was vain, but she could feel that her hair was nice and thick, and it could be styled. So she brushed it back like the magazine showed her. When the steward came with her lunch, he looked at her, his eyes got wide, and she knew why.

It was the ears.

As soon as the steward noticed Sally's ears, he slipped back to the hidden bunk that the stews used to rest on during their breaks on a long-distance flight and sent a quick message to a hotline in London registering that he had seen a lord on his flight, her name, and the details from the manifest. If he was the first to send in the notice, there was a bounty of five grand, and he wasn't going to pass that up! All the workers on the international flights were aware of the bounty, and in every pocket was a business card with the address to claim it. Virgin didn't like it because telling outsiders who was on board broke their privacy rules, but five grand was five grand, and what they didn't know wouldn't hurt them. This lord boarded wearing a wig, and now she didn't care, so he didn't feel the least bit guilty for ratting her out. The Elf Nation reps would be there waiting for her when she got off the plane. He was doing her a favour.

He grinned. His partner would be so happy. The reward money was just enough to top off that kitchen addition they were saving for.

Sally didn't meet the elf when she walked off the jetway. She didn't even get off the plane. As the jet was taxiing in on the long trip from touchdown to her gate, she turned in her little first-class compartment to get her bag, and there was an elf. *A real elf* – holding a clipboard, a business card, and wearing a gentle smile, standing right in front of her, not six inches away.

"Hello! Welcome to Heathrow Airport and London! My name is Elspeth, and I'm your Elf Nation representative!" She waited a minute for Sally to say something, but all Sally could do was stare.

"I know this is a bit abrupt, but the Elf Nation wants to make sure you're okay, and we greet all lords like this. Are you asking for refuge with the Elf Nation, or do you have other plans? We'll help you in either case. There's no charge."

Refuge? Refuge. What a loaded word, and tears came to her eyes. Refuge. That's exactly what she needed. All she could do was nod and whisper. "Refuge, please."

The elf grinned back, obviously delighted, and Sally could swear there were tears in her eyes, too. Sally had never had anyone in their life so glad to see her nod yes, not even Leo when he signed the Ketubah upon their marriage. But then he hadn't taken it seriously, not like she had, and he broke his word the first month they were married.

Elspeth told Sally that she was going to be magically transported and to step onto the aisle.

"Don't worry about your bag; we'll take care of everything." Sally stepped onto the aisle and into another world. She was free.

Judy, Vrt, Sarah

Judy looked at her watch. The plane should be landing any minute, and the greeter elf would pop on board as soon as it was in range. Vrt stood next to her, more out of curiosity to meet this new lord than for any other reason. They were given the alert when the lord was already halfway to the UK, and there was no time for either of the Primaries to come and greet her. That left Conary, who was already up to his eyeballs in VIPs, and everyone else also engaged. Judy and Vrt still happened to be at the Embassy, and the new lords always started there so elves and lords could suss them out before the newbies were ported to Aelfeham House.

They had no idea who this new lord was. No background at all, but that was okay; they seldom had anything to go on. All they knew was that her official name was Sarah Verdugo Ochs, and she flew in alone from Orlando, Florida, on a one-way ticket she'd paid for a couple of hours before the flight. They had a copy of her passport, but that only gave them the information that Ms Ochs had given the US Passport Agency. That could be true or not.

Either she was very rich and last-minute first-class was normal for her, or she was fleeing someone or something, or she was having a last suicide splash before she gave up on everything. Vrt bet she was rich, and Judy countered that she was running away. A box of Krispy Kreme doughnuts rode on the bet.

Sarah Ochs, née Verdugo, ported into the main chamber of the Elf Nation London embassy and froze. In front of her were two lords in dark blue uniforms. Women. They smiled and slowly bowed, but didn't say anything, allowing her some space to breathe and absorb.

Judy and Vrt saw a tired, painfully thin, worn-out woman who seemed to be about sixty-five or seventy with snow white hair and impressive, really gorgeous, elf ears. But what really made them sit up and notice was that this woman was an Elemental – a woman of great power. Both could see it in her blazing eyes and smell the magic that surrounded her just the way Vrt had when she first laid eyes on Conary.

"Lord Sarah, we are so glad to meet you. I am Lord Vrt, and this is Lord Judy. I know you're overwhelmed and tired, so I'd like to offer you a little rest before the next step. A moment for a cup of tea and time to answer any questions you might have –"

Lord Sarah. Not Sally. Sarah straightened up and looked at the lords. Lord Sarah, her true name, not the secular nickname that diminished her. Lord Sarah, it would be then.

She bowed back in imitation of the lords' bow and smiled. The three women went to tea and had a nice, long talk.

Sarah

Sarah was given a very pretty room in Aelfeham House, and from what she was told, she received exactly the same treatment as any newly arrived adult lord. The Elf Nation now had a well-oiled lord familiarisation program developed for incoming lords, complete with elf and lord mentors, a schedule to keep them busy, and a plan of instruction so they would know everything there was to know about the strange new world they were adopting. There was no timeline, no deadlines, just the expectation that the new lords were free to learn and grow at their own pace and become a part of the community. And if it didn't work out, a lord who didn't fit in would be supported if they left.

Only no lord ever left, at least so far. If anything, some lords didn't want anything to do with the human world any more, and getting them to leave to do even minor EN jobs with humans was like pulling teeth. Chi, for one, had a panic attack every time it was even suggested he go anywhere, even

Ukraine. Lowestoft was as far as he would go, and even then he never went north of the bridge.

Sarah was quite happy with all the Lord Lessons and eagerly looked forward to them. Some of the happiest times, before Leo arrived, were when she sat in a classroom, stretching her mind and learning something new, and everything in this strange, uncharted world was new.

The self-defence lessons were loads of fun. Never in her life had she exercised like that, especially not in the shul where they only played at ladylike sports and the girls learnt traditional dances and a few games to teach their children. Certainly nothing like judo or taekwondo! Boy, if she had known a bit of taekwondo when she was younger she would have tried a few moves on Leo! It turned out that even at her age she was very good at it. Victor started to change up her routine just to keep her challenged, and the more he changed it up, the better she got. It was as if her body was spring-loaded for movement, whether it was for fighting, gymnastics, dancing, or anything else. After more than sixty years of being tightly contained socially, physically, and mentally, she was suddenly released, and now she couldn't sit still. She couldn't fly like Alizah, but that was the only thing she couldn't do, and she was giddy with her new freedom both physically and mentally.

Sarah wasn't anywhere near ready to train with Malachi or Vrt, but a few weeks later Victor was talking to Kyrylo and mentioned the words "Warrior Lord". Early days, he said, but –

The only fly in the ointment was her lack of any magical ability. Abilities practise was a disaster, and the elves couldn't figure out what her special talent was. She worried because if she had no magic like every other lord, what if they threw her out? What if she were defective?

After the first week – shit, the first *day* – Sarah knew she desperately wanted to stay at Aelfeham House, and when she burst into tears of frustration and had to leave the room because she couldn't do a simple abilities task like her new friends, everyone was upset. When the instructors saw her melt down she was given a few days off, and Lord Conary came to talk about her lack of talent and explain his story, when he didn't know what he could do. No worries, he said, everyone learns at their own speed, and if it took a century to figure out her ability, that was fine. He made her feel somewhat better about her failure, but only a little. At least no one was going to kick her out.

Sarah's one bit of pride had always been that she was good in school, and she considered herself intelligent and hardworking. She took failure hard, and when the weakest lord in the clan (adult, of course) could move a salt shaker across the table at breakfast, and Sarah couldn't do anything, it rankled. Even Alizah, who couldn't move things, could fly.

The instructor elves considered her failure their failure. As one said, "Your ears have grown to points very early, your eyes glow very bright, and we *know* you have a talent. We can smell it on you. You're unconsciously doing something; we just have to figure out what it is." That didn't make Sarah feel any better either. If she had an ability it was so subtle as to be useless. No one told her they sensed she was an Elemental. At this point it would have just been cruel, and the knowledge would only create more stress. Lord Sarah would think they were making fun of her.

About a month after she landed at Heathrow, Sarah received a message from the London Embassy that said a Rabbi Shulman was trying to contact her and was requesting a call back. Sarah had sent a birthday card to her best friend, Becky, and obviously Becky had told their Rabbi where Sarah had ended up.

The Rabbi wanted to talk in a conference call to make sure she was okay, and since he was a very nice man and she had known him for years, Sarah agreed. The front desk of Aelfeham House set it up so she didn't have to give out her private number, and on the appointed time she found herself chatting with the Rabbi and his wife, Beth. But something was off, she could tell. She could feel other people in the room, and when she thought about it, she was sure Leo and the kids were in there, off-screen, listening.

"I'm glad everything is going well; we miss you here."

"I'm very happy with my life now. People here treat me very well." She didn't say she missed them because that would be a lie. Sarah hadn't thought of her old life in Florida twice in the months she had lived in Suffolk, and even then, it was to thank G-d she wasn't in Florida any more.

The rabbi spoke slowly. "But happiness isn't just for us; it's also for our families. There's nothing more important than a happy family, and a family without its mother can't be happy."

There it was. The Reb was going to try to get her back with Leo. Sarah didn't blame him; that was his job after all, but it wasn't going to happen. She couldn't go back in time; no one had that ability. We only move forward, and Leo and her children were part of her miserable past.

"Rabbi, with all due respect, my family wasn't happy before I left. They especially weren't happy with me. Leo treated me very badly, and the kids weren't far behind. They took his lead on that."

"Leo and I have talked a lot about this. He would like to go into family counselling if you are okay with that. Give it a try, Sally. Thirty years of marriage is a lot to throw away."

Sarah was quiet, and when she spoke again her voice was soft. "Reb, I'm going to turn on the video feed. I know you can't see me now." She pressed a button that replaced her fuzzy outline with an AI-generated deep fake image. Only it wasn't deep *fake*, but a very accurate, animated, lifelike drawing of how she truly looked.

Beth gasped. Sally was a full lord. She had huge ears whose tips met over the top of her head, thick white hair pulled back in a bun, and her eyes glowed like lasers. When she'd left Orlando, she'd looked like she was seventy, old and tired. Now she was a very attractive forty. At the temple, the last person anyone would have thought of as sexy was Sally. What Beth saw today was a woman who wasn't classically beautiful, but a striking one who would make a man look twice.

"As you can see, I'm a lord. I've always been a lord. I'm not human. One of the things a lord can do is tell when someone is lying. We don't always know what the truth is, but we know what the truth isn't. We weren't married for two days when Leo started lying to me. He's lied to me about women, about money, about the kids, about anything and everything. He'll even lie to me about what he had for lunch. He lies for the pleasure of it because he thinks I'm too stupid to catch him. But stupid Leo, I knew every single lie. I have no faith that he is telling you the truth. I'm willing to bet that he's not because lying is what he does to everyone.

"I'm also willing to bet that if he found out I'm a lord, he'd think that he could get me to support him if we got back together. He's flat broke now. Bankrupt. He is now paying for every single lie I listened to for over thirty years, every trashy woman that called me up to tell me he was cheating, every penny he stole from our children's mouths, every nasty comment he made about me, every time he hit me, and worse.

"I gave him thirty years, and that is enough. I'm going to live forever, Rabbi. *Forever.* But I won't give him another ten minutes of my life. That is my truth."

In the background, there was a crash. Yelling – it sounded like JJ, and then Leo filled the screen, knocking the Rabbi out of the way and throwing him to the floor. Beth screamed.

"YOU GET YOUR ASS BACK HERE!" Leo was frothing, literally frothing at the mouth, spitting all over the screen, his eyes glinting purple. "You've ruined my life, bitch. *You owe me*, you bat-eared freak! I –" The audio went off, and all Sarah could see was Leo's rage-distorted face mouthing silently at the monitor in uncontrolled fury. Behind him, Sarah could see the Rabbi and JJ trying to pull him off the monitor where he seemed to be trying to eat her image.

It was fascinating and horrifying at the same time. And funny. Oh, she would love to be a fly in the corner of the room, watching Leo have a full-fledged mental breakdown. Sarah really, really wanted to be there and –

And then she was.

She was in the room. She was in Rabbi Shulman's office, back in a corner, watching the show play out in front of her as they pulled at Leo, trying to get him away from the screen. Everyone – the kids, Leo, Beth, the Rabbi – everyone's back was to her, and everyone was facing the screen, yelling and crying and screaming at Leo.

Sarah looked at her hands. She was glowing white hot. Was this a dream? But she was real, and a corner of a table was poking uncomfortably into her hip and leaving a scorch mark on the blond wood. She had ported five thousand miles away to Florida.

Lords couldn't port.

Only elves could port. That was porting lesson one, day one, hour one, minute one.

She had ported. No elf could port five thousand miles away. She had an ability!

Well, she'd figure that bit out later; now she had other issues.

"*Leo!* You called me back. I'm here."

They froze, all six of them. Slowly, as if they were moving through glue, they turned as one to look behind them, and there Lord Sarah stood, her entire body glowing white hot, her eyes twin orbs of green fluorescence, a small, bemused smile on her lips.

"Do you think you can take me, Leo? Are you as brave now that I'm in the room?"

"Mom – please –" It was Lee.

"Please what, Lee? Are you out of socks? Need someone to give you a twenty for pizza?" Sarah cocked her head. "The last time you said please to me was three years ago. June 15th at three pm to be exact."

"Shit –" Lisa spat out the curse, spun away, and walked out the door. She wasn't going to beg, and she certainly wasn't going to listen to this freak show *thing* that used to be her mother.

"Mom, we're all sorry. We –" JJ started, and then he faded away. His mother's eyes judged.

"I know lies, JJ. When you can tell me the truth, I will listen. You are lying now. None of you are sorry for your cruelty and disrespect. You are spoiled children who are angry at being thwarted. That's all." She cocked her head. "I think it's best you leave now."

The boys backed away and left, leaving Leo swaying, free. He didn't lunge at Sarah; he just stared. Then he took a halting step slowly towards her, his hand outstretched; he was a ghoul in his private horror movie.

"I'm very hot, Leo. Don't touch me."

He moved forward and put his hand against her cheek to see if she was real, a zombie's imitation of a lover's caress, and then he screamed in agony, his flesh burnt to the bone. Screeching in pain and holding up the smoking black cinder that was once his hand, he backed to the door. "BITCH!! BITCH!" he screamed again and ran out.

Beth and the Rabbi were all who were left.

"Rabbi, if you want to go out and call an ambulance for Leo, that would be fine. Beth, if you could do me a huge favour, I need to make a phone call. Could you dial it for me? I'm afraid I'll melt the phone."

Rabbi Shulman hesitated, and Sarah smiled encouragingly. "Beth is perfectly safe with me. I've always liked both of you. You're kind people. Just don't touch me." She looked at her hand in wonder. *Zol er krenken un gedenken*, she was flaming!

With Beth's help Sarah called the Embassy and explained her predicament. She had ported to

Florida and didn't know how to get back. She didn't have any money, passport, nothing. Should she try to port back to the UK? NO! The elves were frantic. *No porting*! Not until you've had proper training!

That evening, after all the trauma of the day, Sarah cooled down enough to join the Shulmans for a good dinner. Then the rabbi drove her to a nearby hotel, where she ordered three large pizzas to snack on while she watched TV. Despite their repeated offers of their spare bedroom, she wouldn't impose on the Shulmans overnight; Sarah knew they couldn't sleep a wink with an inflamed lord in the house. She borrowed a thousand in cash from the Shulmans, who received it back in their bank account within an hour, and by the next day she was in clean clothes, had a new passport faxed over, and was sitting in another first-class seat on her way to Heathrow.

Caddy

"A lord who can port! Have you ever heard of such a thing?" Caddy talked to all of the Old Farts, and none could remember ever meeting a lord who could port. One of the oldest elves said that she had heard of one in the old legends, but had thought it was just a story. She had never met one. Caddy immediately told the elves they needed to write down all of their elders' stories and put them in a book. They needed to preserve the old tales just in case they needed to know them one day, and the Primary didn't want to lose their memories as they passed on to the Void.

The upshot was that when Sarah came back, she was assigned to porting classes with all the other twelve-year-old elves. There was a lot more to porting than the lords knew. She was thrilled.

Victor formally asked the Primaries if Lord Sarah could start Warrior Lord training and, of course, was told yes. A lord who can fight and port halfway across the world – the possibilities were mind-boggling. She still couldn't move a feather, but she didn't need to. The elves were pretty sure she could just port the damn feather if she ever needed to.

Col James Cowen

The presentation "Military Decoys in China - Fake Equipment, Inflatables & Lessons in Deception for Foreign Forces" by the Sandhurst professor was held in a modern lecture hall in a very old institution. It wasn't the big auditorium where the entire school could gather but one of the smaller offshoots. A person would be forgiven if they walked in and mistook the place for the B-movie venue in a modern cinema. All that was missing were cup holders in the sensible blue fabric seats.

Waited in the back for the lecture to start, Col Cowen sat with his friend, Lt Col McGinnis. There probably wasn't much new to discover for either of them today, but you never knew what might come out. The point wasn't to learn something earth-shattering, although that would be a pleasant surprise if that happened. The point was to tick off a professional development box and put another piece of paper in his file for the next promotion board. The more important goal from his boss's viewpoint was networking with all the other senior officers who were also ticking off PD boxes. The audience wasn't cadets; the hall was filled with officers from NATO, EATO, and a few non-aligned friendlies. These sort of lecture-cum-schmooze sessions rotated around, and for some arcane reason, Sandhurst had been chosen for this one over other good locations. Maybe someone in scheduling had their own boxes to tick.

It didn't matter how old or sophisticated you were; when you walked into a classroom you sat with your mates, and the room was filling up with cosy clumps of uniformed officers from different countries. The Germans sat with the Germans. The Finns and Poles and all that Baltic group sat together. As much as they were all, every last one of them, supposed to reach out and network with their counterparts, it was all rather cliquish, and that was just human nature. With still ten minutes to go, and the room was loud with chatter, paper rattling, important people importantly talking too loudly on their mobiles, others climbing down rows to find friends, faux hearty hellos for people whose names they couldn't remember … when down the aisle walked a lord.

A fekkin' Elf Nation lord! She was immediately the centre of attention. Cowen had never seen a lord at one of these things before. He had been in a room with Lord Kyrylo during a NATO meeting as support for General Sheringham, and that was his first time seeing one in person, but he didn't get close. Lord Conary had briefly spoken to him once, but frankly, if he was at anything a lord would show up to, the generals and civilians all got the face time, not mere MI colonels. This one was in the dark blue of the senior ranks, and on her shoulders was a small epaulette that had a quarter moon embroidered on it. Only the very top ranks wore an epaulette.

Cowen wondered how many in the room would catch that detail. It wasn't well-known. Most would know that the Rangers wore black, the RumLot Security guys had dark green uniforms, the everyday lords (if any lord could be "every day") wore the very dark red, and the upper ranks wore the inky dark blue with silver trim. She wore a sabre and knee-high war boots with elf blades tucked in the tops. Even Lord Kyrylo didn't wear a sword.

He didn't see her face, just the back of her as she walked down the aisle to the lecturer, where she bowed and introduced herself. The audience wasn't talking much now, not loudly, at least. They whispered and shifted. A few rude ones pointed.

She had a knot of pure white hair at the back of her neck, and her ears were at least twenty centimetres, rising to points over the top of her head. A fluidity in the way she moved reminded him of a panther, something beautiful and dangerous.

The lecturer greeted her and shook her hand, and even from the back of the room anyone could see he was nervous. But the encounter seemed very pleasant, and he waved vaguely in a "take a seat anywhere" fashion, and she turned and scanned the room, looking for a place. She walked back up the aisle, and this time Cowen could see her face. She was beautiful, but then he'd never seen an ugly lord, not in person and not in the magazines and not in the special files they kept locked up at work. Some were otherworldly, like Lord Vrt; others were more ordinary, and this woman was in the more ordinary category. Again, thought Cowen, what's "ordinary" when comparing lords to lords? To any human, this one was striking.

She sat down directly in front of him in an empty row. As his daughter Chloe would so elegantly put it, OMG! He could look at the top of the lord's head and those ears! The heavy knot of glossy white hair – and those ears! McGinnis elbowed him and pointed with his chin as if Cowen couldn't see what was sitting right in front of his knees.

Suddenly, she sat up, and the ears rotated just a bit, like a fox's. Down at the podium, four officers were standing, gesticulating to the lecturer and some guys in suits. The officers were agitated. He squinted at the BDUs they were wearing; they weren't Brits. Americans. Something was going on, but Cowen couldn't hear what it was, not from where they were sitting and with no microphone on. He bet she knew, though, and he understood then that a lord's ears had a function. Her head tilted, and she gave an audible sigh. That was all the invite McGinnis needed. The man was as bold as brass, he was.

"Excuse me, ma'am. I'm Lt Col McGinnis." And he bent over the back of the seat and held out his hand. "Is something wrong?" She couldn't avoid him if she wanted to, but she was fine; she wasn't offended at his pushy introduction and turned to shake the offered hand.

"Hello. It's nice to meet you, Lt Col McGinnis. I'm Lord Sarah." She nodded towards the podium. "It seems I am disturbing some members of the audience. They don't want to be in the same room as a lord. I'm dangerous, smell bad, not a part of a real country, and not a human. Those gentlemen want me out of here." She shrugged. "It happens."

Cowen couldn't believe it. It was the worst example of bigotry he had ever seen. Every now and then, you'd run across a bad apple in the Royal Army. It was a huge institution, and it took all kinds, but even the worst racists knew better than to walk up to a lecturer and demand that the object of their bigotry be removed. It just wasn't done.

"Lord Sarah, you're not going anywhere," he growled, and he was so upset his Scottish accent was almost unintelligible. She smiled at him and shrugged again. Sarah only had a vague idea of what the man said, but she understood the meaning. He was upset for her.

"I'm not going to make a fuss. If it's an issue, I'm sure there's an overflow room for this hall, and I'll just go there and watch on a monitor." And just as she spoke, a woman in civilian clothes sidled up and began to whisper to the lord.

Lord Sarah stood up, turned to McGinnis and Cowen, and again shrugged. "Mad, bad, and dangerous to know, that's me and your Lord Byron. It was good to meet you, gentlemen." And she stepped to the aisle and headed to the door.

Cowen shot up, absolutely furious, and he wasn't quiet. If truth be told, he was closer to shouting. Roaring in his command voice, his voice flew across the busy room, and he was so upset that his brogue was as thick as oatmeal. Half the room had no idea what the red-faced officer was saying, but they sure could hear him say it.

"This isn't right. Not at all." He turned to the civilian woman, whoever she was; he had no idea. "You should be ashamed of yourself. I'm lodging a complaint as soon as I get back to the office. I won't be a party to such –" and he sputtered, "*un-British* discourtesy. Absolutely appalling. If she goes, I go."

And he followed the lord out. McGinnis gaped at the colonel. He couldn't remember the last time he'd seen Cowen so angry, but fekkin' hell, he was right. And he stood up and followed the colonel.

And then the rest of His Majesty's military looked at each other, mumbled a bit, and then stood up and left – and there were a lot of them; it was Sandhurst after all.

And then everyone else left except for the Americans, the lecturer, and some civilian officials. The chaotic hall in front of the lecture room was packed tight with indignant officers, who could barely move but they could certainly voice an opinion. Every single officer out there seemed like they had a very important reason to shake hands with the lord, tell her their country didn't agree with such bigotry, and generally feel righteous and outraged on her behalf. A few minutes after the kerfuffle, someone in a grey suit announced that an overflow room was to be used by the delegations who wished to sit "with the North Americans," and the main hall would welcome the return of the rest of the audience. It wasn't a good solution as it permitted racism, but officers from any military tradition aren't by nature rebellious, and it was a compromise.

Cowen didn't see the lord again or shake her hand; there were always too many others crowded around her, and when she re-entered the lecture hall, someone gave her a seat in the front. But he had the satisfaction of having done the right thing and the renewed respect of his peers. He was a top man.

The next day, Jamie called him while he was on his way home from work. The lad was so excited that he was sputtering. "Ded!! There's an *elf* at our door! You've got to come home *now*!" And so he raced home, and, yes, indeed, in his lounge he found all three of his kids sitting and having a nice chat with a very fierce-looking Warrior Elf holding an elaborately carved wooden box. When he walked in, the elf bounced up, bowed to him, and handed him the small coffer. "Lord James, a mark of the Elf Nation's gratitude from Lord Cadence," and the little soldier blinked out right then and there in front of them to the delight of the kids.

Inside the box was a note thanking him for standing up for Lord Sarah, signed by the President Lord Cadence herself and a really lovely elf knife. On one side of the handle was an engraved thistle, and on the other side was a trout. How did they know?

He hadn't said anything to his kids about yesterday, so he had to explain the whole incident to them, and they were so proud of him and excited about the elf that it brought tears to his eyes. It ended up being a brilliant day.

Caddy

Caddy had a problem and that was Scotland and Northern Ireland. She had always promised to finish up the rest of the UK, and the elves themselves had pushed north from York and managed to get all the way up to Dundee. Despite their best efforts, there were still large areas that needed coverage if all the coastline of the UK was going to be brought under the EN umbrella. Besides, every time Caddy looked at the satellite photos, she knew in her heart that there were loads of elves sleeping in the north, and she felt guilty for not finishing the job. She wanted to wake them up. There was also pressure from elves who wanted to visit relatives and friends in the Safe Haven, and pressure from the UK government.

So she conferred with Kyrylo, Conary, and Jameson, and at the next mapping meeting with the EU government reps, she informed them that Lord Mordecai would be waking up the rest of the British Isles with forays into Canada, and she would be working on Europe at her usual one location a week pace. What could they say? Not much, and while there was some pouting, it wasn't as if countries like France and Spain were being ignored; it was just that they weren't going to benefit from the increased capacity the new lord brought to the table.

Mordecai and Malachi were fine with the new schedule. Scotland didn't involve as much travelling for the lords to get to the target areas, and it was easier on Gangster Jack. He didn't mind the trailers, but flying wasn't his favourite mode of transport. It was hard to sleep on them.

The King and the Prime Minister were informed that the EN planned to resume awakenings to finish up Scotland and then move on to Northern Ireland and the Channel Islands. If that was okay with them, could they please provide the extra military security that was usual in the European countries? The reply was yes and came so fast that Caddy looked for scorch marks on the email.

When Caddy first awakened elves in England, there was no military involvement at all. The entire process was secret. In Europe, by the time countries like Germany and France were involved, the existence of the EN was well established, and the militaries were eager to help.

That meant while many, many European soldiers of all types could wear the "EN" medal and ribbon on their uniforms, no one in the Royal Army or Air Force could, which was a bit of a sore point. Soldiers do like their medals!

Locations halfway between Dundee and Aberdeen were scouted, and in the meantime, preparations were made.

Cowen and McGinnis

Col Cowen found the email ten minutes before Lt Col McGinnis did, but McGinnis made the most noise, whooping down the hall as if he'd won the fekkin' lotto. And maybe he had.

They were to attend a training session with fifty other specially chosen military members and ten alternates drawn from all the forces. Training would take one day and be in preparation for attending and working at an EN awakening in Scotland. They would have specific duties assigned later.

Cowen couldn't stop grinning all day. More tick boxes for the personnel file, another ribbon (and a nice one, too), and a story for the kids.

"That's what happens when you sit in the right seat," McGinnis crowed. "I told you we needed to sit in the back! And you wanted to sit up front like some brown-nosed head boy. If we'd done that, we wouldn't have been near Lord Sarah!"

"You just wanted a way to sneak out for a vape, you bastard, if it got too boring."

"I didn't say I wasn't motivated to choose that place for personal reasons. I'm just saying I'm a bloody genius for choosing it."

McGinnis bragged about the assignment to everyone in the section until they were thoroughly sick of him, but the day before they left for the training session, the sergeants presented him with a fairy wand to use on the day, complete with ribbons and glittery stars, which was thoughtful.

The training was at the EN embassy in London in the embassy ballroom.

Cowen walked down the long halls to the ballroom, escorted by a cute elf who giggled the entire way about his uniform. "And what does the green beret mean, sir? And this patch?" She found his entire work uniform fascinating, which was funny because she was dressed in a costume that looked like a Morris dancer had just thrown up. Maybe she needed more ribbons.

In any case, the place was teeming with humans and elves, all running around looking busy.

Inside the ballroom, the embassy spread out a huge buffet, which was as welcome as it was unexpected, and more elves were taking orders for tea and coffee and doing their best to make everyone feel welcome. In the front of the room, casually sitting on top of a long table and drinking coffee or tea, were a gaggle of bluecoat and redcoat lords. Lord Sarah and Lord Vrt were two of the bluecoats; the rest he didn't recognise. Piled next to them was a pile of little boxes and other demo items.

At exactly five til nine, Lord Sarah put down her coffee and gave the room a five-minute warning. At exactly nine on the dot, she started talking. When someone in the back wouldn't shut up, she stopped and glared at him, and her eyes glowed like lasers. *He* stopped in mid-word, and she then continued. There was no messing around with this one.

Once she began her lecture was fascinating, and the room stayed dead silent. She started with some history, how and why the elves were hibernating, and pointed out that every single elf they saw today was over 3,500 years old and came from that same hibernating process.

Then she told them what would happen on the day and why the EN had certain procedures. Again, there was a reason for everything, and she explained them all. She spoke about the dangers of orcs, how the pheromones of the elves would make anyone with orc blood go crazy, and why they tried so hard to keep unauthorised people away.

Then the soldiers had elf throwing practice, which meant about fifteen elves of all sizes, ages, and shapes wearing bathing costumes popping into the ballroom and everyone picking them up from the floor and tossing them into the sky to see them port away. It was hugely fun, and there was a lot of giggling and laughter. None of the humans had ever touched an elf before, and that was strange, too. It made them seem real and oddly delicate. To pick up an elf meant that you could feel its heartbeat, and your connection was with a living creature. Suddenly, they weren't cartoonish dolls any more.

It was then that the day began to get really weird for Cowen. When it was his turn to pick up an elf, a middle-aged matron of some weight (for an elf), she went into fits of giggles and wiggled away. "I'm sorry, Lord James, but I'm ticklish! Can you pick me up by the waist and not under the armpits?"

McGinnis laughed. "Cowen, she called you a lord! It must be the blue eyes. Or else she needs her specs."

The elf woman laughed, too. "But he is a lord! C'mon, Lord James, let's get this done." And Cowen picked her up and threw her as hard as he could in the air, and she ported away.

Cowen scowled at McGinnis. Now the man would tease him about the "Lord James" thing for the rest of his career; he just knew it. Once it got around the section, the nickname would be like a virus. It would spread, and everyone would use it.

After the porting there was a demonstration of how to open the egg sacs. Lord Sarah then showed them how to hold the knives, and just for entertainment, showed them how an elf warrior threw them. The elves hauled out a wooden board with an outline of a man drawn on it, and from across the room – and it was a massive room – she threw five knives at the board so quickly that they blurred, and each knife pierced the board to the hilt in a straight line down the centre of the man.

"Ladies and Gentlemen, I'm going to give you each a knife to keep for your own. They're not steak knives, but killing and cutting knives, so always treat them like a loaded gun. The knife will know you and won't work for other people, so don't give it away! Please don't throw them here in the embassy! Safety first! You're all trained weapons handlers, so I think I can stop talking at this point."

Then they were all issued elf knives, a new toy for the soldiers which caused no end of joy. Cowen was secretly pleased that these knives were utilitarian, and the knife from Lord Cadence was certainly not.

That was the end of the day. The lords walked around and thanked the attendees and had little chats, and as Lord Sarah worked her way around the room she deliberately looked for Cowen and McGinnis, and when she found them in the crowd, she walked up with a big smile, holding out her hand. And then the next weird thing happened.

She stopped and gasped, and the most confused look flashed across her face. "Excuse me, gentlemen, I'll be right back– " And she spun around and trotted off.

Cowen looked at McGinnis and shrugged. "You always have that effect on women."

McGinnis was aggrieved. "It was you, you fekkin' tube. She didn't even look at me."

Then the utterly fascinating Lord Vrt walked up, smiled, and Lord Sarah was temporarily forgotten.

"Ah, the wonderful colonels! It's so nice to finally meet you! Lord Sarah told me all about how you stood up for her –" Her eyes narrowed, and she studied them both, and then back at Cowen.

"I hope Lord Sarah is okay! She ran off quick –"

"Oh, that's why I'm here. She asked me to take care of you two and give you both her regards. She'll be fine; she just had a spell at an awkward time. It's a girl-lord thing. Nothing you guys did." She smiled at Cowen. "One day you'll know what I'm talking about. In the meantime –"

And she chatted about the day, asked them a few questions, and generally fascinated two men who were happy to be charmed by the Angel of Death and who really didn't want to know anything about the mysteries of female plumbing, lord or otherwise.

Col James Cowen and Lord Sarah

The awakening in Scotland was well organised, as it should be with all the practise the RumLot people had by now. The location chosen was the estate of a stately home that was rented out for weddings and business conferences, and the massive fields surrounding the listed mansion were now used for grazing picturesque sheep and as a backdrop for pretty wedding photos.

Sarah ported to Dundee, and from there she and Althea and Mordecai took the helicopter to the grand house. While they waited for the rest to arrive they had breakfast. Malachi was on his way up with Gangster Jack and some of the RumLot crew.

She and the other lords discussed over breakfast the conundrum of Col Cowen. It was the cautious consensus of the lords that the Scot was also a lord. The elves insisted he was, although no one had seen his eyes glow or any indication of points on his ears. They said he smelled lord and felt lord. There was no doubt in their elvish minds.

If he were a lord in his mid-forties, he wasn't showing any signs at all. Mandy was of the opinion that the lords with hard lives showed their magical maturity, or "ripening" as the elves put it, the earliest. Those who lived a calmer and more placid early life didn't ripen as quickly. In other words, stress hurried up the process, probably as a survival mechanism. Althea had had both major stress and the cauldron, so her skills came to the forefront amazingly early, in her mid-twenties. Mordecai was over one hundred and thirty before he fully ripened, even though the process started in his fifties. Caddy was over one hundred.

While elves said that historically most lords grew into their abilities between fifty and seventy, there was a lot of natural variation, and from what they knew of Col Cowen, he'd had a happy childhood and a rather smooth career. His only major stress the lords knew about was suddenly losing his wife to cancer, and while that was a major blow, it wasn't a lifelong stressor that would cause a fearful lord to jump-start their ability simply to survive.

The issue was when to tell him? Not today; they had other business to attend to. Jameson was the usual lord whisperer, but he was busy in Ukraine. Unpleasant things were happening by the Wall, and he was needed there. Ditto with Kyrylo and Caddy.

Revealing that his tribe was lord and not human needed to be done at a calm time and with due consideration that he had a houseful of young kids to deal with, too. They had, from all indications, adapted to the death of their mother as well as could be expected, but how would they take finding out that

43

their beloved dad was not human? Would that be a gain or another loss?

In the meantime, Sarah asked that she be shielded whenever possible from the man's scent. She'd had a good whiff of him at the embassy, and that was enough to scare her. She did *not* want to bond with anyone at this time in her life, and she certainly didn't want to get involved with someone she didn't know.

She was training to be a Warrior Lord, and she was ready to face anything in battle. What she didn't tell her friends was that the only thing in the world that scared her to death was a man in her bed. Her faith had kept her sane, but it had also kept her married, and it had taken her thirty years to walk out of an abusive marriage that had destroyed her self-worth as a woman. The last thing she wanted was to enter another relationship with all of its risks of vulnerability and intimacy and find out she'd made another horrible mistake. Sex outside of marriage was not something she would do for religious reasons, and since she wasn't going to bond or marry, she wouldn't be bedding anyone.

Althea was bonded, so whatever pheromones that James gave off wouldn't bother her. He didn't know he was a lord and didn't know about their customs and the multiple showers a day. The soldier was perfectly clean, but to a human nose, not to a lord's.

Althea also pointed out that he might be orc-bait, too, if he were a one-shower-a-day guy. They just didn't know.

After breakfast Mordecai and Althea walked the field they were using just to get a feel for it. Sarah walked around "the circus" and inspected the marquees that were used to hold water and snacks for the soldiers and waited for Malachi to show up. The staging area was busy with their RumLot personnel, and the buses with the UK military soldiers, sailors, and airmen pulled up, so the place was now a hive of activity. Sarah found her two colonels and chatted with the guys for a few minutes. She felt bad about rudely abandoning them to Vrt (even though she knew that any man would prefer a five-minute chat with Vrt over any hour-long conversation with her), and since she was outdoors and could angle herself upwind, she was comfortable talking with McGinnis and Cowen.

They were both nice guys, and her five-minute chat lasted a lot longer than it should have. McGinnis in particular began to get that look in his eye and started to flirt, and she saw Cowen roll his eyes at the man more than once. Then McGinnis, in his usual bold way, asked her outright if she had a lord boyfriend, and Sarah blushed hard, which made her blush even harder.

"If you're asking if I'm bonded, no, I'm not." She shrugged and smiled at the men. "Single lords are thin on the ground, and in my role, well, men like more approachable women. Demon-eyed valkyries don't get the hits on lord dating apps."

Cowen scowled at McGinnis; hitting on the lord had obviously made her uncomfortable, so he tried to turn the conversation. "Oh, I think men like all sorts of women. What exactly is your role? I see the shoulder boards, and other lords aren't wearing them. What do they mean?"

Back on more neutral terrain, Sarah turned to James. "I'm an Elemental who is a Warrior Lord. The blue uniform means I'm a full, working lord for the Elf Nation in a leadership role. The epaulettes mean I'm an Elemental. Lord Cadence is the only person with a full moon on her shoulder. Lords Kyrylo and Conary have half moons and rank over me as they have major areas of responsibility, like the military and diplomacy. I have a quarter moon as I don't have a major area of responsibility but work where I am needed for all three of them."

"What's an Elemental? And what's a Warrior Lord?" McGinnis asked that, so at least his mind was back on business and not on hooking up with valkyries.

The corner of Sarah's mouth turned up. "An Elemental is a lord of great power, and I'm going to leave it at that. A Warrior Lord is a trained killer, and we train all of our lives. I'm a soldier – a lord who protects and keeps the peace – like you guys. You'll know us by our swords. I am the only Elemental who also trains as a Warrior Lord, and that's why I'm the only one wearing the boards and a sword." She grinned at the expressions on their faces. "And that's why I don't date. When a guy finds that out about me, they all have the exact same expression you guys are wearing right now. Terror. Which is a bit of a romantic downer."

Cowen snorted. "You don't scare me, Lord Sarah. I have two teenagers at home and one on the cusp. I live with abject terror."

And Sarah had to laugh. "Oh, a man with stories to tell! Let's go get a cup of coffee before we start forming up, and you can tell me about your demon children." And off they went to see if the caterers had anything interesting, leaving both Cowen and McGinnis wondering what her "great power" was, what her "work" was, and if she really could use that sword as a trained killer would. Cowen bet she could.

While Malachi stepped into the Kyrylo role of protecting Mordecai while he was waking up the hibernating elves, Sarah had fallen into the Jameson role. This meant she stood outside both the ring of regular soldiers who guarded against intruders and the inner ring of those who freed the elves from their sacs and boosted them in the air for an easier port to the Safe Haven. Her job was to help centre the circle, to keep everyone focused on the job at hand (especially at the end when the "joy juice" was most potent) and troubleshoot any problems that arose.

At the appointed time one of the RumLot cadre blew a whistle, and the soldiers and RumLot security humans, the trained and vetted Royal military members, and the redcoat lords formed up into a large rough ring about the size of a football pitch. Mordecai walked the area and quickly found his centre. Sarah and Malachi (on Gangster Jack) ran the circle, pulling people where they wanted them to stand and rearranging as needed. Sarah put a RumLot security soldier between Cowen and McGinnis and moved a few of the outer ring of guards out a bit further.

Then she called Malachi over, and the entire circus had to wait and watch while they conversed. There was a heavy tree line and a fence almost touching the side of the circle, a perfect place for elf-parazzi to hide, and Malachi nodded. He knew all about that risk. But they weren't going to move Mordecai from his chosen spot, so they moved some extra soldiers in that direction. Sarah spoke into her mic, and a minute later a drone flew in and positioned itself over the trees.

Cowen watched the two lords talking, and he could see where Lord Sarah was pointing and where they were looking, and from his background in battlefield tactics, he could understand what they were talking about without being there. She was concerned about the circle moving so close to the treeline.

With the drone in position Mordecai was given the thumbs-up, Malachi handed over Gangster Jack to the groom, and the awakening commenced.

Cowen and the other new participants knew what to expect, but knowing and experiencing are two different things. James had never felt magic before, not real, gut-wrenching, spine-tingling magic that rattled his bones and rang in his ears. He wasn't a musician, but listening to Mordecai's song as he woke up the elves and drove the clan to the surface was an emotional experience he wasn't expecting. He wasn't just listening to the music; he was inside the music, a part of the song, along with everyone else.

When he felt the ground tremble under his feet and the vibrations travel up his legs and into his spine, the anticipation that something wonderful was about to happen was almost orgasmic. It wasn't sexual, but damn close to it, and the aching power of the song as it reached its climax was a mix of pain and joy. Then the elves erupted from the ground.

He would never forget releasing his first elf. He had helped birth all of his children, and this was what it felt like. Wonder. Joy. Relief. The little woman was an older matron, all round, wet bits topped by a fluid-soaked mop of grey hair, but when James lifted her from the collapsing sac, she looked into his eyes. While he didn't know his own were glowing bright, she smiled at him, and they connected. He knew if he ever saw her again they would know each other because at that moment they became clan. They were family. He threw her in the air as hard as he could, and she ported out.

And then there was another and another and another, and for the next half hour, James and the rest of the circle attacked the egg sacs and released elves to be reborn in this new world. Then it was over as suddenly as it had begun. Mordecai gave his victory cry that rolled and echoed over the heath, and James experienced his reward, the blast of exhilaration that came as the rebirth was completed.

Dancing with joy, people were screaming and crying around him, but he just stood there, his body a sponge soaking up the joy into every cell.

A hard punch (really hard!) from Malachi, who leaned over from the saddle and yelled over the roar of the exultant crowd. "James! Go that way and get your people back on the ground. We're not done yet!" And he rode off.

James blinked and suddenly saw the soldiers of the outer ring absorbed in their own pink fog of exhilaration, and he became Col Cowen once more, running at full speed to the soldiers who were supposed to be guarding the outer edge to wake them up and get them back on duty. On the other far side of the ring, barely visible through the masses of milling people, he saw Malachi, McGinnis, and Sarah doing the same thing – waking people up and separating those who had gotten a little too friendly during the final pheromone burst.

He ran from soldier to soldier across the field and then up to the fence. On the other side of the fence he almost tripped over a couple of soldiers who were supposed to be patrolling the woodline but instead were getting much, much too intimate. James jumped the fence and bopped one on the helmet.

The poor guy woke up and looked up at the colonel and back down at who he was about to screw, appalled, and the woman under him squeaked and rolled away, thoroughly embarrassed. She wasn't being raped, far from it, but she certainly wouldn't have bedded this guy if it hadn't been for the joy juice. In real life, they didn't even like each other.

James just grinned. "No one saw anything, no one did anything – right?" And the red-faced soldiers nodded as they fixed their uniforms and pretended the other one wasn't there.

Looking around for other patrolling soldiers lost in the woods, James saw a movement in the brush about fifty yards away and ran to it.

He didn't find soldiers rolling on the ground. He found a RumLot Security guard and two civilians digging up three elf eggs and putting them into a small trailer hitched to the back of an ATV. They were stealing elves.

James and the RumLot guy saw each other at the same time. The traitor drew a pistol and shot at James, but James was already diving away. Was there some latent lord magic involved? James would never know, but somehow he evaded the shot by throwing himself to the side. Unfortunately, where he threw himself was right off an embankment and down a muddy cliff edge into a small burn.

As he tumbled down to the water, two things popped into his mind. One was that this would be a great stream for trout. The other was "Where the shit is Lord Sarah when you need her?" James was unarmed except for his elf knife, and he desperately needed something to fight back with if he was going to rescue those trapped elves from the egg thieves, and Lord Sarah always seemed armed to the teeth. The water hit him with the force of a fully loaded lorry and knocked all the air out of him.

On top of the cliff the RumLot traitor looked over and saw the colonel lying face down in the water, motionless. He turned and went back to his friends. He had more important things to do than rescue nosy regular Army idiots. Let him drown.

Sarah and James

Sarah froze. She was standing in the middle of the water tent talking to Judy when she heard someone calling her. Judy looked up at her friend, and she didn't have to read her mind to know something was wrong.

James Cowen.

He was in trouble, and for a brief moment electric fear fired through every thread of her body. He was falling, and then she felt the air being knocked out of him. Water.

Instinct kicked in, she ported to his voice and found herself waist-deep in a wide stream, James floating face down in front of her. It only took her a second to flip him so he could breathe, and by the time she dragged him to the rocky shingle, he was already sputtering and moving on his own.

Then a spit of water erupted next to her, and she looked up to the cliff edge and saw a man shooting at them with a pistol. The silencer on the weapon told her this wasn't a crazy farmer scaring off trespassers. This one was out to kill.

Dodging bullets, Sarah and James scrambled out of the water to the bank and sheltered under a small eroded overhang. Whoever wanted them dead wasn't a very good shot, or maybe the two lords were just really good at evading the bullets. Either way, they made it to the hollow, and there they huddled, James pushing her high into the dirt, shielding her with his body, his arms holding her tight, and his face buried in the knot of hair at the nape of her neck, breathing like a spent racehorse. Sarah could appreciate his instinct to protect her, but really, she was the Warrior Lord here, and he was the one who needed to catch his breath after almost drowning.

"What's going on?"

James was still trying to force air into his lungs, but he got it out. "Three egg thieves. They have elf sacs in the back of an ATV. Digging out another egg. A RumLot guy. Uniform. Big man and a woman."

Sarah looked up, listening. She could hear them still working; then she heard the ATV start up. She pressed the alarm button on her shoulder radio and called for Malachi, and repeated what James had told her. Then she pushed her pistol into James's hand.

"You stay here. I'm going up." And before he could say anything, she was gone, porting to the top of the cliff, and he was left holding nothing but Sarah-scented air and her pistol.

The RumLot traitor was standing by the edge of the cliff, looking down. When Sarah ported in behind him the bang of her port spun him around, and the last thing he saw in this world was the glowing lord and the edge of her sabre as it decapitated him.

She turned, and in front of her was a nightmare. By the ATV stood two orcs – a huge man and a woman. The woman was sitting on the ATV, revving up the motor, but with true orc stupidity she had revved it up too hard and fast, and instead of moving forward the drive wheel dug into the soft, wet earth and buried itself up to the axle. There were three full-sized egg sacs piled in the ATV's trailer.

The orc man had an elf baby in his hand. He licked it and grinned and then tossed it on the ground behind him, a snack for later, where the tiny boy screamed a high-pitched, insulted wail. Neither of the orcs noticed the dead RumLot guard or the glowing lord as they concentrated on freeing the ATV from the mud.

Sarah ran to the baby, scooping him up in her hat so she wouldn't burn him, and yelled, "Mother!"

But the mother didn't come. The mothers always came; they were tied to their children, and all they needed was the call to home in on. *The mother didn't come.* No elf came.

She held onto the baby, and the massive orc suddenly discovered there was a lord next to him. Screaming in fury, he lunged at her, and she rammed her sabre into his gut and twisted, disembowelling him. He looked at Sarah with a quizzical expression on his face and then at his guts as they slowly oozed to the ground and moaned. His last words before falling to his knees were, "Shit. That hurt."

Behind the orc a banshee shrieked, and the orc woman pulled her gun on Sarah. As Sarah turned, she saw James at the edge of the cliff aiming his pistol at the woman, but it was too late. The woman's bullets were on their way, and Sarah watched them fly towards her in slow motion because she was already bending space and time and porting away.

There was a great crack of lightning, and the bullets sped through the plasma – but there was no lord and no elf baby. They were gone.

In the Safe Haven, the blue-painted dome with the artificial stars that made the sky roof snapped with sparks. With a boom that rattled bones, a bolt of lightning snaked down the needle of the Spire and burnt into the floor of the busy market. Panicked elves screamed and ported or ran away, and the air crackled with electricity and reeked with the chlorine smell of ozone.

Sarah fell hard to the tile floor of the market, and her knees buckled as she collapsed from the fall of porting in too high. The baby howled, its tiny face as red as all hell and rage could make it, but it was alive, nestled in her hat like a very angry baby bird in its nest. Sarah pulled herself up, her body glowing white hot, swaying and gulping great barrels of air, and she was surrounded by elves peeking out from behind market stalls, some Warriors poised to attack, all of them with shocked eyes wide at the sight of a lord in the main square of the Safe Haven.

She tossed the baby like a sack of flour to the nearest elf. "Find its mother." Jamming the hat back on her head, she looked around and up to get her bearings – and the needle of the spire swayed, sagged, and then shot down like an arrow, aimed directly onto Sarah's head, and she saw death. But a millisecond before it hit, there was a tremendous explosion – and there was no lord for it to impale because at that moment, Sarah ported out.

The elves never found a body. All that was left under the rubble of the spire was a black mark on the melted tile that the elves could never scrub out. But after that day, they never wanted to.

And there was no soul. No Lord Sarah. She disappeared into a ball of plasma as if she had never been.

Malachi and James

No one could tell Malachi differently; Sarah's death was his fault. He was in charge of security, and an Elemental Warrior lord, a friend so close to him she was his sister, died on his watch.

Sweet, salty, bruised Sarah had come so recently to her full, glorious ripening, and Malachi knew she was ecstatically happy with her new life. He knew because she'd told him.

One day they were sitting at a picnic table at the target range after pistol practice, in a bone-chilling mist, cleaning their weapons, when she turned to him and just grinned. "G-d has blessed me. Here I am with a great friend doing fun things and living my best life. How many people will ever say that?"

Malachi grinned down at his pistol, but he understood. He understood perfectly. But he had to tease. "Oh, some people would say that gettin' beat up daily by Victor and his Warrior Elves is not exactly a blessin'."

The tiniest of shadows crossed the sunshine of her face, but she shrugged. "The elves? That's not a beating; that's a privilege. I know what a beating is; they're training me hard so I won't get beaten again. I learn every time they hit me, and I think I'm very close to leaving them behind. I win most of the time now. I'll start training with Vrt next week."

She turned back to the pistol and cleaned out the barrel, humming to herself. They didn't have to clean the pistols; elves would have done it and probably better. But a marksman always maintains their own weapons, and field cleaning might have to be done one day out in a battle, so this was practice, too.

When Malachi charged up on Gangster Jack, Sarah had killed the human traitor and disabled an

absolutely massive orc and then disappeared. Malachi
heard the bang of her port just as he rounded a small
copse. In front of him was James Cowen rolling on the
ground with a screaming, blood-spurting female orc.

James shot her centre mass, just like he did on
every firing range target during his military career,
emptying his pistol into her chest and gut as he walked
towards her. It didn't work with the orc, and with a
roar she leapt on him, all teeth and fury.

Throwing away the spent pistol he stabbed her
in the gut with his elf knife, but in her orc frenzy with
battling a lord, she still wasn't ready to die. Screaming
in rage, she jumped on top of him, and that was the
opening Malachi needed. Gangster Jack didn't even
break stride, but flew by her with Malachi leaning over
like a fucking Tatar, and with one smooth slice of his
sabre he lopped off her head. James kicked the orc
woman's body off, and he wobbled up and stared,
stunned, at the orc. Fifteen rounds at semi-auto, a
stabbing, and yet she still needed decapitating before
she died. He couldn't fathom it.

Gangster Jack spun around like a barrel pony,
and Malachi jumped off and ran to the ATV, James
right behind him. They scrambled to free the
struggling elves from their sacs before they drowned
while being born. One almost didn't make it. They
pounded on the poor man's back trying to get fluid out,
but the two they freed must have called for help
because two naked, exhausted Warrior elves ported

back in and rescued their brother, taking him to the
Safe Haven where the healers saved him.

Suddenly the elves were gone, and there was
nothing more to do but decapitate the orc Sarah had
killed, who was still moaning on the ground despite
the fact that his guts were no longer attached to his
body. Malachi managed that clean-up task, and it only
took a second.

Riding double, Malachi and James trotted to
the central gathering point, where it was all chaos as
Mordecai and the other non-warrior lords were
evacuated, and the RumLot guys combed the area for
any evidence of other traitors and egg thieves.

James left Malachi in the crowd but wouldn't
leave; he kept looking for Sarah, calling for her.

Everyone was leaving. The military contingent
had loaded up, and McGinnis ran up to Malachi,
yelling, "Where's Cowen!! He's not on the bus! We're
waiting for him!" The lord yelled back to leave;
they'd take care of Cowen. McGinnis hesitated, then
ran back, and all the buses pulled out.

And then there was no one left but James,
standing in the middle of the huge field, stock still. He
wasn't calling for Sarah.

Malachi rode up and dismounted. Cowen
didn't move. "James! It's time to go. She's ported

someplace. We'll find her. She's probably back at Aelfeham House now."

James slowly turned to Malachi, and before the lord's eyes Cowen was already turning into a zombie, his dead eyes staring at nothing and everything.

"She's gone. She's gone."

Malachi hustled James to Gangster Jack's trailer, and they sat in the straw in the empty stall next to the horse for the ten-hour drive back to Suffolk.

James never said a word. He was right. Sarah was gone.

Lord Sarah

No one, lord or elf, could feel Lord Sarah's spirit, and with no spirit in this world, it meant she had died. The elves mourned Lord Sarah with the heart-shredding grief that they would mourn any beloved family member.

While all deaths were mourned, this was a lord whose spirit had burned as bright as any star, an Elemental who gave up her life to return a baby to his mother. She didn't know that the baby's mother and father had died in the last great battle before the clan had fled to hibernation, so there was no parent to find.

Lord Sarah had followed the parents' trail to the only place she knew would hold a reborn elf – and it killed her. The elves were convinced of it, and Lord Sarah's death only proved that no lord or human could survive a trip to the Safe Haven.

The small clan of lords was in shock. For all the dangers Caddy warned against, for all the obsessive security concerns of Kyrylo, for all the dangerous missions, they had never lost a lord, and now one was gone. Someone who should have lived forever had died.

The Old Farts were grim; they had suffered through this tragedy before. While the elves had had their own horrible experience with genocide – and there wasn't an elf family who didn't have their own to mourn – the Old Farts had, to a lord, lost everyone during Gaia's suicide and the aftermath. Every parent, every brother and sister, every friend had been killed. Everyone. Losing Sarah reopened old wounds that they were sure had healed, and Caddy had to assign an elf to Chi for three days just to watch him until he was able to put his memories back in the box where he kept them hidden, and he was able to function again. He didn't know it, but Talia slept in the hall outside of his room the entire time.

The new lords, the ones born in the modern era, were shaken. No one really believes they will die, not even humans who know better, but now the immortals were shown that they were vulnerable, too. Death was a theory but was now a fact.

In just a couple of years, their fragile clan had grown from one lord to more than thirty, but that was still a tiny group, and Sarah's loss ripped open a jagged hole.

Adem

The elves were firmly convinced Sarah was dead because she had ported the baby to Safe Haven. Weren't they all told from birth that the Safe Haven was only for elves?

When Malachi and James walked into the stables at Aelfeham House the place was already in mourning. James was ported back to his home where his kids were waiting, and Malachi went back to his room, slammed the door, and wouldn't talk to anyone, not even Mordecai.

The next morning, at five, he had an elf port him to Dover, where he took the first RumLot helicopter to Calais and was ported to Ukraine. He was at House by six-thirty, just in time to meet Caddy and Kyrylo for breakfast, where he formally resigned.

Caddy went full-on Warrior Queen and absolutely would not accept any resignation. Malachi said she had no choice, and he turned on his heel to leave, but Kyrylo was standing in the doorway and wouldn't let the Warrior Lord out until he had his say, too.

"Kai, I know. I know how this feels, when you lose your people." Kyrylo's voice broke."I've done it. I've stood at funerals of good, good people I've sent to battle and thought – no – I *knew* it was my fault. They might have died from a Russian bullet or something else, but they wouldn't have been there if I hadn't sent them. But I sent them, Kai, because the cause was greater than they were, greater than me."

Malachi stood there, his eyes glowing bright blue, whether with tears or the fire that burned in every lord, it was hard to tell. Both.

"She was my sister, Kyrylo."

"Yes, doing something she loved. She loved us, Kai, she loved the elves. She'd be devastated to know she was the cause of you quitting. You know that in your heart." Kyrylo sighed. "Listen, I'm not going to go around in circles talking to you that this is not your fault. Shit happens, and crap like that. You would just say no. But do one thing for Caddy and me – and for Sarah. Stay here for a few days and rest with us. If at the end of the week you still want out, I'll talk to Caddy, and we'll move on. We can't make you stay in a job you don't want."

Malachi stood there, frozen, the only movement that said he was still alive was a twitch of one muscle in his jaw.

"Sarah would want you to think it over."

Then he broke. Tears streaming down his face, he nodded. Kyrylo hugged him, and they went outside and sat on the wide porch and talked about Sarah all morning.

Adem listened to all of this, his own worry and upset about the news of the dead lord pushed aside by the intensity of Malachi's grief. The man, who couldn't say two words during a chess game other than "your move," couldn't stop talking about the lord. And they weren't even bonded!

He'd met Sarah a couple of times, but mostly she worked out of England. Adem knew as soon as she walked in the door that she was an Elemental of tremendous power. She radiated it.

She'd popped by a couple of times on her way back from some assignment to rest and get something to eat, and she ate an enormous amount of food to fuel her equally enormous energy requirements. Adem had never seen an Elemental burn so hot, but then what she did needed a lot of strength. Even Caddy and Kyrylo, as impressive as they are, weren't as strong as Sarah. They could bend waves and energy, but Sarah could bend time, and time controlled everything. She couldn't stop time or leap into the past or future, but she could harness time, and that was an almost godlike power.

Adem didn't think anyone other than himself had any idea how much effort it took her to port. Lords looked at elves popping in and out and thought it was easy. But elves, if they were athletes at it, only ported about fifty miles. Usually, they ported about twenty, and the holes they made in space and time were very small. Anyone could tell that by the pops the elves made, which sounded more like crackles of static. Sarah could go huge distances, maybe infinite distances, and the sounds she made as space and time were displaced were massive booms that shook windows and made people look in the sky for fighter jets.

She could port other things, too, whereas the elves could only port themselves or create a porthole for goods, humans, and lords to move through. A lord had to walk through the elf-created porthole. Sarah could look at something, and it would suddenly find itself someplace else, whether it wanted to be there or not. That took a tremendous amount of energy, and she wouldn't do it with living things – yet. She was afraid of porting a living being to a dead zone with no air or high in the sky or entombed inside a mountain. Porting was pretty complicated, and the landing zone had to be just right. Figuring it out hundreds of miles away took a lot of practice and would take centuries of experiments and learning to reach her full potential.

Now she'd never get that time to grow.

Malachi, though, wasn't mourning the loss of a military asset but the loss of a friend. Adem listened to Malachi and Kyrylo talk, and Caddy joined them after Kai had settled down a bit. They sat and reminisced, and then the painful conversation turned to her last minutes, and they talked about how she died. Then Caddy made an observation that startled Adem, driving everything else out of his mind.

"The elves say that Safe Haven is off-limits for lords and humans because they'd die, but House is a Safe Haven, too, and lords and humans come here all the time. I wonder what's different."

House wasn't *a* Safe Haven. House/Adem had *made a* Safe Haven for his Caddy; that was his ability. Inside the Safe Haven bubble Adem made with his magic, Adem built a house.

When he thought about it, he remembered making the huge bubble for the elves they named the Safe Haven. He had given it to them he-couldn't-remember-how-many-thousands of years in the past, literally generations of elves ago. But he'd never told them that if they ported a lord or a human (or an orc, for that matter) into Safe Haven, the non-elf would die. That was something they'd made up themselves and now took as fact.

Probably the first nameless elf, the one Adem gave the bubble to, said it was *just* for elves to use, and that morphed to *only* elves should go, and then that evolved to "only elves *could* go." Their immutable fact was the product of a millennial game of telephone.

The more Adem thought about it, the more he was convinced that Sarah didn't die because she ported to Safe Haven. She died because she ported back out when she saw that spire thing falling on her and to someplace where she couldn't live. Maybe she accidentally ported to the bowels of the Earth and died in a pool of magma. Or she ported to the moon and died of asphyxiation, too exhausted to port back out. Something like that. She had only been porting long distances for a very short time and was still learning. Porting accidents happened all the time with young elves, but Sarah's power could make a porting accident fatal.

Or maybe she was alive somewhere in time where the living creatures of the Earth couldn't sense her.

Adem, just to make sure, started scanning for Sarah's soul. Like all lords and elves, he could think about a person and get a sense of their well-being, and that meant whether they were alive or dead. If a person was very close to death, their soul might be so weak they might not be felt, but that didn't mean they were dead. And people with no meat at all and on their way to the Void could still be sensed; that's how ghosts were made. Vrt's husband, Prana, was such a ghost. He had no body, but until he walked through the Gates, his soul was still on this Earth and he could be heard and felt.

Adem the fungus was still huge. Oh, not anywhere as big as he was before he went on his diet, but still bigger than any human, lord, or elf. He was about as big as a sperm whale now, having dieted down from his chubby forty-three tons to a more svelte, but still too big, fourteen tons. Fourteen tons of biomass spread over a few acres could pick up a lot of very faint signals, and what he picked up was that Sarah was not dead.

Sarah was at the Gates. She even had her body, so she wasn't at all dead, just very, very far from home.

If she was at the Gates, they weren't letting her in.

If whoever was manning the Gates wasn't letting Sarah in, she would port back to Earth, no one would know when or where, because the Void's Gates were outside of Earth's space and time. The Gate area was like the inside of the bubbles Adem could make, so he understood how it worked. She could come back in an hour or in a century; no one could predict.

Sarah was alive!

Adem was so excited that he flew to Caddy in the form of Spoon and started bouncing up and down and spinning. She looked at Spoon and smiled. "Kai, Kyrylo, I think lunch is ready."

And that's when it hit Adem. He had something of vital importance to say that was very complicated and subtle, and he couldn't do it. He was a fucking fungus communicating through a wooden spoon.

His family was grieving, and they didn't need to.

So why was he staying as a fungus anyway? Caddy, Kyrylo, and Ivana didn't need him to build rooms or clean or cook or anything like that; that's what elves did. Caddy had stopped needing Adem days after she first walked into his outhouse and called up the first clan of Ukrainian elves. He just built things for fun; the elves did all the work keeping Caddy and Kyrylo happy, and that was as it should be. It was so natural that Adem didn't even think about it.

In the last three years, he'd just flitted around entertaining himself, having fun, chatting and playing games, and generally falling back into his old social butterfly habits, living off his friends. He wasn't being useful to Caddy anymore, and now that he could, he couldn't because he had been lazy.

Adem felt horrible about how he was letting them all down. They didn't know he was the creator of Safe Havens and understood how Sarah's great abilities worked, but he did, and he couldn't tell them.

That night, Malachi was alone in his bedroom and sobbing, grieving for his friend, and all Adem could do was sit in the corner and use the spoon to bring the man a towel to wipe his eyes. He couldn't even give him a hug, much less tell him Sarah was still alive, just too far away to feel. And if he did, would he be believed? To his family, Adem was Spoon, a bit of weird entertainment. After Malachi finally fell asleep, Adem made up his mind. He was going to change back. No screwing around this time. He was going to lose the weight and get to under a thousand pounds and reform into a proper lord man.

He hoped he would remember what he looked like.

Sarah

The old woman poked at Sarah with a stick, and when the lord stirred and moaned, she stepped back about ten feet and squatted, never taking her eyes off Sarah's battered body.

Sarah opened her eyes. She was floating, or maybe just lying, inside a cloud, and the mist ever-so-gently swirled around her. She could see swirls of colour, very faint, and little trails of tiny sparks, and it was the sparks that gave some definition to the vapour. It was like lying inside an opal.

"You have to go back. You're not done. *I'm* not done." The old woman waved her stick towards some vague point, and the disturbed cloud swirled around the tip of it like smoke.

The lord's bones hurt. Her eyes hurt. Lights danced behind her eyes and formed into shards of glass that pierced her brain, gelling into a molten migraine from hell. Every part of her screamed pain, but she sat up anyway.

Sarah looked at the old woman, and the hag morphed into a beautiful, haloed, and crowned queen in a blue cloak – and then into a black-skinned, bejewelled siren with a thousand arms – and then back to a crone, if a different one with her own unique ugliness. Every few seconds, she changed, always a woman, though, but in some different fantastic form. Some Sarah recognised, but most she had never seen before.

"Who are you?"

The crone shrugged, and from her shoulders fell millions of tiny babies like grains of sand. "No idea now. Many names and none of them matter. What matters is that we aren't done. We still owe. You have to go back. Don't be selfish."

Sarah struggled to her feet. She was so, so tired. To go forward was to rest, to sleep, to painless oblivion; to go back was to return to everything hurtful, to pain, to fear. But now she was angry – who was this woman to call her selfish? She wasn't selfish. Sarah always gave everything –

"No, you don't. You don't give everything, not at all. You give only what you want to. You put your love in little sealed boxes and ignore it. Instead, you fondle your hoard of pain and glory in it like it was some virtue. You feel sorry for yourself a lot. It's very selfish of you."

"What right do you have to judge me? What do you know about my pain?"

The old woman sighed. "I know your pain because I was – probably still am – selfish like you. I destroyed my world because my pain was more important to me than everything else. Now I'm atoning." She tilted her head, which now had a lovely face but hair of snakes and eyes as dead as cinders. "You're Jewish; you know what the Rebs say about atonement."

"Atonement! You might have to atone, but –"

"You have been given great power and an equally great love; now you have a debt that you haven't even begun to pay back. You have Kippur. If you leave now, you will leave the world and those you love worse off than if you had never been born. You have not paid back the debt you owe for your gifts."

Sarah was stunned. Was she a debtor? A debtor who didn't pay back their debts was a thief, and thieves were the definition of selfish. Was she being selfish? She had gone from being a clinically depressed, battered housewife married to a fucking orc, and now she was a lord, a woman of huge power – and not just any lord, but an Elemental. And what did she do with that power? The minute she had a bad day, she gave up, and here she was at the Gates of goodness knows where – heaven, hell, or the Void – whining that she had a migraine and needed a nap.

She most certainly still owed Kippur.

Sarah pressed her lips together and frowned. The old woman nodded and smiled. Now she looked like the Venus of Willendorf.

"Go back." The hag gently said.

And as Sarah gathered her energy up for one great leap back, she heard the woman yell after her. "And for all the stars, bed –"

The lord was gone, and the crone's voice trailed off. " – the man and make some Scent for your elves. He's a good one."

The old woman sat back down and guarded her door, the mist of the universe swirling around her, and she took a nap. It had been a busy eternity, but there was still much to do. And she was old.

Sarah

Oh fucking hell. Sarah sat up and looked around her; if this was hell, it had most certainly frozen over. She was in the middle of a vast grey and black desert of wind-tortured rock, and the cold – it wasn't just below zero, it was double digits below zero. Negative sixty-five, she found out later. Even with the white hot internal heat she carried from the incalculable port from the gates of the Void, she could still feel the cold. Was she even on Earth?

It would be utter irony for her to miss her entire planet and port to some rocky death orb like Pluto. But she could breathe; there was air even if the unearthly cold hurt her lungs, and if she listened hard, she could hear the hum of life. It just wasn't anywhere near where she was.

It was – and she turned slowly, her ears twitching and rotating like a bat's.

There.

She could barely move, but move she must. With porting, she could keep her heat up and maybe avoid becoming a lord-cicle, but it took energy, and she didn't have much left. There were people; she could hear them. And slowly, in little hundred-mile limps, she ported towards them.

On the third port, she had to stop and rest, and the gods favoured her. Sarah practically tripped over a desiccated, wayward penguin frozen solid in the snow. A little guy, but he had frozen to death before he starved, and there was a bit she could cut off with her elf knife, and after thawing it in her white hot hands, she ate the nasty, fishy birdflesh raw.

The penguin's calories were just enough to allow her two more ports, and then she saw them. Lights. She made one last port, and she staggered up to a door. A sign said, "Entrance 4, Closed for the Season, Please use the Front Door. *smiley face*"

Fuck that, Sarah thought, and she banged on the door. Just as she was about to despair and make her way to wherever the hell the front door was, she heard a creak, and the door opened.

James

The black despair was more than he could bear, and if it wasn't for his children and the experience of being flayed alive once before when Lauren died, he surely would have finished his misery in some more efficient way than this slow death by agonising inches.

But he had survived it before by grimly deciding to endure the next minute, the next hour, the next day, and do whatever it took to make time pass. Like any zombie whose heart no longer worked, he survived on habit and muscle memory. He woke up, he kissed the kids goodbye when they went off to school, and he ignored their stricken faces and hollow-eyed alarm at the state their dad was in; he ate, he went to work, he repeated the process. He would get through it. He had no choice.

James didn't understand this black despair, not at all. When Lauren died, they had known, loved, and lived together for fifteen years. Her cancer was sudden, furious, and fatal, and when she died the entire family was bereft, and his personal tsunami of grief was overwhelming.

But Sarah –

He had only known Sarah existed for two months and had barely talked with her. The only time he'd touched her was during that disastrous battle at the awakening, and he'd held her tight during the firefight with the orcs. James knew he'd never forget the feel of her and the smell of her, but it was just the one time. And yet her death felt just as bad as if they had known and loved each other for decades. It made no sense.

Tonight, they were going to light her pyre, and since they didn't have a body, they'd burn all of her possessions. It was inadequate, but the elves insisted, and as one told him, they had to honour her somehow on her journey to the Void. If a single hair clung to a pillow or a skin cell lived in a seam of her clothing, it was all they had to turn to carbon and send back to the stars. They asked him to light the pyre, and he had no idea why, but they insisted that he was the only one who could. Not Lord Cadence or any of Sarah's lord friends, but the one who last held her and, in the end, couldn't protect her.

He laid his dress uniform out on Lauren's side of the bed and checked it over once again. For Sarah's funeral, it had to be perfect, even down to the new EN medal he'd earned for being at the disaster. When he was done, he lay on the other side, a weak imitation of a corpse, and stared at the ceiling and waited for the hours to pass.

One foot in front of the other.

Amundsen-Scott South Pole Station

Hebe called for help on the intercom and pressed the emergency button; she heard footsteps running towards her as she put her parka on before opening the fire door. In the Antarctic, you just didn't open the door without protection. She mumbled the mantra of all Antarctic explorers, *Dorothy, you aren't in Kansas anymore*. The camera showed a shape at the door, but that was impossible. No one should be wandering around out there.

Behind her, she saw two of the guys trotting up, putting on coats and gloves as they ran, and she yelled that she was opening the door. She did, and in tumbled a body. Working fast, they pulled it in and slammed the door shut. Amazingly, the person wasn't in cold-weather gear! Nothing! Not even gloves.

Then the body moved, and Hebe saw flashes of an eerie green light trace over it like St. Elmo's fire. Mark and Ben stepped back, and the body turned to its back, sat up, and an emaciated death's head smiled and whispered, "Thank you."

Then they saw the ears. Even at the South Pole, they knew what lord ears looked like.

James

The elf punched him hard and yelled in his ear. "Lord James!! Lord James!! Wake up!!"

James's reflexes were good, but the elf Manfred's were better, and when James punched back, the elf easily dodged.

"Wake up!"

"Och, away an bile yer heaid, pal." James looked at the clock; he had plenty of time. "Bolt ya dafty."

"I'm not going anywhere!" And he punched the lord's arm again. "She's *ALIVE*, you fekkin tube! Lord Sarah is alive!"

James bolted up. Alive? Sarah was alive?

"Can't you feel her?" Manfred was in tears. "We got word about ten minutes ago –" And he blathered on, but James wasn't paying attention. He was listening, feeling really, and then he could *feel* it. He could *feel* her. The jagged Sarah-shaped hole ripped in his life was no longer there. Instead, life was just normal. Better. The agony was gone.

He leapt off the bed, whooping and hollering, and the kids shot in from their bedrooms, terrified that their dad had finally fallen off the cliff edge he had been dancing on. But Ded was laughing and crying and jumping around with a soldier elf and acting absolutely insane. Then they were all hugging and crying, even though none of the kids knew Sarah, but they were so happy for their dad, especially after the last black week they had watched him suffer through, that they had to whoop and holler, too.

It took a few minutes, but when everyone calmed down, Manfred told them that Lord Sarah was at the Amundsen-Scott South Pole Research Station in

Antarctica. She had walked across the South Pole in negative 65-degree cold and knocked on the door of the research station. She was in pretty rough shape, but Dr Mandy was on the phone with them, and that was all the elf knew.

He would take the entire family to Aelfeham House if they wanted – and of course they did. So the kids dressed as fast as they could, and Manfred started the port chain to Aelfeham House, where they could wait for more news.

Dr Mandy

The doctor's phone call went to the embassy in London, and within minutes, Dr Mandy was screaming into the link, trying to make sense of it all. The healer was too professional to cry on the video call, but it was hard. The doctor at the research station was very good and very nice, but dealing with the medical needs of one of the magical creatures was just not in his portfolio. But then the purpose of a doctor in such a remote place was to deal with every kind of emergency, so he tried.

"Just keep her comfortable and force as many calories into her as you can. Put a tube in if you have to. She'll recover very fast, but it will take an enormous amount of food. Wake her up every two hours *minimum* and feed her. You're American. Stuff her like a Thanksgiving turkey."

He nodded; he'd thought as much from her emaciated condition. Amazingly, there wasn't any frostbite, and Dr Mandy told him that Lord Sarah generated her own internal heat to battle the cold; just feed her and let her sleep. Lord **Sarah** would leave as soon as she was able.

When the doctor pointed out the problems with getting a medevac plane into the South Pole, Dr Mandy just laughed, a little hysterical herself.

"No, she won't need a plane; she'll leave on her own when she has the strength. You couldn't stop her if you tried."

The Cowens

Lord Sarah's personal items were removed from the pyre, and that turned the huge pile of wood into a bonfire. With a bonfire, there had to be a party, and when the Cowen family walked through the last port to Aelfeham House the party was well underway. James introduced the kids to everyone he knew, and Lord Farah bustled up and shooed Richie, Jamie, and Chloe to groups of lords and elves more appropriate to their ages.

"Don't worry yourself, Lord James!" she trilled. "I'll take good care of Lords Richard, James, and Chloe! They'll have fun, and everyone is dying to meet them!"

The place was a madhouse of screaming, laughing, crying, hugging celebration. A beer tent was set up on the huge lawn, and elves were popping in and out like firecrackers. Every human who worked for the embassy and RumLot was porting in, as well as close human friends like Conary's family.

Everyone insisted that James light the bonfire, and when he threw the torch in, it went up like a Roman candle. Elves, lords, and humans all danced and sang around it until the ridiculous hours of the morning.

Kyrylo told James that RumLot Security had sent the big jet to Argentina to wait for Sarah to get strong enough to port herself to Ushuaia International Airport. If she could manage that leap, then she could rest and eat on the flight back. If she couldn't do it, they would send a local plane to get her. Dr Mandy thought that Sarah should be feeling better in about four days if they fed her enough.

Kyrylo didn't say he was worried about the cadre at the research station. It was an American facility, but all he could hope was that the scientists there weren't influenced by the politics back home. An extraction team was also on the plane flying to Argentina. Just in case.

The Cowens

The next morning, for the first time in years, James called in sick and rolled back into bed. At forty-six, he was getting too old to party until three am and drink the amount he had drunk. It wasn't healthy. It wasn't a good example for the kids. Someone was pounding nails into his head.

Kids.

He had misplaced his kids. Fekkin' lost'm. All three.

Running from room to room he accounted for them all, although for the life of him, he had no idea how or when they got there. Richie's room smelled suspiciously of beer, and Jamie still had all of his street clothes on, and they were filthy. There was a Chloe-sized lump under the duvet, and James didn't go check on her. She was getting too old for her Ded to go barging into her room, but she snored, so he knew she was there.

He took a moment of quiet time in the hall, leaning on Chloe's door to steady himself, his epic hangover not helped by his panic at losing his kids. Actually, the panic from the running around did the hangover a lot of good, and it was now the four-piece marimba band that had lodged behind his eyeballs and was even more epic. It was surely the reason he didn't see the elf standing next to him and why he tripped over her and fell flat on his arse.

"Lord James, yer lookin' a bit peely wally," she said, her hands on her hips and looking at him with a cross between bemusement and disgust.

"Sorry?"

"Hey, I'm just trying to talk your lingo – going native, I guess. You often switch back and forth between English and Unintelligible."

"Who the hell are you?"

"My name is Jean, and I'm your housekeeper. Two others and I will rotate in and out, but I'm the lead housekeeper. If you or the kids need anything, just yell *"Jean!"* And we'll take care of you."

"I have a housekeeper –"

"Yes, and a lovely lady she was. Mrs Willis has taken the offered pension and is now planning a holiday in Benidorm." Jean sighed. "But we will leave her to do that. We have other issues. You have an appointment with Lord Cadence and Kyrylo in London in an hour, and we need you to clean up a bit. You stink. If you could please get in the shower –"

"I can't be in fekkin London in an hour!"

"No need to swear, Lord James. Of course, you can. We will port you."

"Port?"

"Yes, port. It's an elf thing. Now, if you can get into the shower, we would very much appreciate it."

And with that she glowered at James in a way that made him decide that maybe he did need a shower after all.

An hour later, after his army speed field shower and gulping something strong and disgusting in a teacup that Jean insisted he drink, he was dressed in clean civvies and sitting in a very posh office in front of the Primaries and learning that he, James Cowen, was a lord, too.

"A lord. Me? You have to be –"

"Crazy? Off my rocker? Daft?" Lord Cadence looked over the rim of her teacup, and he could see her glittering eyes smiling.

"Yes, ma'am." Then he paused. He had just called the Queen of the Fairies crazy. And then thought, the hell with it and ploughed on. "I don't have anything that's 'lord' about me. No powers, no ears, no nothing."

"Your eyes are glowing right now." Kyrylo gave James an appraising look. "Pretty bright, really."

It took another half hour of convincing and explaining before James would even consider the notion. Then the real bombshell came.

"And all of your kids. All three. They're lords, too." Caddy turned serious now. "You have no idea how much of a blessing that is. Only two of mine are lords; the other two were human. None of Conary's kids are lords, only two of the grandkids. It's so hard to watch your children age."

Then Kyrylo explained the issues of growing up a lord and living in the human world and the decisions the Cowen family would have to make.

James was stunned. What do you say when you're told all three of your kids are magical creatures who'll live forever – if orcs don't eat them first? He had seen what an orc could do; he'd fought one at the awakening.

"I need to talk to my kids."

Caddy nodded. "I think you'll find they have already figured it out. They've all had trouble at school, from what Lord Farah has learnt. And they spent hours with lord kids and elves last night. That's why we insisted that you come in first thing this morning."

James glared at her, and he had no idea his eyes glowed bright blue. "It appears I'm the last to know what's going on with my own kids."

"Your children didn't want to worry you. They love you." Caddy put her teacup down. "It's hard being the weird one. That's the biggest issue every single lord who has grown up with humans has faced. Being the oddball. Sometimes it's teasing and bullying and saying mean things. Sometimes they kill you. You go and talk with your kids. Any decision you make about your future is up to you, and we'll support you fully. No money worries at all. None. Lord Jack will come to your house this evening for dinner to answer any questions, and he'll be your mentor."

Kyrylo added a few more words about military career decisions, and James was ported back home, where three anxious kids were waiting for him in the lounge. He discovered that they weren't worried about being lords at all; they thought it was really cool. They worried about what their dad would think about it and if he still loved them even though they weren't normal.

Once they were assured he would love them even if they were Oompa Loompas, James found out quite a few disturbing things – like the problems Richie was having with one of his college teachers and the pretty severe bullying Jamie was going through. Chloe seemed to be doing fine, but she had to walk Jamie home from school every day. That was more disturbing than the lord thing, really, and James felt really bad that he'd had no clue that his kids were having problems. He thought that after Lauren died, they coped extremely well, but it turned out that what they did really well was hide their problems from him.

Lords Jack and Alizah ported in for dinner, answered questions and talked well into the night until Jamie fell asleep on the sofa, and even Alizah was yawning. The next morning, Col James Cowen submitted his resignation and applied for terminal leave, citing family concerns. Jamie was immediately sent to Aelfeham House to board and go to school there with the plan to come home every weekend while things were sorted.

A day later, Lords James, Richard, and Chloe ported in from their home and started attending lord classes and a week later, self-defence training. The fifteen-minute porting commute from their family home wasn't a problem.

Sarah

When the jet pulled up to the gate at Heathrow the only people to disembark were the London-based crew. Somewhere over Ireland Sarah ported to Aelfeham House on her own, and it was loads of fun to walk into the breakfast room for lunch and sit down as if the intervening two weeks had never happened.

Oh, the squeals, the screams, the tears, the hugs!

Sarah was painfully thin and still recovering from the severe energy drain that came from the fighting and extreme porting between Scotland and the Antarctic research station. But overall, she was back to normal and didn't look like a skeleton any more. She didn't tell anyone about porting to the Void and her encounter there, and only Kyrylo asked why they couldn't feel her alive for a week. All she told him was that to her the missing time wasn't a week but just minutes, and that was true. He didn't ask her where she was during those minutes; he just looked at her for a long time and then nodded and left.

Alizah said later she had never seen so many elves in Aelfeham House in her life, and every one of them was there to see Lord Sarah. Malachi didn't give a shit if he was rude; he wasn't going to let any three-foot runts get in the way, and he waded through the elves and gave Sarah a massive, tearful bear hug.

He felt so bad that his Sarah had died (not really, thank goodness) on his watch and now was so happy he could hardly speak. Sarah couldn't talk much either because she had tears of her own, but she didn't blame anyone for the entire incident, especially Malachi, and she gave him a huge hug and a kiss back.

And that was the only kiss. When Lord James came up, she grinned and said that the last thing she saw was him shooting at the orc woman, and how did that turn out? She was so happy he came out of it okay, and she admired *Lord James* in his new redcoat uniform. She shook his hand and turned to talk to Vrt and the rest of the people crowding around. And he was fine with it!

She shook his hand.

Lord Sarah shook Lord James' fekkin hand!

The odds makers in the Safe Haven pubs were gobsmacked. The elves were absolutely sure these two had bonded. Maybe they hadn't completed the entire mating dance, but they were bonded. And now, after the trauma they had both gone through, they both acted like they were cousins or something.

Not even cousins – work colleagues from different departments. Their eyes didn't even glimmer when they looked at each other. Nothing.

Elves didn't know what to think, but there were a lot of things to gossip and wonder about with Lord Sarah's return, so the two lords' utter lack of sexual tension was just one of many topics.

The next morning, the housekeeping elves left Lord Sarah's bedroom disappointed. Her sheets were fine and no different from every other night since she first left Orlando and landed in the UK.

Richie

Richie Cowen started taking Ranger training as soon as he moved to Aelfeham House. He wasn't sure if he really wanted to be a Ranger and still had plans to enrol in a normal, human university eventually, but a gap year learning to be a lord was just fine.

He certainly could see the value of getting good at the self-defence part before he struck off on his own; besides, the guys and girls he trained with were cool. Several of them were human, and no one cared if he couldn't move a grain of sand or didn't have pointy ears. The elves just shrugged and said all that would come in good time and not to worry about it, so he didn't.

He had his own room at Aelfeham House, and while his dad insisted they eat dinner together at least twice a week, Richie was growing up and away as all young adults do. Chloe and Jamie seemed to be doing well – thriving, even – and were now teasing Ded to be allowed to stay at Aelfeham House full time. Neither saw any reason to go back to the old house when they had their own rooms in the school wing, but Ded was resistant. He didn't want to give up the house he and Mum had bought when he made Captain and started a family.

Richie and Chloe worried about Ded a lot. The man was really old, forty-six, and his auburn hair was painted with white streaks at the temples. Oh, he seemed healthy enough, and now that they knew he was a lord and not susceptible to diseases like Mum's cancer, it looked like he could go on for a while. They worried about who was going to take care of him when they grew up and moved away, and they wondered if he was lonely. At least he didn't have to worry about sex, not at his age.

The teenagers dated, and they had friends, both human and now lord. But who did Ded hang out with? No one other than Unc Ham. Hamish McGinnis was a guy Ded had known since he was a cadet, and they'd more or less had parallel careers. Yes, there were times they were assigned to different posts and jobs, but sooner or later, they would move back to the same office and pick up where they left off. McGinnis had a brief "practise marriage" and a loud, messy divorce, and after Lauren's death the old friends just became bachelor buddies who complained about their subordinates, moaned about the generals, watched rugby, drank beer, and farted.

At least, Chloe pointed out, McGinnis *dated*. The older two were well aware that their father wasn't looking to upset their little family by bringing in a stranger and during the first couple of years, they appreciated his reticence. Losing Mum was too hard and too raw a wound to allow someone in who had their own issues and might not be right for Ded. None of the kids wanted a mum substitute; they just wanted a friend for their dad – the way Mum had been a friend.

Ded had never even asked anyone out for a coffee, not that they knew. The kids suggested a couple of times that he ask this pretty neighbour or that clever teacher out and said a date with a nice lady was perfectly okay with them, but then Ded would just explode and go "full on Scot" if they said anything. The more upset he got, the more backcountry highland his accent became, until no one who lived in the civilised world could make heads or tails of what he was saying.

But the kids were moving on, and now Richie was moving out. Ded, however, was Ded, and he wasn't moving anywhere.

Richie knew that Ded and Lord Sarah had fought the kidnapper orcs when they thought she had died, and the kids had all worried a lot when he went into that black depression while she was lost. The old guy had taken it all very hard, and then when he heard she re-emerged, he went off in the other direction and was (uncharacteristically) hysterically happy. Then the next day, they found out they were all lords, and that just blew everything out of the water. Lord Sarah was pushed out of the kids' minds totally. They had never met her, never talked to her, and had no idea what she looked like. Since Ded didn't talk about her, she wasn't even a blip on their radar.

So when Lord Tuân walked in at the end of PT one morning and told the trainee Rangers that Lords Sarah and Vrt were going to have a bit of pike practice and they were going to watch, Richie was happy to follow the order to observe the experts. Very happy. What healthy, heterosexual young man wouldn't want to go watch Lord Vrt do anything? He'd watch her sort laundry if he were allowed. All the boys had a crush on Lord Vrt. And as an added bonus, he'd finally see this Lord Sarah, the Elemental Warrior Lord.

The trainees ran over to the practice arena and lined up around the iron pipe fence that made a roughly circular fighting arena. He wondered what a Warrior Lord woman would look like, and when they got there, Lord Sarah wasn't at all what he'd imagined. In his imagination, she was muscular and stocky, a fierce Amazon. And butch. Weren't all women warriors butch?

In reality, she was a bit shorter than Vrt and quite a bit curvier, and while she was not as ethereal or as beautiful as the Angel of Death, Lord Sarah was still very attractive with full, smiling lips, a long, straight nose, and wide, amused eyes. She had the most gorgeous ears – tall, mobile, and beautifully shaped. It was hard not to look at them.

The women smiled and waved to the trainees and then did a few stretches and showed off a bit, throwing the heavy pikes high into the air and catching them like batons, giggling and calling to each other, and it was obvious to all that they were good friends. When Victor was ready and rang the bell to start the round, they squared off, the giggling and joking stopped, and suddenly they were all business.

Richie thought they would have some formal, choreographed dance as their pike practise like the Ranger trainees did. But no. At some unseen signal, the lords suddenly flew at each other with the rage of the Furies, the pikes banging against each other with bone-jarring intensity and moving so fast they were a blur. They used the pikes as levers, as poles to balance and spin from, as bats, as anything that would give them an advantage in their frenzied assault. If either woman had misstepped or ducked a second too slowly, the damage would have been fatal, but they were so fast, and they seemed to know what the other would do before they did it. Neither held back, and neither gave quarter; they were out to kill. Then, as suddenly as it had started, it was over, and the two combatants froze in place with Lord Sarah holding her pike to Lord Vrt's neck. A gentle tap, and she won the point.

There were two more equally furious rounds, and Vrt won both of those, so she won the day, two to one.

When it was over, both women were panting like racehorses, and sweat dripped down their backs. They stood, arm in arm, while Victor critiqued the rounds and they talked about the battles. Then they had a few minutes of formal, choreographed practice to correct mistakes before they walked over to the trainees and chatted a bit, smiling at their awed compliments and showing the Rangers some of their moves in slow motion so they could learn.

When Richie told them his name, Lord Sarah looked at him and grinned. "Oh, so you're Lord James' son! How nice to meet you! Your father is a very impressive man, and I'm sure you're proud of him. Your whole family is going to be a great addition to the clan, and if you're half as brave as he is, I expect great things out of you."

All Richie could do was grin back and enjoy the compliments for his dad. After the women walked away, Lord Tuân turned to him, confused. "You've never met her before? I thought Lord Sarah and your dad were bonded."

"Bonded? My old man?" And he laughed. "No, we can't even get him to go on a date!"

Tuân shrugged and smiled. "And that's what I get for listening to gossip! Boy, was that wrong!"

Ded and Lord Sarah? That was brilliant – he'd have to tell Chloe as soon as he could. They'd have a good laugh over that one.

Chloe and Richie

Chloe howled with laughter. Richie always told a good story, and with the retelling, Lord Sarah became prettier and prettier and more and more awesome, and the idea that their old dad had become bonded to such a woman he barely knew was hysterical.

Yeah, Ded was great, and you don't get to be a colonel in the Army if you're not clever, but – as Richie said to Chloe – he was *Ded*. Grumpy, goofy, loving, worried, old, grey-haired, broken-down gutties with holes in them, soft in the middle, dad-bod, kilt-wearing, Scottish Jew Ded. The man who might be brave on the battlefield but was a coward when it came to asking a woman out to Starbucks for a coffee. Ded.

Everyone had to admit it; Ded was lovely, but he was weird. Grandma and Grandpa were London-born Jewish hippies who moved to middle-of-nowhere Scotland, where land was cheap and set up an organic farm raising kosher beef cattle. Ded, being Ded, set his life course 180 degrees away from that and walked into an Army enlistment office at sixteen, passed some tests, and was sent to a military academy.

Being Jewish, Scottish, and rural poor, he struggled to fit into the rigid class structure of the Royal Army, but he did. No one ever said that James

Cowen wasn't clever and adaptable. He had a great head for languages, and if you heard him in the officers' mess speaking with his cut-glass Received Pronunciation accent, you'd never know of his rural Scottish roots. He could even be charming when he put his mind to it.

But the more they talked about how funny it was that anyone would think their dad was bonded – married in the human world – to an Elemental Warrior goddess, the more Chloe started to wonder.

"I mean, Ded is really cool! He's a brill dad –" She looked at Richie, suddenly serious. "Doesn't he deserve the best? I mean, why shouldn't he go out with Lord Sarah? What's really so stupid about it? They're both lords, and he might be a new one, but that doesn't matter, does it? Is she bonded to someone else?"

Richie had no clue. He had just seen her for the first time today, and Tuân thought she was bonded to Ded, so probably she wasn't bonded to anyone else.

Chloe chewed her lip, thoughtful. She would check into this. Her Ded needed someone, and there was no reason not to aim high. That's what he always told them anyway.

Chloe

Chloe needed information, and she didn't have to think long and hard about who to ask. Talking to the principals, her dad and the mysterious Lord Sarah was out of the question, of course, and she didn't want to talk to another lord. The lord kids wouldn't know anything, and the older ones would say that the other lords' personal lives weren't any of her business. Of course, they were wrong; her dad's love life was most certainly her business, but being right wouldn't get her anywhere.

That left elves, and elves loved to gossip. She'd already figured that out with Jean, who was as chatty as she was lovely. And so she strolled into the kitchen after she was back from school, ever so casually, and hopped up on a stool and let the elf bring her a plate of cookies and a big glass of milk.

"So, how was your day, dear?" And with that, they were off to the races. Her day was fine, school was great, and Richie had a really interesting story to tell about seeing Lord Sarah and Vrt practise fighting with poles. Then she mentioned what Lord Tuân said.

"Jean, why do people think that Lord Sarah and Ded are bonded? They don't even talk to one another!"

Jean hauled herself up on the other stool and thoughtfully ate a cookie. In her tiny hands, it appeared the size of a dinner plate.

"We elves think they've bonded. When lords bond, their smell changes. It matches. They also lose interest in everyone else – they actually can't smell the sexy bits of another lord. Their scent only works on each other. Elves are the same way, so we know how this goes. We can smell that your dad and Lord Sarah have the same smell, and they're not looking for other mates, so it looks to us like they're bonded. But they're not frustrated and longing for each other, not from what we can see, so they're not lovesick. If they are, they're hiding it really well. It's a puzzle."

"I don't see how they bonded if they've never been alone –"

Jean laughed and laughed. "Oh, dear child, bonding and sex are two different things! You can bonk, and you can bond, and when they both happen at the same time, it's wonderful. But you can bonk without bonding, and you can bond without bonking!"

Wiping her eyes and chuckling, the elf continued. This was an interesting subject!

"I think Lord Sarah got a good whiff of your dad the first time she met him. He wasn't cleaning up the way the lords are taught to do. I'm not saying your dad was dirty, but one five-minute shower a day isn't enough for an unbonded lord, not unless he's trying to snag a woman. So she met him, and he was not only right, he was ripe, and that started the process. She didn't even have to know his name.

"We elves are pretty sure that's what happened because she kept asking the other lords to keep him away, but then she would end up going up and talking to him. She couldn't help herself, and she probably thought she had it all under control."

Chloe looked at her plate. "But Ded isn't bonded to her."

"Oh no, he must be. They smell the same. Something happened somewhere that hit him with her scent, and he physically changed. The only time we know of was when they were in that battle with the orcs stealing the elves. She was probably sweating like a racehorse then, and she sure wasn't in control of her scent."

Jean looked at Chloe and smiled to herself. She wondered if she should place a bet at the Dirty Hen in Safe Haven. Their board always had good odds.

"They're bonded and don't know it. Or they know it, and they don't think the other likes them. Or maybe they don't know each other well enough to trust and love. Your dad doesn't seem the least bit interested."

"No, he's afraid of girls, I think."

"Oh, I don't think your dad is afraid of anyone but himself. He's certainly out of practice with girls,

I'll give you that. But if he's bonded, there's only one girl he needs to practise on."

Chloe nodded. She thanked Jean for the cookies and left to do her homework. Some of it even had to do with school.

Chloe

So Ded needed to have some time with Lord Sarah so he could have some girl practise and learn to talk to one again. If they weren't talking then they couldn't find out if they were really made for each other, so the problem was getting them in the same room so they could talk.

It was like spotting a cute boy you see across the campus but don't have any classes with. First, you looked over his mates to see if he hung out with idiots. Then you found out a bit about him using the Girlfriend Spy Network, and if he wasn't a total loser, you started getting into his face space.

Chloe knew how that worked; basically, you "accidentally" bump into the cute guy in the hall and make sure you both have lunch at the same time. You get friends to pass notes and get you added to his WhatsApp. You make sure you are available if a bunch of mates are going to the cinema. There were ways, and obviously poor, clueless Ded didn't know any of them.

She looked around the house. Ded wasn't going to move to Aelfeham House, or so he said. That meant Lord Sarah would have to come here if they were going to manage some F2F time that didn't have the pressure of a real date. Maybe Richie could invite her to dinner to talk about the Rangers or something. The elves kept the place clean, so that wasn't a problem. The problem was Mum.

One of the last things Mum had said to the kids was that they weren't supposed to get in the way if their Ded started dating again. She'd made them promise. She'd said that he was too young (Mum was always sweet that way) to live alone forever and that she was sure he'd find someone nice, so don't get in the way; it wasn't disloyal to her. Everyone could love more than one person. Just like she could love three kids who all came at different times, Ded could love another wife when one showed up and not forget Mum. She'd told them all that over and over and even wrote it in her last secret letter to each of them.

Mum died, but she never left. Mum was everywhere. Her photo was on every surface, every wall; in every nook and cranny there was a reminder of Mum. Chloe could almost cry. You couldn't sit on the sofa without squashing the needlepoint "World's Best Mum" pillow. There was even a framed picture of the family at the beach on the wall of the bathroom. It was like going to a guy's locker and finding it plastered with pics of his old girlfriend.

If she went to Ded and said they needed to thin the photos of Mum out a bit he'd go full Scot on her, and she knew it. He wouldn't listen to any of the kids on that score. It would have to be someone a bit more neutral, and the only person Ded would listen to would be McGinnis.

But would he listen to McGinnis?

Well, all she could do was find out.

Hamish

When Hamish McGinnis received the text from Chloe that she would like to talk (PRIVATE! NO DAD!!!! *multiple emojis*) to him on the phone, he called back in five minutes. He had known the child since she was a baby, and he relished the "naughty uncle" role he had with all three of the kids. But for her to call him that meant something important was up, and with the massive upheavals in their lives in the last month, he was worried. Learning you weren't human must be a shock.

After establishing that she and the boys were fine, McGinnis asked her directly why she had called.

Chloe sighed. "Uncle Ham, it's Ded. Look, we kids are all fine with the lord thing. It's brill, really, but Ded is – well, he's clinging on. I know he quit the

Army, and that's a big deal for him, but it's time we moved on in other ways, I think."

"What do you mean?" Privately, Hamish agreed with the "moving on" bit. Jamie Sr. had needed to move on from Lauren a good two years ago. The woman had been lovely, wonderful, perfect – but she was also dead. And Jamie was not.

"Well, the boys and I want to live at Aelfeham House. They'd give us our own flat there, so we'll still be a family, but Ded won't leave because this is his and Mum's house. But if he won't move, maybe we could bring people here. But –"

"But what?"

Chloe tried to phrase this delicately. She was worried about how this would get back to Ded. "It's just between you and me, Unc Ham – *please*. But let's say Ded wanted to date one of the lords, and he brought her over here. Like for a family bar-b-que or something –"

"And she saw the living shrine dedicated to your mother that you guys live in? Yeah, that would turn any woman off, lord or not."

Chloe let out a big breath, relieved. Good ol' Unc Ham got it.

"He won't listen to us. Mum would be fine with all the photos and such gone; she'd probably think it's all creepy. But it's time to move on, Unc. Maybe you can talk to Ded? If he won't give up the house and put it all in storage, maybe we can clean it out a bit?"

"Luv, I'll try." And with a few more assurances that the kids were all doing fine, Hamish signed off.

He thought about it for a while and then went to the computer and looked up the rugby fixtures. There must be a game on the telly this weekend that they both desperately wanted to see. There always was.

Chloe went to bed that night quite happy with her day. She had revised two English papers, found out more about bonding and bonking, and had a good talk with Unc Ham. Tomorrow she had a Lord Class on Elf Clan Structure, A levels Biology, and World History, and she would try to track down the elusive Lord Sarah and accidentally bump into her in the hall.

If this woman was her bond-mother, it was time she met her.

Chloe and Sarah

After PT, Chloe went back to her Aelfeham House room to shower and put on her uniform for her Lord Class.

It was a very pretty, grown-up room and made her old bedroom in Catterick look a bit tatty. She wished she could stay in it all the time and hang out with the guys after classes instead of going back to the old house. Her old bedroom hadn't been updated for over seven years now, and until she was given this new bedroom she hadn't noticed. But really, did a sixteen-year-old still need a Frozen-themed bedroom? When the housekeeper elf first showed her the room, Chloe was as pleased as she could be and noticed only one framed family photo on the bookshelf, which was perfect. And she had her very own bathroom. Even more perfect.

On her way to breakfast in the Youth Breakfast Room, she walked down to reception and asked the lady at the desk if she knew where Lord Sarah was and was helpfully given a copy of the lord's schedule. Just to be thorough, she also asked for a copy of Ded's schedule. The receptionist didn't seem to think it was the least bit odd that Chloe was asking; after all, everyone was busy. Then she showed Chloe how to access everyone's schedules on her phone and told her that if anything was whited out that time was private;

otherwise it was all an open book. *That* was really useful.

Over breakfast, she compared the two lords' schedules. There was no overlap. Lord Sarah did Important Things, blocked out as AM Meeting- LE256 (for London Embassy) and AM Meeting- L Kyrylo/ Malachi. She had time blocked out for training in the afternoon, for training with Small Arms and H2H (hand-to-hand), along with time blocked out for showers, eating, and "free". There wasn't much free time at all. Her day started at five and ended at five.

Ded had PT, Lord Class, and H2H in the morning, and all afternoon he was scheduled to be with Mr Hadid in Lowestoft, along with meals and showers scattered in there, and then back home to Catterick for dinner with the kids.

Chloe frowned. How were they going to meet and have a chat when they weren't even in the same county? How was Chloe going to accidentally-on-purpose bump into Lord Sarah?

She went to Lord Class, where she bumped into Ded for an hour, but that wasn't going to do either of them any good. It was hard to concentrate on elf clan structures and organisation when she couldn't even get her own clan organised.

It took three days before Chloe could accidentally-on-purpose bump into Sarah. At the end of her PT, she noticed that Lords Vrt and Sarah had a Krav Maga combat session scheduled, and so she sneaked out early and went to the practice arena they were setting up. Anyone could come and watch, and there were a few of the soldier elves standing around waiting to watch and make bets. She was the only girl and the only lord watching, but no one said anything.

She was gobsmacked at the speed, power, and sheer violence of the two women as they battled. Richie had tried to describe the pike fighting, but the most he could say was "awesome" over and over.

Valkyries, angels, Amazons – whatever they were – they were beautiful as they danced the line between life and death. For a few exhilarating minutes, the sound faded away, and it was just the two furious women dancing a ballet of annihilation.

And then Chloe was back in the real world. The elves hooted and hollered and loudly made side bets. It seemed that the crowd was evenly divided between the Lord Sarah side and the Lord Vrt side. This time, Lord Sarah won the day, and when it was all done the women were again fast friends.

"They're pretty good, aren't they?"

Chloe spun around, and behind her were Lord Conary and Lord Malachi. Both came up and leaned on the metal fence.

"Yes, sir, but that's a bit of an understatement." Chloe turned back to watch Victor run them through a couple of practise moves he felt needed fine-tuning. "Can you fight like that, too?"

Conary laughed. "Oh, hell no. My speciality during a fight is to disappear!" Malachi snorted. "Now, my dear friend Lord Malachi, he can give the women a run for their money."

Vrt saw her bond-man, and the two women walked up, all smiles and sweat. She gave him a kiss and asked what had brought the men here.

"We had a few minutes to kill, and since we were in the killing mood, we thought we'd have a look at you two killing each other. And this lovely young lady asked if I could fight like you, which did my ego a world of good."

"Shhhh – we don't talk about Conary's fighting techniques. They are –" started Vrt.

" – eclectic," finished Sarah.

"Oh, definitely unusual. Maybe even eccentric." That came from Malachi.

Conary looked pained. "I'm being dissed in front of impressionable youth." He turned to Chloe. "By the way, who are you? You look familiar, but then all you teens look familiar."

"I'm Chloe Cowen, Lord James' daughter."

Sarah grinned, obviously happy to see the girl. "Ah, now I've met two out of three! How wonderful! So, to what do we owe the pleasure of your visit today?"

Chloe didn't know she was going to say it and immediately regretted it once it popped out of her mouth.

"I want to learn to fight like you and Lord Vrt."

The four lords all looked at Chloe and fell silent. Chloe knew that the lords around her were probably the most deadly of the entire lord clan. She hadn't been around a long time, but she'd heard stories. She didn't blink; she didn't say anything; she just kept eye contact with Lord Sarah and held her breath.

Lord Sarah's eyes glinted, and she cocked her head.

"I can arrange that."

McGinnis

The game was between New Zealand and Ireland, both good sides. Hamish flipped a coin and won the toss, so he chose Ireland, leaving Jamie to cheer for New Zealand, whom he didn't like.

A good start.

The elves had put out a very nice spread on the coffee table, and if Hamish could envy his friend one thing, it was the elves. Oh, to be a bloody lord and have elves waiting on your hand and foot! The little buggers actually seemed to like Jamie. And they were pretty. Gawds, they were gorgeous, the women at least. The man elf was a stocky, bearded bulldog who didn't take shite from anyone, especially the lord's human friend. The women, though, they were class.

Once Lord James and his half-wit pet human were fed, watered, and carefully positioned on the sofa to watch the match, Jean and Alex ported out to wherever home was and left the beautiful, but tragically much too tiny, Annabelle sitting in the corner knitting, just in case they needed anything important like another beer.

Hamish sighed. Absolute class.

Little Jamie wandered down for a few minutes, got bored with the pre-game nonsense, piled up a big plate, and left. Ham didn't know where the other two were. Probably at Aelfeham House with their mates.

"So, how is the lord thing going?"

Jamie perked up. It was working out. He'd only left the Army because of the danger his human lifestyle put the kids in, and he'd really feared it was the end of his professional life, which he loved. But after a few days with Rashid Hadid, he was offered a role in the RumLot Security organisation. They needed another Rashid/Jameson type to work under Kyrylo, and RumLot Security was a massive, multinational organisation. Kyrylo and Caddy wanted a lord at that level (humans, after all, were fragile creatures), and from what James could see, the position would put a Brigadier General slot to shame. A dream job. As soon as his lord classes were over he would be a bluecoat and shadow Hadid and Jameson for six months each; then they'd figure out a new command structure.

Hamish grinned. He was genuinely happy for his old pal and knew if he ever left the RA, he'd have a good job somewhere interesting. Gawd, choosing that seat at Sandhurst was the best fucking decision he'd ever made in his life. And to think he almost gave up smoking.

"That's really, really good. I know it's all up in the air now, but those RumLot people will move you, and the kids tell me they're doing great at Aelfeham House."

"Don't be daft. I'm not moving."

Hamish took a drink of his beer and watched the game.

"Where's Chloe?"

"She's with mates at Aelfeham House. They're having a movie night."

"And Richie?"

"Aelfeham House."

Hamish didn't say anything. Just sipped on his beer.

"And little Jamie, he's up in his room texting or playing games online with his friends at Aelfeham House?"

James glared at him, and Hamish could see the telltale glow that told everyone this man was a lord. It was funny; he hadn't noticed it before, but then he'd never looked deep into Jamie's eyes; he had no desire to date the man. He'd just thought his friend had bright blue eyes that caught the light.

"Tell me, if Lauren were here, you'd still be a lord, wouldn't you? Your kids would still have the magic genes, wouldn't they? What would she say about keeping this house?"

"Ah dinnae ken."

"Oh, you ken. You ken good. You know what she'd say. She'd say, Jamie, you tube, this place is just bricks. You're not married to bricks. Take care of yourself and the kids. That's what she'd say."

"That's enough, Hamish."

Ham shrugged. He knew his friend, and he'd known him longer than anyone, even Lauren. If he had a brother, it would be Jamie. He'd let Jamie stew a bit. Besides, the game was getting interesting.

James

Chloe went into Ranger training. Her dad raised an eyebrow, but he didn't say no – mostly because he was sure she'd drop out in the first week.

But he also let her stay full-time at Aelfeham House as long as she was in training so she could make the early morning classes and then have a place to crash when she dragged herself home at night. Yeah, the port to and from Catterick was only fifteen minutes, but James wasn't going to have Chloe come up later when she washed out and say he didn't support her.

This meant that it was just the two Jamies at the old house, which started to get pretty lonely, especially when younger Jamie started dropping broad hints that he would much rather stay at the boarding school even on weekends. Maybe, he asked James, you can stay at Aelfeham House on the weekends, too? Then he could hang out with his friends.

By then, James knew that Jamie hadn't had any friends for the last two years, and now he had good ones, just not where he lived. And he was getting to the age where mates were starting to edge out parents.

At the end of the first week, James asked Chloe how the Ranger training was going and said there was no shame in putting it off and moving back home. None at all. Maybe it would be better to wait a couple of years and try again; she was awfully young. He said this as she was grimly wrapping up her ankle in an attempt to keep a bad scrape clean.

"Ded, you signed up in the Army when you were sixteen. I'm not going to quit. I'm pure dead brilliant."

What could he say to that?

Chloe survived the first week and then the second. Richie told James she was doing really well and that either Lord Sarah or Lord Vrt came to check on her almost every day.

Chloe was the one he'd worried about the least after Lauren died; James always considered Chloe the most placid of his children, but here she was, full of surprises. It seemed that the easygoing middle child who never caused any worries had a core of steel in her spine.

When James finished the last module of his Lord Classes he found a blue uniform hanging on the back of the bedroom door the next morning along with instructions on his phone to shadow Rashid for the next six months.

James stood in his new blue uniform in the kitchen with a cup of tea, and it was very quiet. Dead quiet. Lauren had loved this kitchen so much; it had meant family to her. And like he did most mornings, he looked at the wall of family photos she had framed and mounted over the kitchen table. For three years, she'd watched over them every morning as all four of them had come to terms with her death, grew up, and moved on. Now the kids were gone, and so was Lauren.

The house felt empty. It was just a pile of bricks, after all.

James looked at his watch; it was time to go.

He called for Jean and asked the elf to send his personal stuff to the flat at Aelfeham House, and he thanked her for the excellent care she, Alex, and Annabelle had given to him and his family. But he wouldn't be needing them any more.

"It was a pleasure, Lord James. Really, it was. Do you want the house mothballed or sold? I can do whatever you want."

It took a minute, but he choked it out. "Put it up for sale. A house needs a family to live in it, I think."

The elf nodded and agreed.

A team of elves packed up the house and put everything in storage. It only took them a day. The house was sold three days later to a sweet couple who were pregnant with their second baby and needed the room. It was a lovely house, and they were thrilled. It had good bones.

James told Chloe and Richie that he and Jamie were now living at his flat at Aelfeham House, and he expected them to have dinner with him at least twice a week. They were happy now, he could tell, and that was all that mattered.

Chloe and Sarah

Victor pushed Chloe hard, but then that was the point. The trainee Ranger gets pushed right to the breaking point, and then the new Ranger learns in their tired bones that they could do so much more than they ever thought they could, and that builds the foundation for further growth. It really didn't matter if one trainee could do fifty press-ups and the next could do one hundred. It mattered that they pushed to their personal limit and developed the mental capacity and confidence to leap to the next level. Stressing the tree produced stronger growth, and that was the same for humans, elves, and lords. Victor was the master of stress.

The elf was pretty sure Chloe would do fine, and he was quite happy with starting her at sixteen. The elves started comparatively young, too, and Victor could adjust his regime for young bodies and growth spurts. Like Wendell, Chloe started at a low level and gave the impression of being soft, but she was stubborn and didn't like being told no, which in some circumstances would be characterised as "determined" and in others would be "goddamn mulish". He privately thought she would do better than her brother, but he only said that to his bond-wife.

Would she end up as a Warrior Lord? It was much, much too early to say. A lord needed to be fully ripened and have their abilities to really get to that Warrior stage, and Chloe had decades to go. But like Tuân, she would be offered the training when the time was right and if she still wanted it.

Lords Sarah and Vrt never interfered, but they watched. Occasionally, if Chloe seemed down or was struggling, they would offer a kind word or even a quickie demonstration, which they always generously gave to any of the trainee Rangers who were around.

But they both understood the power of stress. As Vrt once said to Sarah, their horrible early lives made them stronger lords, and it was so much better for Chloe to have her stress inflicted in training in a controlled, neutral way by Victor than to have to endure the crushing mental agonies she and Sarah had gone through.

Sarah and Chloe became friends. Chloe was in awe of the two lords, and there was a lot of hero-worship there. You can't be real friends with someone you think is out of your league, not to mention the age and experience differences between the two, but like the mentoring relationship between Caddy and Ellen that slowly grew into a firm family bond, Sarah and Chloe were walking down that same path.

They laughed a lot, Chloe learned a lot, and both got comfortable with the knowledge that the other liked them a lot. Chloe trusted Sarah with her heart. It took a bit more time for Sarah to return the feelings; her rocky relationship, to put it mildly, with Lisa coloured her attitude to a true mother/daughter bond, but slowly the bond grew despite Sarah's reticence.

It was that new and fragile family bond that alerted Sarah that something in Chloe's life had turned sour. She knew it wasn't the training as that was going as it should, and Chloe seemed happy with her morning PT and afternoon classes. But there was a cloud in the Chloe-verse, a bit of forced cheerfulness that didn't strike Sarah as true.

Was something with her family bothering her? Her father was spending a lot of time in Lowestoft now with his new job. Did she miss him? Her brothers? Chloe always worried about them more than she should, but they seemed content with their new lives, too. A boy? Was the entire lord, moving house, re-aligning of her family just too much, too fast?

When an unusually dispirited Chloe left training one morning to make her way to breakfast, Sarah watched her walk away and thought that it was time she found out what was going on with the girl.

Sarah found her in the horse barn, brushing down one of the big Suffolk Punches, a lovely and hugely pregnant mare named Hillary Farm. The elves or the human stablehands would have done that, but Sarah knew the comfort of work, and she didn't interrupt Chloe; instead, she walked to the corner of the stall, lowered herself awkwardly on a too-low stool, and unbuckled her belt.

"Y'know, this sabre is dramatic and bad-ass, and I have to wear it, but it does get in the way sometimes."

Chloe didn't say anything; she just kept brushing.

"You're unhappy."

Chloe paused, just a second. There was no point in saying no; she couldn't lie to Sarah.

"I'll be okay. I'll get over it. There's nothing you can do anyway."

The lord sighed. You can have great power and still be powerless, and whatever was bothering this sixteen-year-old was most likely out of her power to make better. That was life.

"Probably not. But I can listen, and if I'm not the right person, maybe you have a friend who –"

Chloe spun around, her face scrunched into tears. "I don't have any friends! My so-called friends don't want anything to do with me any more."

Sarah jumped over to hug the girl, the sabre falling to the floor. "Then they're idiots. Why? What happened?"

And then it was all tears, and Chloe and Sarah sank into the clean hay of the stall, and the woman hugged and rocked the girl and listened to her heart break.

Chloe had two inseparable girlfriends from her old school, Maeve and Liddy, and like many teenage girls, they were as close as sisters. The crux of it was that her friends didn't want to be friends with a lord; they were jealous and had ghosted her. And to add insult to injury, Liddy was now dating a boy who Chloe had long fancied. The teenager had lost her social anchor at her old school and hadn't had time to replace it in her much tinier new school and was now alone and adrift between the two.

What could Sarah say? That this was normal teenage stuff, and Chloe would get over it, everyone always does? That wouldn't be helpful or comforting. So she just hugged her and told Chloe she was a wonderful, beautiful girl, and her friends were jealous idiots who would one day realise how hurtful they were.

"You're a lord, and that's a great gift, sweetheart, but every gift has a price. I guess your price is a wall between you and your friends. Can the wall be broken down? Would you forgive them if they came back to you?"

Chloe sniffed and wiped her eyes. "I don't know. They've been pretty mean."

"You have two choices. You can send them a text and say that you are what you are and can't change that, but you will always love them, and if they want to be friends again, you're around. But don't be a doormat, Chloe. I know from experience that doesn't help. They need to love you for who you are and on your terms, not theirs. Or you can be sad for a day or two and move on. Make new friends here with kids who are like you and love you for being the wonderful Chloe. That's a choice only you can make."

"What would you do?"

"Both. You can do both, really. Send them a text, and then leave them to stew over it, and in the meantime, move on. They have broken your trust, and that can only be patched over, not disappeared. Maybe y'all can be stronger friends for this. Maybe it's the end of an era, and you'll move on. But you're a wonderful, sweet girl, and you'll make new friends, I know it."

"Did your friends dump you when they found out you were a lord?"

Sarah laughed and hugged Chloe. "Oh, child, my life before I came here was pure, unadulterated misery. My old life didn't dump me; I dumped it. I had a couple of girlfriends, and only one is still in contact with me, and now it's just a call now and then. We lead separate lives, but, y'know, she loves me and told me for years to leave my miserable marriage, and now she's very happy for me. That's a *real* friend. They love you for who you are, the good with the bad. But the friends I have made here! Oh my, they are precious, too. I wouldn't go back for the world."

"Well, Liddy didn't turn out to be a real friend but a back-stabber. How could she date Nicky? I like Nicky, and she knows it."

"Well, she isn't loyal, that's true. But Chloe, Nicky has agency, too. He has a vote in who he dates. It's not all Liddy. Are you sincerely broken-hearted over Nicky not liking you best, or is the hurt really that Liddy saw an opening after you left and took it?"

Chloe thought for a minute. "Liddy. If Nicky went out with someone else, it wouldn't hurt so much."

"Liddy moved on. You had left, you and Nicky weren't a pair, and from what she could see, you'll never come back. She sees Nicky probably every day, and they have an attraction, and they didn't fight it. It really wasn't about you in the end. Let's say you went back, and Liddy and Nicky broke up; would you still want him?"

"Probably not." Chloe sniffled and smiled ruefully to herself. "I guess I'm just being a bitch. A dog in the manger thing. Maybe Liddy ghosted me because she knew I liked Nicky and she felt bad." Sarah smiled at the flash of maturity.

"We're lords, baby, and that means *different,* and you weren't brought up to understand how lords look at love and lust. You were brought up human, but they have their own ways. Nicky and Liddy will date, and maybe it will be intense and last a long time, or not. Humans flit from lover to lover. You will find men who will be fun to date, but one day you'll walk into a room and someone's special scent will hit you like a truck, and he'll steal your heart. There's no point in fighting who we are, and there's no point in trying to be human. Nicky and Liddy will move on, together or apart, and I think you're moving on, too."

"Yeah, I guess so." Chloe stood up, and Sarah followed. "I need to blow my nose." She hugged Sarah, and they walked to the lav to look for tissue. "Thanks, Sarah. I'll be okay."

Then she turned to Sarah, and a wistful expression flashed across her face. "I wish you and Ded had hooked up. Everyone thought you did, y'know."

Sarah froze. Instead of looking at Chloe, she put her sabre back on and fiddled with the buckle. "Your dad and I are friends, but he doesn't love me. I'm not the sort of woman men fall in love with. That's just the way it is and the way it's always been."

"Oh, Sarah – that can't be true. I heard you were married once! You had kids! He must have fallen in love with you!"

The lord's eyes glowed, and she threw Chloe a tight smile.

"It was an arranged marriage, and I had thirty horrible years married to an orc, and with him I had three horrible orc children. So, no, not a lot of love in that family."

She didn't say that sex and love were two different things and that a woman didn't have to consent to sex if the man was determined enough. All three of Sarah's children had been conceived through rape, and that was just a brutal fact.

"An arranged marriage? In the US? Isn't that illegal?" Chloe was shocked.

Sarah leaned against the door of the lavatory and blew her nose, happy to leave the subject of James. She didn't want to talk about Chloe's dad, not at all.

"Oh no, not illegal if everyone is a consenting adult and agrees. I was over thirty when I married. My family was Jewish, what the goy call ultra-orthodox. I was the only girl, and I had one younger brother, and we had good, observant parents who loved us. I worked in my dad's electronics firm, and my brother was going to take it over. It was important to my family that I marry someone who could be an asset to the business and take my place in the firm when I left to be a wife, and they wanted to find the perfect boy. Well, they were very picky, and I was very ugly – not a good combination – and time passed, and I essentially aged out of the marriage market."

Sarah looked at the ground, remembering those humiliating meetings with the few men the matchmaker had found with an electronics background and who her parents deemed good enough for their beloved daughter.

Two families awkwardly sitting and having a nice, painfully curated lunch; two young people meeting for the first time and chatting; one hopeful, the other disappointed in the tense, dumpy, plain girl with the disgusting skin and fierce eyes. Of course, the acne flared up with stress, and there was nothing more stressful than the first time meeting a new prospect.

"When I was twenty-eight, my mother and brother died in a car accident. That left my dad and me to carry on with the business, and I took care of him, too. It takes a lot of adjusting for us 'leftovers' when the mom dies; you know that yourself. Anyway, a couple of years passed, and I was really, really old for a new bride. Then, unknown to me, Papa got lung cancer, and, again unknown to me, decided to find me a husband so I wouldn't be alone after he died.

He called the *shadchanit*, and she found a man who was good in the electronics field and didn't mind an old, ugly wife with a nice little business and a fat dowry. Absolutely the worst person for me, but hey, I didn't know it at the time and neither did my Papa. Papa thought he had stumbled on a gem. He was so happy he had taken care of me." Sarah's voice broke, remembering her father's joy when he'd told her about Leo. Her Papa had loved her so much.

"Leo and I met a couple of times, and he was very nice. The rabbi told me I wasn't getting any younger, and it was not right for me to be a celibate old maid, and of course, he was right. Celibacy is not the Jewish way, and I was, and am, observant. So I got married. Papa died four months later, and I was already pregnant. I lived in my personal hell until my youngest graduated from university, and then I walked away.

And that was my life, Chloe, until I found this place. So no, I never had a man who loved me, not in a romantic way, and I probably never will. But I'm so much happier now with what I have been given. I have been blessed beyond my wildest dreams. I'll never go back."

Chloe sniffled. "I don't want you to go back. We love you. And you're not ugly! Why would anyone say that? That's mean."

Sarah hugged her, and they started their walk back to the main house.

"I love you, too, sweetheart. You are my star, really, you are. And if you don't think I'm as plain as an old boot, that's extremely sweet of you. At least the acne cleared up! But I don't worry about my looks. I have no idea what I look like, and that's for the best; I don't even have a mirror in the bathroom. But what I *do* have is a ravenous appetite. Let's go have some lunch."

Vrt and Chloe

The text was short and sweetly formal.

"Lord Conary, could you please ask Lord Vrt if I could have a word with her at her earliest convenience? – Chloe"

Vrt resisted anything to do with phones and computers. But at least, Conary thought, I know what's going on in her life because *everything* comes through my phone. So he got up and went to find Hell's Anachronism and relay the message.

Vrt sent an elf to fetch Chloe and port the girl to her and Conary's flat. That was best, she thought, because whatever Chloe wanted must be pretty important.

Vrt's flat was odd, but then so was Vrt. It reminded Chloe of the inside of a Gypsy tent or maybe some Arabian Nights fantasy. Every luxurious surface had pattern, colour, and sparkle, and sometimes all three. The elves who designed it must've been on crack, that's all Chloe could think. But as chaotic as it was, it all worked.

"What's up?" Vrt handed Chloe a soda and leaned back on a huge pillow, and tucked her legs under her. She had a juice glass of wine with a straw.

"It's this embassy ball. Are you going to it? The one in Kyiv?"

"We're *all* going to it. It's required. Lord Cadence rotates the big yearly embassy bash, and Kyiv is this year's venue."

"So if everyone's *required* to go to it, does that mean my dad and Sarah will be going?"

Vrt sat up and cocked her head at the very, very clever girl.

"Yes, your father is now a bluecoat training for a top-ranking military position, directly reporting to Kyrylo. Sarah is number five in the ranks; if she's not there, Caddy will want to know why. Personally."

Chloe shifted in her seat. Vrt was Sarah's best friend, so she could be speaking out of turn. She didn't want to offend anyone.

"Did you know that Sarah thinks she's a dog? I mean, super ugly. So ugly that she doesn't even own a mirror?"

Vrt narrowed her eyes. All she ever saw Sarah wear was either workout gear or uniforms. She saw her once in jeans. But never dressed up, never with make-up on or her hair done. She didn't even get manicures. Vrt thought it was just a lack of opportunity; the woman was a hard worker, and playtime didn't come often. She didn't know Sarah thought she was a troll.

"Tell me how you know this."

And Chloe told her about what Sarah said regarding "I'm not the kind of girl men get romantic over," and the acne and being ugly as an old boot.

When she was done, Vrt was blinking back tears. She'd had no idea. Sarah was gorgeous! No wonder she wasn't chasing after James; she thought she wasn't attractive enough for a man to pay attention to. Well, if anyone knew how to dress to make a man sit up and pay attention, it was Vrt.

"You just leave Sarah to me. You work on your dad. She's going to be a goddess at that dance, or I'll cancel my subscription to Vogue. I guarantee it." She narrowed her eyes, already plotting. "Your dad won't have a chance in hell."

Chloe squealed and bounced up to hug the lord. That was exactly what she wanted to hear.

Vrt and Sarah

"What do you mean you're going in your uniform?"

Sarah shrugged. She was loading up a pistol for target practice and was determined to give Malachi a run for his money. "I'll dress the same as all the guys. If they're in uniform, I'll be in uniform. I guess the elves will give us a sash or something since it's a ball."

"The *guys* will be in dinner jackets, tuxes to you Americans. *We* will be in formal ball gowns."

Sarah pulled off three careful shots and peered at the target. It wasn't as neat a hole as what Malachi would do, but they were all in the black. Then she looked at Vrt, frowned, and then shrugged again.

"I guess the elves will lay out something for me. As long as it's modest, I don't care."

"Oh, if you don't care, let me deal with it. But it won't be modest, I'm going to make sure of that. And you'll have your hair and makeup done. And court shoes."

"Court shoes? Am I playing basketball?"

"High heels, you barbarian."

Sarah laughed. She could already see Vrt salivating over dressing her up like a doll. "Okay – tell you what, I'll let you take care of everything. I trust you. But you have to agree to one thing. I don't want my boobs to bust out on the dance floor. That would irritate me."

"You dance?"

"Vrt, I'm observant, not dead. I used to dance all the time at temple when I lived in Florida; it was an exercise class. Swing, Latin, ballroom, folk, modern – as long as it wasn't too 'lascivious', we did it. I didn't dance with men, of course." She aimed and pulled off three more shots, this time pretending to put them in Leo's black heart. Ohhh – perfect! She would remember that trick for the next time she was up against Malachi.

Vrt promised that any outfit she put together would be fit for dancing, and the fast friends left the range quite happy. Sarah pushed the dress thing right out of her head, and Vrt couldn't get it out of hers.

Sarah

The email sent out over Ellen Hadid's name was quite firm. There was going to be a red carpet parade, and the list below had the order they would walk. A strict order of precedence was given, everyone was instructed on what to do, and a practice session was held so that everyone knew how to walk, wave, stop and turn, and gracefully go up to the reception line. The email reminded everyone that photos of their outfits would be on social media, print media, and video worldwide.

The top of the order was

1- Lord Cadence will escort Lord Kyrylo
2- Lord Conary will escort Lord Vrt
3- Lord Sarah will escort Lord James

And then on down the pack.

Sarah was upset. Couldn't she be further down the pack? Like at the end? It was bad enough she was paired with James and having to deal with him and his scent, but as the number three couple they would be one of the most photographed (i.e, drawn by sketch artists), and the interviewers wouldn't be bored yet. What if she had a scent attack in front of the press? What if she tripped and fell from the court shoes? What if she said something mind-bogglingly stupid?

She was getting very nervous about the whole thing.

Then she found out she had to be one of the people in the reception line who shook hands with all the guests. Like she was a friggin' Primary! She and James would have to stand together, shoulder to shoulder for almost an hour, making nice to all of the guests as each one in turn walked up and had a good, appraising look at her.

Guests from all over the world, the great and the good, as they say in the UK, all looking at her and wondering what the hell *she* was doing there.

Staring at her.

Sarah had a flashback. It was time for her monthly mikva, and Sarah went to the temple for the ceremonial bath. She always enjoyed it, walking naked into the mikvah was a peaceful, purifying, *solitary* ritual where she could pray to herself and be alone with her thoughts. The attendant was a sweet woman. Rochel was her name, and Rochel was very careful not to look at the bodies of the women she helped into the bath, only looking when they were fully immersed to make sure not even a hair of the unmarried floated to the surface.

But that day when Sarah climbed the steps out of the water to take the towel from Rochel, the attendant was distracted or turned or something, and she saw Sarah naked. Naked and a mass of bruises, cuts, and bites from the beating Leo had given her two nights before. Oh, he made sure he never hit her face, but her body was fair game.

Sarah would never forget the expression on Rochel's face. She was so ashamed; all she could do was take the towel and wrap her battered body, and leave as fast as she could. Later that day, the Rabbi's wife called her and asked if there was anything Sarah wanted to talk about. Sarah said no. The next day, three men from the temple came and had a private talk with Leo. It only made the beatings worse.

And when she went back to the temple, her one place of refuge, the women looked at her. They judged. They pitied. They whispered.

They stared.

She had a full-blown panic attack and found herself pounding on Vrt's door. Vrt said all the right things and pulled her friend back from the ledge, but she could see that Sarah was terrified.

"Sweetie – I don't see why you're so nervous! You do fine at the embassy stuff. You never seem nervous there!"

"I guess it's because I'm okay in uniform. It's a role, and I know I'm good at it. If I have a crumb on my jacket, people still think I'm competent. No one cares what I *look* like; they're looking at the lord, the uniform, not at *me*. But this – I'm not good at the girly stuff. I'm not good at being *looked* at. You don't understand, Vrt. You're gorgeous, and I know you had a long time under a mask and not being gorgeous, but the *exposed* time of your life, when you were a young woman, and now, you were always beautiful. No one is going to make fun of you in a ball gown. Plain women like me – people aren't nice, Vrt. They look. They judge."

And Sarah sat on Vrt's pouffy sofa, head bent, silent tears fell on her hands, and it broke Vrt's heart.

"Do you trust me, Sarah? You're going to look perfect. Absolutely beautiful, and I want you to feel beautiful. You're not plain, not by a long shot. But you have to trust me on this. You'll be fine."

Sarah sighed and nodded. "I trust you, Vrt. I know you'll do your best, but you have to work with the clay you're given. I'm not going to flake out. I'll try, anyway. On the day I'll be there, but –"

"No buts. Listen, you're one of the bravest people I know. You can get through a reception line, and everything will be fine. And if anyone says anything mean, you need to tell me who. So I can decapitate their stupid orc head off."

Sarah smiled and sniffled. "If you're decapitating in court shoes, make sure you adjust your centre of balance and don't overswing."

Oh, Canada

It was two in the morning, and Minister of Foreign Affairs Monet waited in the deserted hangar office along with her security and staff. From the observation window she watched the huge unmarked cargo jet pull in. Ground crew guided the airstairs to the passenger door, but the massive rear hatch was opening, too. They must be going to unload something big. She expected an armoured limo.

Off to the side were two unmarked buses and other vehicles. Uniformed Canadian RumLot Security employees, with their maple leaf shoulder patch, were hanging around them.

Something was up for the EN to fly over unannounced and, fingers crossed, it was good news. Ottawa had been asking – very politely, because they were Canadian – for the EN to establish a firmer foothold in Canada because it seemed every time the Americans turned around they got a little bit crazier. Trump had made "jokes" about Canada becoming the 51st state, but when he was asked Meechum didn't smile. Canada's huge border with the US simply could not be defended if the Americans took a notion to walk over, and wacko QAnon worshippers would not shut up about having a "European" nation as their northern neighbour. Not to mention the demon thing. The nut jobs online really frothed at the mouth when elves and lords came up.

So if they were going to froth, they might as well have something to froth about, and if the EN truly established a presence, the Canadian government would have an ally, a powerful one, that would, the Canadians hoped, keep the Americans sane and on their side of the 49th parallel. That's all the Canadians wanted – sanity and peace.

Elves would be nice. Canadians, civilians and government officials spent a lot of time in Europe observing the integration of elves with local populations, and they could see nothing but advantages for the Canadian people. Monet visited relatives in Provence, and they were certainly elf-o-philes. Elves planted a lot of flowers around their houses and had great market stalls. Excellent cheese, Tante Marguerite said.

Then out of the rear cargo door emerged a horse trailer! Monet raised an eyebrow and glanced at her aide. But he was pointing to the passenger stairs; the door was swinging open, and it was time for the ministry people to head to the bottom of the stairs and greet their guests.

First down was Lord Ratna and Lord Tuân; Monet heaved a sigh of relief. Lord Ratna was Canadian, and she was coming home. That meant something. Right behind them were the twins, Lords Mordecai and Malachi. And that brought a very unprofessional grin to Monet, and she heard the staff murmur behind her. An elf raiser! Intelligence sources had known for a while how the elves came to this world; the lords raised them somehow. They tried to keep it secret, but a secret with almost a thousand human witnesses didn't last long. Lord Cadence was one elf raiser, and Lord Mordecai was another. They had no idea if other lords were doing it, but those two were the main ones.

And so here was Mordecai, with his brother Malachi, who managed his security when the elves were raised. Behind them were a couple of unknown redcoat lords – they'd figure them out later – and a bunch of RumLot Security soldiers. She saw General Jameson.

"Lord Ratna, so good to see you back on Canadian soil. Welcome!"

Tiny Lord Ratna trotted up, bowed, and then shook hands and greeted the entire staff as did the others in turn. Lord Malachi ran off to check on his horses, but Monet had a moment with Lords Ratna, Tuân, and Mordecai before they went to the buses that would take them to the EN embassy.

Lord Mordecai grinned at the delegation. "So are you ready?" In the subdued light of the hangar, his eyes glowed bright. All the lords' eyes glowed.

Monet had no idea what he really meant, but she had hopes. "We Canadians are always ready, Lord Mordecai."

Mordecai nodded, "The concert is starting, Minister, and today you're hearing the orchestra warm up. Thank you for coming by and welcoming us. Now, if you'll excuse us, we'll start out for the embassy while there's no traffic on the roads." He bowed to her and followed the soldiers and RumLot staff to the buses, and within minutes the convoy drove out of the hangar and into the dark.

The Canadian welcome delegation clapped and waved as the EN people left and then went to their offices, where they spent the rest of the night writing reports. They also drank a lot of champagne, which they really shouldn't have done at work, but the Minister turned a blind eye to the celebration. She had a glass, too.

Conary and James

James had no idea why Conary asked to see him, but he liked the guy, and they worked well together. It was just odd. Conary was diplomatic, and James was military; all of his orders came through Kyrylo.

He walked into the lord's embassy office, and immediately Conary jumped up and led him to the sofa and offered him a beer. So nothing serious then, thought James, and the elf brought him a Blackshore Stout. He hadn't tried any of the local beers before he moved to Suffolk, but this was becoming a favourite.

"Okay – I'll get right to it. I'm here under strict orders not to tell you who sent me." Conary took a sip of his odious Vietnamese beer. "But the first initial is V, and the last one is T, and that's all you're getting out of me."

James nodded.

"It seems that this year's embassy ball will be in Kyiv. Are you aware of it?" Conary didn't even bother to wait. "Good man, I knew you would be. Anyway, you're escorting Lord Sarah through the clown walk – sorry, red carpet – and then the reception line. You know about that?"

And this time, he paused and shot James a sharp look, gauging him. James nodded again and lifted his glass. Yep, no problem. And there really wasn't. He was quite sure he could walk down a carpet, no matter what the colour, and not trip. And he was equally sure he could handle himself around the fearsome Lord Sarah. It wasn't as if he hadn't had to go to some formal, terribly stuffy, mandatory fun thing every fifteen minutes when he was in the RA. He knew what to expect. And he said as much to Conary.

"Well, you're used to it, but Lord Sarah is having a bloody meltdown. She's terrified. Stage fright."

"Really? The woman is a Valkyrie! Everyone is afraid of *her*!"

"Our women are titanium on the outside, but have soft squishy middles, which can be fun at times, but not now. Sarah is convinced she's a dog's dinner when it comes to looks, and Vrt thinks this is triggering some old abuse memories. She won't talk about it, but she had a pretty rough time before she came here."

James was shocked. Sarah was abused? What on Earth?

"So I'm asking you, as a friend, to be nice. To be supportive if she seems wobbly. That's it. We're worried about her."

"You don't have to worry about me." James looked away, collecting himself. "I had no idea."

"I know, but many of our lords have some pretty horrific backstories. Most probably. Whenever a new lord comes on board Rashid does some background checking just so we know what to expect. We just have to watch out for each other. So that's it. I just wanted to talk to you in person. And I would appreciate it if you kept my involvement to yourself. Remember, I go home every night to the Angel of Death, and I want to keep her happy. "

The men shook hands, and James was ported home to sit all evening and think about Sarah, abuse, and wonder what Rashid had found out.

Sarah and James

The dress was a dream. Sarah had never seen anything so beautiful. It was dark orange silk that some otherworldly artist had painted on so that the overall effect was that she was dressed in flames, with just enough crystals sewn on that the fire sparkled when she moved. The full skirt floated around her, and when she danced, she would be on fire. The wide, low neckline was certainly not modest, but when Sarah tried it on the dress fit like a second skin. Her boobs couldn't go a-roaming if they wanted to.

She didn't have any jewellery, so Virt insisted that she order some ear cuffs to complement the dress. A pair of silk dancing shoes and a ridiculously tiny handbag to wear at her wrist, and she was ready for the red carpet.

On the day of the ball, there were *five* elves in her hotel room just to get her ready. Sarah had never seen such a palaver over putting on clothes. But she endured the hairdresser, the makeup artist, and all the rest, right down to the dresser who slipped the shoes on her feet like she was Cinderella.

She almost walked right out to go meet James, but they insisted on her having a last look in a full-length mirror, and Sarah was stunned. Just like Vrt promised, she looked beautiful. She had to look twice. Was that really her? Sarah truly didn't have any idea what she looked like now; the last time she'd seen a reflection of herself had been twenty years ago, back in Florida, when she'd had to nurse a black eye and a split lip when Leo lost his temper and forgot to keep his fists away from her face and down on her body where nosy people couldn't see the cuts and bruises. She hadn't looked very good then.

She almost cried; she was so relieved, but that would have messed up the make-up, so she just had to content herself with effusively thanking the elves, and she left them beaming and quite proud of themselves.

She wondered what James would think.

She was supposed to meet him in the hotel bar, and they would be ported to the embassy together, but he changed his mind. Sarah didn't know it, but James was waiting for her down the hall from her room by the elevators. In his black dinner jacket, he blended into a dark corner and from there he watched her door.

Sarah walked out of her hotel room, and the overhead spotlights of the hall caught the crystals and the jewelled ear cuffs. With her graceful panther walk, she looked like a flaming angel floating down the hall.

He'd thought she was beautiful when she was walking up the aisle of the conference room at Sandhurst, but this creature –

Sarah walked to the elevator, but she didn't see James standing in his dark corner. He saw her stand in front of the doors, and then she looked at her feet, and he could see her steady herself. She was getting up the nerve to press the button and go on stage, and she was scared stiff.

"Sarah?"

And then he was there, standing next to her, grinning down, absolutely delighted with her.

"Bloody hell, girl, you're gorgeous! You should wear this dress every day!" He took her hand and did something he had never done before to any woman – he kissed it. There was a sharp breath, and he felt it. Had he gone too far? Well, in for a penny, in for a pound, and he stepped back and admired her again.

"You are stunning – look at you!" And she smiled shyly at him, blushed bright red, and he looked into her glowing eyes and was lost.

That was the moment James realised he was bonded. He finally figured out what everyone else seemed to know, and it hit him like a freight train, the certainty in his soul that this woman was perfectly matched to him and he was hers. Forever.

"Thank you, I'm so glad you –" And the elevator door opened, and the spell was broken. James guided Sarah in, and they went on their way.

He held her hand through the entire red carpet nonsense, and whenever he felt her tense up he'd bend down and whisper into those wonderful ears that she was beautiful, or something funny, or anything to put her at ease. And the miracle was that she would look up and smile, and she held his hand back. James was her anchor.

James couldn't hold her hand while he was in the reception line, but he stood very close, and if he moved away, she would move in closer. After the first few minutes of "hello, how do you do, so glad you could come", Sarah got used to it, and it all became rather rote. A few people asked for selfies even though they were told not to, and Lord Sarah and Lord James smiled and looked blurry for them.

After that chore was over, they moved to the ballroom, and the band was already playing.

Sarah glanced over at her escort and whispered, "James, do you dance?"

"Of course, I can dance. What do you want? A Scottish reel? Texas line dancing? Ballet?"

Sarah beamed at him, her whole body radiating happiness. "A waltz? I'll let you lead."

And so they waltzed and laughed and danced all night and had a wonderful time.

President Meecham

There were elves in Canada. Elves had jumped the Atlantic Ocean and were now in Canada, threatening all of North and South America. They even threatened Central America, but who cared about them?

Credible reports in the media and in intelligence briefings said that elves were now openly working in the EN embassy in Ottawa and were seen on the streets of the city. One was sighted in Montreal. The CIA reported that lords had stayed in the EN embassy in Ottawa for a week and then returned to the UK. They were pretty sure elves were hidden in the horse trailer the lords brought with them under diplomatic cover. They could also have been hidden in a suitcase; they *were* small.

Meecham looked at the intelligence report, and the first thing that passed through his mind was "how is this going to affect my re-election campaign?" The second thing was "how are we going to keep the nasty little shits out of the US?"

He was pretty sure they burrowed, and they could make tunnels right under the border and infest the Land of the Free like a virus. He had no evidence of that, but it seemed like something they could do. Vermin in Vermont … (Meecham wrote that down on a notepad. Clever! It would make a great meme on social media for his campaign.)

But back to the problem of burrowing elves – putting a wall along the 49th parallel and up to New Brunswick wasn't going to work because no one had any idea how deep the little mole rats could go.

At the moment, the polls said that only twenty-three per cent of the American population leaned anti-elf and lord, but that could quickly sink if they realised that elves and lords were now in North America and they proved to be a positive thing. If Meecham's campaign lost that twenty-three per cent, the President's anti-elf, pro-orc stance would quickly become a campaign liability. He would have backed the wrong horse.

He pursed his lips and then took a sip of his Diet Coke. The best thing would be to go on the offensive and make sure the people knew the real problems that came with immortal beings with unchecked magic making decisions that affect American lives.

What decisions, you may ask? It didn't matter. Decisions. Meechem was a master of the vague statement that let the average voter fill in the blanks with whatever they liked. What was needed was to give humans (like himself) unchecked power to make decisions that affect American lives.

He called in his campaign advisors, and they went to work.

First, a strongly worded letter was sent to the Prime Minister of Canada *emphatically* condemning the importation of an invasive species known as "Elves and Lords" into North America by the Canadian government. Canada was reminded of the United Nations Intergovernmental Platform on Biodiversity and Ecosystem Services (IPBES) Assessment Report on Invasive Alien Species and their Control (known as the "Invasive Alien Species Report"). Target 6 of the adopted Kunming-Montreal Global Biodiversity Framework was designed to "eliminate, minimise, reduce, and/or mitigate the impacts of invasive alien species on biodiversity and ecosystem services."

That would surely make the Canadians sit up and pay attention! They were into that eco-crap.

Then an executive order was written to require the Border Force to check every single car, truck, rail car, and plane coming into the US for elves and lords, which would, unfortunately, cause a huge backlog and disruption at the border, constraining trade. Meecham only expected that to last for less than a week, but the point was going to be made. Elves were going to cost the Canadians money.

When a comment was made by an advisor that no elves have ever been seen trying to enter the US,

Meecham just nodded wisely and said, "Yet. And we plan to keep it that way." He was going to sell himself as the protector of American borders, and to do that he had to make sure the elves were seen as a security and biological threat.

The Chiefs of the National Guard and Homeland Security were called in and ordered to make plans for closing down the US Border in case of an elf invasion until the Army could be called up. When one expressed confusion as to exactly how they were supposed to capture creatures who could disappear the minute anyone tried to grab them, Meecham snapped, "That's why you have the stars on your shoulders. You figure it out." When one grumbled that the only threat elves presented to humans was as a trip hazard, Meecham fired him on the spot. One had to be firm with rebels, and that made the others toe the line.

Of all of Meecham's advisors, only three had ever seen an elf during a vacation in Europe. None had ever talked to an elf. None had a clue about *terrior.* None had any idea if an elf could even defend itself. There was no instance of an elf harming any human; at least no evidence existed. The CIA had questions about a decapitated mugger in Portsmouth, UK, but no hard evidence, and from the UK police's perspective, the case was closed because they thought it was done by one of the accomplices.

They had no idea if they could keep out the elves who wanted to come in, but that didn't stop them from simply making stuff up. And that's what they did.

Sarah and James

It was a disaster. It was supposed to be so simple, really. An easy, stress-free lesson on a lovely day, doing something James loved – fly fishing in one of Scotland's remote and pristine streams.

The elves found a perfect place, a fly fisherman's dream, and on a grassy bank in the dappled shade, they placed a massive picnic basket packed with all sorts of surprises and a couple of bottles of really, really good wine. All of his rods, reels, flies, and kit they needed were ready and waiting.

What could go wrong?

He was nervous; this was suspiciously close to being a date, and he didn't want to push things too hard and scare her off. Catching a Sarah was a lot like fly fishing – it required finesse and patience. James wanted a nice, casual day out where she could get used to being around him and relax, and then they could progress to dinners and dates.

When he proposed the outing he wasn't sure if she would bite, but Sarah was happy to learn about fly fishing with all of its esoteric customs, superstitions, and cheerful insistence that the fish were fine with being hauled into a net by a hook piercing their lower jaw. None of the fish ever complained, not that anyone reported.

They ported in together, and the elves left them to it. James showed her how to put on the waders, which made her giggle, and he set up a rod for her and showed her how to cast.

Sarah, the Warrior Lord, was very strong, and she whipped the rod much too hard. James watched her and gently suggested that she throttle back a bit and develop a lighter touch, and then he messed up the entire day. He could trace it back to the point when he said, "This is how Lauren would do it."

Maybe he could have recovered at that point, but he missed the first clue and didn't stop there. He cast and got into the rhythm of fishing and didn't look at Sarah standing about twenty feet away. Instead, he concentrated on the fishing and chatted about how he and the kids and Lauren would go fishing, and how he and Lauren would tie flies, and how Lauren was really good at putting a picnic together –

And then he glanced over at Sarah, and she was just standing there with a stricken look on her face. She wasn't fishing.

"Is something wrong?"

She blinked and said, "I'm not feeling very well right now," and he sensed she was telling the truth. Then, without a word, she ported out, and James was left standing in the stream alone, puzzled and concerned and not a little pissed at being abandoned like that.

He gave up after about ten minutes and called for a very surprised elf to port him back home. Back at Aelfeham House, he went to look for Sarah to make sure she was okay, but there was no answer at her door. The reception desk didn't know where she was, and he started to get the nagging feeling this was not just an upset tummy.

He went to the flat and found Chloe and Jamie playing a racing video game on the TV; when he walked through the living room to the kitchen Chloe looked up, surprised.

"What are you doing here! What happened with the fishing thing? Where's Sarah?"

Now he was really pissed and growled at his daughter. "Ah dinnae ken. She scarpered." He didn't look at her as he got a beer from the fridge.

"Oh, Ded, what happened?"

He threw himself on the sofa, popped the top of the beer, and took a long drink.

"We were fishing. It was nice, but she didn't say much. I thought she was good. Happy. I told her about how we used to fish as a family. Told her how your mum used to tie flies. Showed her how Lauren cast, thought it would help her –"

Chloe looked at him, stricken with the exact same expression on her face that Sarah had had before she ported off. And it hit him.

"I screwed up, didn't I?"

"Ohhhh, yes," sighed Chloe, and she turned back to the game. When a sixteen-year-old shakes her head at you and sighs, you have definitely screwed up.

Oh. Yes.

He must have rattled on for a good half hour, comparing Sarah to Lauren, before she just reached her full snoot and left. Shit, he wasn't even missing Lauren; it wasn't that at all. His late wife was just such a huge part of his history; it was like talking about his mom or dad and what they said and did.

But Sarah, she was his bond-wife even if they weren't all there yet, and she was fantastic in her own right, and he wanted to make this work. No, he *had to* make this work. But no one wanted to be compared to a past lover and found wanting. "I'm not feeling very good right now." No shit. The expression on her face – the more he thought about it, the worse he felt.

He had screwed up from the beginning. He should never have asked her to go fishing for the first time out; fishing was too full of old memories, and he and Sarah needed to make their own memories. He'd thought it was neutral, but it was anything but neutral. Not for him.

James wondered where she was. He hoped she wasn't in Antarctica.

Sarah

Sarah was praying.

After she left James standing in the stream, she ported herself back to her room, but she couldn't stay there; he would come looking for her; she knew that.

She was so upset she couldn't think, and when you can't think, the best thing to do is to find a quiet place and pray. Praying, meditation, whatever it was fashionable to call it, would always sort out your soul and give peace if you let it.

So she grabbed something to cover her head, took off the disrespectful jeans, put on a modest skirt, and ported to a temple. There were a lot of beautiful temples in the UK, and she had, on various Shabbats, visited many of the largest ones. She would find a large congregation where no one would notice her in the crowd, hide her ears under a wig, put on something to cover her head, and sit in the very back of the women's side. She could absorb the beauty and peace, listen to the rabbis, and if she was lucky, enjoy the cantors.

Only a couple of people other than the elves knew she was observant because she didn't make a big deal out of it. Flaunting your holier-than-thou observance was stupid; it was prideful and vain.

The elves cooked kosher meals for her and made sure she ate correctly. There were candles in her room if she needed them. If something of life or death importance came up, she would work on the sabbath, but most of the time she managed to do the right thing. It wasn't hard. G-d never asked too much, no matter what Job said, because in the end, all that was wanted was for people to be respectful and to do the right thing, and they were given brains to figure out what those things were.

Bevis Marks in London was beautiful, and Sarah was sure she wouldn't be followed there; she could sit in peace and have a think.

In the late morning, the old temple was empty aside from three old women tidying up. They were volunteers doing regular light cleaning as a mitzvah, and when they saw the stranger come in and quietly take a seat in a dark corner of the women's side and start her prayers, they left her alone. They understood without being told.

Sarah sat and prayed, and as she reached a meditative state, she began to chant the Torah aloud. The women paused their cleaning and listened. There were no men around to fuss over a woman chanting the megillot. She perfectly chanted from the book of Ruth from memory, her clear soprano turning the words into music. The women came and sat near Sarah and prayed with her because that was a mitzvah, too, and the dusting and polishing could wait.

When Sarah finished and the last syllable faded away like a lover's whisper, the women thanked her.

"So beautiful," one sighed. "But why Ruth?"

Sarah thought – why did she choose Ruth?

"Because I am the outsider asking to be let in, I guess, in many ways. Because I have a man who loved his late wife and now is trying to love me, but doesn't know how to let go of the past. Because I can't let go of my past enough to trust him."

The women nodded. Been there, done that. The Book of Ruth was old, but Sarah's song was older.

"Ruth, the outsider, went to Boaz and gambled it all that he would be a good man. But he was an outsider, too, and he gambled it all that she was a good woman."

"What do you mean? Boaz was the ultimate insider. He was powerful."

The woman looked at this stranger sitting in the darkest corner of the Temple, an outsider, and the outsider's eyes glowed green.

"Ruth went after Boaz, and the story seems to be all about Boaz accepting her, but flip it around. She had to let him enter her heart, too. She had to trust him to do the right thing. He could have taken her (and we all know what "lie at his feet" means) and cast her aside, and who would blame him? She wasn't his responsibility; she had another male relative to take care of her. But he didn't. He had to bargain for her, work for her, and he did the right thing by her. They had to trust each other, but to do that, she first had to trust this new man, this stranger to her, this outsider in her life. She took the first step, though; she was the driver of this story. It's the Book of Ruth, not the Book of Boaz."

Sarah listened and thought about the story. Ruth's story was so subtle, so many layers, and that's why it has survived for thousands of years. Ruth was accepted, but she was also accepting. Boaz was as much a stranger to her as she was to him. She gave up her old life for him, but he fought to marry the poor widow when he didn't have to. She gave him something, and it wasn't just sex; it was her heart. And she took the first step. A brave woman.

"Thank you. You've given me a lot to think about." She stood up, smiled, bowed, and the shawl she used to cover her hair fell off, and they saw she was a lord. And Sarah ported out, the bang from her exit making the dust from the chandeliers sprinkle to the floor.

"Blimey! We'll have a story to tell at dinner tonight!" And they went back to finish their dusting and talk about Ruth and Boaz and strangers.

Sarah and James

At eight, James walked over to Sarah's door. He could see a light under her door, and he heard the telly on; someone was extremely excited about bake-offs. He hesitated for a second, let out a sigh, and knocked.

Sarah opened the door, and she wasn't surprised to see him. He would ask why she ran off, and she already had an explanation thought out. It was hard because she had to be honest, but she didn't want to make him feel bad or get angry at her.

But James didn't ask why she'd ported out. He stood at the door, oh so handsome, and oh, so sad, and apologised. He knew why she ran off. He'd been nervous and had rattled on about the past, and it had taken an hour to figure it out, but when he did he –

Sarah threw her arms around him and kissed him, which was certainly unexpected, but James wasn't going to argue, and he kissed her back.

He kept kissing her (fekkin' hell, how could he stop?) and stepped into her room and pushed the door shut, and that's when he felt her tense up as stiff as a board and back away.

Sarah's eyes were as wide as saucers, and he could see tears welling up. And he thought about what Conary said about abuse.

"James, I can't –"

He stroked her cheek. "Love, I know that. I thought we could watch *Bake-Off* together. Who do you think is going to win?"

Sarah gaped at him. Absolutely gobsmacked. And then she just howled with laughter and took a couple of steps back, collected herself, and then glanced at the telly and started up again.

James strolled over to the sofa and threw himself on it, clasped his hands behind his head and put his feet up on the coffee table and grinned. "My bet's on the little Asian girl. They're fierce bakers. Do you have anything to drink that's caffeine-free? It's getting late for coffee."

Sarah could have kissed him, but that would just get the man going again. Instead, she wiped her eyes and in the back of the fridge, found him some orange juice, the best she could do. She curled up on the couch next to Jamie and watched TV until the news was over, when he left to go back to his flat.

Sarah and James started dating. Cautious little dates about once or twice a week. James had a full-time job and still had kids at home, and insisted that even the two older ones have dinner twice a week in the flat. As he told Sarah, they'd be leaving, but they weren't gone yet, and they needed the foundation of a good family.

Jamie still slept at the flat, but most Saturday nights he played computer games with his friends and stayed overnight in the school wing. Keeping him off the games and tablets was a constant struggle during the week, but if he did his school work and kept his gaming in bounds, James let the boy blow off some steam with his mates on Saturday. It seemed fair.

Sarah had her own full-time job. She attended military and security conferences and lectures to listen, learn, and be a visible member of the Elf Nation. When she was needed at one of the embassies to help Conary, she was there. And she did mysterious jobs for Kyrylo.

When James discovered she would totally disappear for a couple of days and then reappear without a word, he asked her what was going on. She just shrugged and said that when he did his Ukraine stint Kyrylo would let him know, but she wasn't at liberty to say. When you say something like that to a career military intelligence professional, they will do two things. They won't ask anything directly because secrets are what the trade is all about – and then they'll start to poke around to find out for themselves, whether they need to know or not. The MI tribe are all nosy bastards.

So Sarah and James had Saturday nights and Sundays and an occasional day in the middle of the week if their calendars and the moon and stars aligned.

Then one Friday, James found one of those rare blank spaces in his schedule, and he took the afternoon off. Sarah's schedule had been whited-out since Wednesday, but she was due back from one of her mysterious jobs by four thirty. The kids were all doing whatever it was they did during the day, so he wandered down to the Breakfast Room for lunch and to see who was hanging out there.

Chi, Ratna, Tuân, Sam, and Grace were there, and that was a good group to have lunch with; they were happy to see him. After a nice lunch, he was just getting up to leave when, with a huge bang that rattled the windows, Sarah ported into the room. She was covered in snow and looked like she had just walked out of some sort of firefight. Literally. She was covered in dirt and soot, and the knee was torn out of her uniform, which James noted was the field uniform, not the blues she usually wore. She was armed to the teeth, including some sort of nasty-looking baby machine gun, which she threw in a corner along with her sword.

She ran to the buffet, and James had never seen anyone gorge like that. She was shovelling the food in without bothering with plates or even utensils.

Elves popped in with trays of sandwiches. Big ones. She grabbed a couple and plopped into a seat with her eyes closed, took a couple of big breaths, and ate them as fast as lordly possible and then looked up to see the amused faces of her friends looking at her.

"Feeling peckish?" asked James.

She had the grace to look a bit sheepish and grinned at him. "I missed breakfast."

An elf popped in with a huge glass, almost a vase, of something thick and brown, which turned out to be a full-fat chocolate milkshake. He stuck a straw in it, swirled an entire can of squirty whipped cream on top, and Sarah thanked him, looked back over to James, and winked.

"I've given up on my diet."

"So, Warrior Queen, was it a successful mission? Kill any orcs? Fuck any foreign spies? Did you save the world as we know it?" Chi was curious. They all were, but he was the only one with the nerve to ask directly.

Sarah looked at Chi and finished up the milkshake, her eyes amused and glinting. James wondered where the hell she put it all.

"Oh, Chi, you are the twenty-second star of my constellation, you are. I had a good day. Others did not. And that's all I'll say."

Chi was pleased for her and grinned. "Very good! And I'm so happy to hear I've risen from twenty-five to twenty-two. Nowhere to go but up!"

She leaned back and eyed the buffet again. "What's the time here anyway? Do I have time for another plate?"

"Well, I don't know what your schedule is, but it's four-thirty –"

"SHIT!" And she jumped up and ran out. An elf ported in and started to mop up the floor where the snow and dirt had all melted into a big, dirty puddle. When he was done, he turned to James. "Would you mind, Lord James, taking Lord Sarah's weapons to her room? I'm not a warrior, and I'm afraid to handle that gun thing. I wouldn't know which way to point it."

James smiled and gathered up the sabre and the machine gun. It had been fired, he noticed, and he walked to Sarah's room. The door was an inch ajar, and he nudged it open, and there she was. She was in a bathrobe, still dripping from the shower, in front of two Shabbat candles, her hands over her eyes and chanting the blessing. *"Barukh attah adonai, eloheinu, melekh ha-olam, asher kidd'shanu b'mitzvotav v'tzivvanu l'hadlik neir shel shabbat."*

Sarah was Jewish. He had no idea. Religion had never come up. There was so much to learn about her –

"May the peace of Shabbat fill our hearts, fill our home, fill the world. Amen." She spun around and saw him. She stood up straight and exhaled.

He walked up and shifted the machine gun so he had a free hand and traced his index finger down her nose and then kissed her forehead. *"A woman of valour who can find? For her price is far above rubies. The heart of her husband safely trusts in her, And he has no lack of gain. She does him good and not evil all the days of her life."*

Tears came to her eyes. Sarah whispered, "I'd kiss you, but you're armed. Please check the safety.

Careless of me, but I'm not sure I set it. I was in a hurry when I ported out."

James chuckled. "Here, you do it. I don't think I've ever handled one of these, much less used one."

She took the machine gun, disarmed it, and broke it down. "I probably shouldn't be doing this on Shabbat, but I don't recall learning anything about weapons in my shul. It never came up."

"I'm sure it's okay. A safety thing is not optional." James leaned the sabre against a corner and went to sit on the sofa. There were no lights on in the flat except the candles, as it should be. He had forgotten how peaceful and nice it was to sit and wait for full dark to come and the Shabbat candles to burn down.

"So we might as well get the religion thing out of the way. I can't think of a better time." She brought him a beer and curled up next to him, and told him about her family and how she was brought up in a very orthodox, some would say ultra-orthodox, household and that she was still as observant as she could be.

And he explained that he was brought up in a conservative, observant family, but when he married Lauren, who was not of any particular religion like many modern humans, he let his Jewish side fade away. It had faded but wasn't forgotten. Lauren had properly converted so that James' family would be happy that the kids would be born Jewish, but they didn't practise because her parents suddenly became more Christian when Lauren converted and when the kids were born it became an issue.

"I'll admit it, I was lazy. When you're brought up in rural Scotland, the only Jew kid in school, and then join the Army, which isn't exactly teeming with Jews, it's easier to just go with the flow."

Sarah was snuggled up to James, and her fingers traced his jawline and then his lips. Was he growing a beard? He needed a shave, that was for sure.

James bent down to kiss her, and his hands started to do their own roaming.

"You're naked under this dressing gown."

"Yes, I'm naked under all of my outfits. So are you."

"I can be more naked. I can stay the night." His breathing was getting faster.

Sarah sighed and pushed him away. This was going too far. "No, you can't. I'm doing way more than I should with you. I won't do anything more until my divorce is final."

James made a face. "Oh, I think that —"

"No, I won't; don't even ask." Sarah looked at him sternly. "I had a lousy marriage, but it was the guy that made it lousy, not the institution. I take marriage very seriously. As horrible as Leo was, I never cheated. Not that he didn't deserve it, but because I won't cheat on my own values."

James sighed, "Of course. You're in charge, Sarah. But it's hard –"

"If it's hard then go to the bathroom and take care of it."

"*Sarah!*" James laughed and shook his head. He could see the corner of her mouth twitching up, and so he had to kiss it.

"Okay, Pet, a wee bit longer celibate – so when is your divorce final? Can I make a countdown calendar?"

"I really have no idea. I wasn't fussed about a date because I thought it would all happen in good time, and that was all before you and I bonded. I'll call up the lawyers on Monday and find out what's the holdup."

With that, they snuggled and talked until the candles burned down to nothing and played with each other until Sarah's own breathing got a little ragged. But before things got out of hand, she sent him on his way. Values were values.

The news on Monday was not good. Not on the religious side and not on the civil side.

When Sarah told James that night what she'd found out from her American lawyer she was in tears of frustration, and it had nothing to do with aborted foreplay.

The problem was that the bastard Leo was not going to agree to a divorce. In Orthodox Judaism, only the husband can permit a divorce by giving his wife a Get, which must be accepted willingly (and goodness knows Sarah would accept it with open arms). Then it would go to the Beth Din, a rabbinical court, that makes sure both sides agree and all the i's have been dotted and the t's crossed. So while Sarah thought her civil divorce was proceeding through the Florida courts, Leo was the holdup in the rabbinical court.

No divorce, no single Sarah who could get on with her life.

Then the Florida civil divorce went all cockeyed.

Leo's attorney in the Florida court argued that since Sarah wasn't a human, she couldn't sue for divorce because, essentially, she was never legally married. Insultingly, he wrote in his argument that you can't marry a dog, so you can't divorce one either. When that made the papers, a group called Friends of the Elves filed an *amicus curiae* brief disputing that humans and non-humans couldn't marry, and then everything went to hell.

Instead of a nice, clean civil divorce, the case was bumped to higher courts, and Leo found that he had some support in high places; the public started to donate to his cause. There were fundraisers on the internet. He started to make a nice bit of change on his status as an aggrieved husband whose fairy wife ran off with all of *his* money *and* his hand. Serena came back. The kids went on right-wing talk shows and podcasts. Lisa came out as an orc.

In the meantime, the actual civil divorce was being held up in bureaucratic limbo because everyone and his brother stuck their nose in it.

Sarah wasn't bothered about the civil divorce; she figured it would come eventually, and it wasn't a religious bond. But, she told James, now she was getting neither one and was still tied to Leo whether she wanted to be or not. She was a chained wife, an *"agunah"*.

James hugged her and thought about it. He didn't ask her to forget about courts and councils; he wasn't going to ask her to set aside what was clearly important. Sex would become fornication, and she wouldn't be a wife but a concubine, and that was not going to happen to his Sarah. Simply living together while she was still married would put an ugly shadow on their relationship that would eventually have to be wiped clean anyway, so they might as well do it right from the beginning.

"Would you mind if I got involved? Talked to some lawyers myself? We have some good ones here that Rashid has on call." He pulled her close. "You don't have to deal with this idiot orc by yourself. We're a team now."

She sniffled and nodded. Anything to get this moving. Anything to get rid of Leo.

The Get

There were ten people on Leo Ochs' screen. Leo, the three kids, two lawyers, an expert in rabbinical law, a finance guy, and an unknown man who was there as an "observer". Neither James nor Conary liked the idea of an unknown sitting in on this meeting (Was he from the press? The US government? One of Ochs' financial backers?), but they were told that their list of participants was non-negotiable, and they ceded that point just to get them to the table.

Conary hated these massive video conferences, but they were a fact of life now. He liked to see people's faces in person, judge their body language, see what they were doing when no one was looking. But the alternative was to put this meeting off for weeks while one side or the other cleared their schedules for a trans-Atlantic flight. And then the lords would be sitting in a room with at least four hostile orcs. Not good.

On the European side of the pond, there was James as Sarah's advocate, a lawyer who specialised in US divorce cases, Conary as the EN rep, and their expert consultants for guidance on rabbinical law – a posek and an Av Beth Din, a man who advises the Beth Din judges.

The way Conary looked at it, and everyone on their side agreed, since Leo was willing to talk at all, he was ready to negotiate a settlement, and it probably was simply a matter of finding out how much money it would take to buy him off.

The EN lawyer started the meeting with a scripted intro that stated Lord Sarah's side and formally asked Leo to sign the Get "because the marriage was irretrievably broken and so that both sides could get on with their lives."

Leo's lawyer replied that Leo would not sign the Get because he wanted Sally back, that he loved her, and her leaving had been a great shock to him and his children, and that if she indeed was a good, observant Jew, she would be committed to keeping her family intact. They had been, he said, married thirty years, which showed a strong commitment on both sides.

The lawyer turned to Leo and asked if he had anything to say, and of course, Leo did. "Please tell Sally this from my heart. She can come back, and I'll forgive everything. I know we had some rocky times, and I wasn't the best of husbands, but I've changed. I'm in counselling now. We have three kids and four grandkids, and we can have a happy family if she gives us a chance. I won't sign the Get because she still is a beloved member of our family."

James raised his hand and leaned forward. "May I have a word? Leo, I'm Lord James, and you know I'm speaking for Lord Sarah today. She thought everything would be less emotional if she sent an agent to speak for her. Lord Sarah said you got pretty upset the last time she spoke with you, and you tried to attack her. How's your hand, by the way?"

Flushing bright red, Leo snarled, and his eyes turned purple, but his lawyer shook his head at Leo, and the orc steadied. "I know I was upset, but like I said, I'm in counselling. I'm learning to control my temper."

James smiled sympathetically and nodded, the picture of commiseration. Tempers are hard to keep under control.

"Counselling is good. I'm sure you need it. I want to make sure you understand that if Lord Sarah returns she will lose her position in the Elf Nation and won't get any financial help from us while she's living with you. Unfortunately, she committed all of her money she took as her share of the joint household accounts to battered women's shelters in Florida. It's a good cause and one close to her heart. So you and your children will have to take up the slack in supporting her. Are you okay with that?"

Leo's eyes glittered. "What do you mean, she has no money?"

"Not much, I'm afraid. And no money from us either if she returns. I think there's about a thousand in her bank account now. You see, we lords don't get paid; we get everything in kind. Our clothes, our food, our lodging – everything is provided by the elves, and there aren't any elves in the US to support Lord Sarah. As a tribe we lords are as poor as church mice."

JJ shot up and yelled at the screen, "If you don't have any money how the hell can you make any settlement? You guys are rich!"

James nodded. "The Elf Nation is indeed rich. But not lords. We're like monks. Vows of poverty and all that. The elves take care of us. But of course, you want Lord Sarah, not money, right?"

There was silence. Conary raised an eyebrow at their lawyer, and she had to smile down at her papers. No one had expected this from James.

Leo's lawyer looked grim. "Of course, Leo wants Sally back. That's what he said."

"Okay." And James stood up. "I guess that's the end of this meeting then. I'll go tell Lord Sarah that Leo wants her back and that he's in counselling and that I recommend she go back to Florida and try to patch things up. You guys are prepared to feed and house a lord? We eat a *lot*. And you *do* have medical insurance, right? How's your hand again?" Then he waved and turned. "I'm sure you've thought it all out. Bye!" And he switched off his video feed.

"WAIT!" Shooting her hand up, Lisa yelled. Wide-eyed, she looked over at Leo, who sat stunned. "Pop! You have to –" And then her sound went off.

"Ummm – yes, Lord James." Leo's lawyer cleared his throat. "This is a happy and unexpected turn of affairs. There might be some adjusting that needs to be done on this side. May we have a few minutes? A short break?"

James turned his monitor back on. "I'm fine with a break; see you back in ten minutes then? I'll go get a coffee. EN side, could you please turn your audio and cameras off? Everyone?"

Conary looked at James and whistled. "Well, that was bold. Remind me never to negotiate with you." The lawyer laughed. "The expression on his face when you said she'd go back to him!"

James grinned. "I just want a happy Leo. He's in counselling, after all, and in a fragile state. It was good to hear they didn't want any money." Conary barked a laugh.

Ten minutes later, the video conference resumed, and this time Leo's lawyer spoke first.

"Leo and the family welcome Sally's return, but they have concerns about supporting her. Funds are very tight now. When she left she took more than three hundred thousand dollars in cash from the bank, and that was spread between retirement, business, and household accounts. The cash flow position of the business was severely affected. There's a lot of debt."

James looked pained. "You say she took three hundred thousand? From a business *and* the house? That's not very much in the big scheme of things. A pittance. I understand the house was hers anyway. Inherited from her parents, mortgage-free. And the business was her parents, too. Leo was given a pretty good dowry when they married. What exactly did he contribute anyway?"

"THE BITCH OWES M –" Leo's feed abruptly went black.

"Oh, dear, I think Leo is getting emotional. We'll move on while he gathers his thoughts. So what you're saying is that it's best if Lord Sarah doesn't go back to Florida?"

The lawyer spoke through gritted teeth. "The family feels that now is not a good time."

James nodded. "Okay, here's the deal. Leo? Can you hear me? Time is one thing we lords have in abundance. Lord Sarah is immortal. A lord. She will live forever. If she waits long enough, she won't need a Get because she'll be a widow and everything in her life will be kosher. What's Leo's life expectancy? Fifteen years? Twenty? He could die tomorrow. Decades are nothing to a lord. I know lords who are *three thousand* years old. Lord Conary, how old is Lord Vrt? About that?"

"My bond-wife is about 3,500 years old, but I've never asked her the exact number. I doubt if she knows for one thing. And it's rude."

"So let's say we leave today, and Leo says he doesn't want Lord Sarah back for whatever reason, and he also says there's no Get. Then there's no reason to negotiate any settlement. She can just wait it out here, provided with everything she needs here by the Elf Nation in luxurious comfort, and Leo can live with his present circumstances until he dies of old age. You've paid into Social Security, haven't you, Leo?"

James paused, and his voice became hard.

"I am authorised to settle this today. But Leo, I'm not going to fuck around with you. I don't like you. This shit is not going to be drawn out. I'm going to give you a number, and if you want the money, you're going to sign the Get today. Voluntarily and in front of witnesses. It's today or never. If you fuck around, Leo, you get nothing, and Lord Sarah waits for you to die of either frustration or old age – in poverty."

James held up a bank draft to the screen. "If you sign the Get and fax it to us, the money will be in your account within half an hour. You have ten minutes to make a decision; in fifteen minutes, I'll be heading home. There's football on the telly tonight." He turned to the room. "Cut off the feed, please." And the EN screens went blank.

James grinned at Conary and then yelled out the door. "Did I do good, Judy?"

Lord Judy poked her head in and gave him a thumbs-up. "Ninety per cent?"

"Seventy-five. He's an orc. He can't do maths anyway." James turned to Conary and the lawyer. "Judy told me what she thought his bottom line was and suggested I offer him ninety per cent of that. If he fusses, I can raise a wee bit."

Ten minutes later, Leo's lawyer came on video. Leo and the kids were gone. The lawyer had the Get signed and witnessed. Copies were sent to everyone who needed one as well as the Beth Din, along with a video of Leo surrounded by JJ, Lisa, and

Lee attesting that he had signed voluntarily. He didn't look happy, but the kids sure did.

All Sarah had to do was wait for word to come back from the Beth Din, and then she and her Boaz could get on with their lives.

James and Sarah

James was happily sitting on the sofa in Sarah's flat, feet up on the coffee table, beer in hand, footie on the telly, and a huge pizza within reaching distance. That morning Jamie had been allowed to stay overnight at the boarding school wing because Ded had no idea when he'd be coming home. You never had to worry about getting a sitter when you lived with elves, but Jamie was happier near his mates than sitting alone with an elf in the flat. Elves were rubbish at computer games. They always won.

Now all James had to do was wait for Sarah to get home from work. He wondered what she did; he'd have to ask her directly one day.

She walked in normally, not porting, and this time she wasn't ravenously hungry, but being a lord she wasn't going to turn down any junk food, either. After giving James a kiss and grabbing a piece of pizza she went to shower. She was filthy and covered in dust and dirt from head to toe, her green eyes sparkling out of a clean patch on her face like she had been wearing goggles. James noticed she wasn't wearing her normal dark field gear but was in a mottled light brown like desert camo. Curiouser and curiouser.

When she finally came out from a very long shower, at least by Jamie-standard, she was wearing a silky kimono thing as a dressing gown and still combing out her damp hair.

"Okay – time to dish. What happened at the conference call?"

James lifted the pizza box. Underneath was a legal envelope, and he handed it to her. "Your Get. Signed, sealed, and sent to the Beth Din. Both the posek and the Av Beth Din we hired say it's watertight. No worries."

Sarah looked down at the paper, and James could see it shaking. He leaned over and pulled her onto his lap. "Pet, you don't have to worry; it's over." He tilted up her chin and kissed her nose. "No tears."

She nodded, gulped, and wiped her eyes with the back of her hand and then began to read the paper. There it was, Leo's signature, witness signatures, all that was needed, with a settlement of –

"Two point five million!" Sarah stared at the paper and then back at James, who grinned. "The Elf

Nation paid my settlement to Leo, and it was *two point five million*!"

She looked at the paper again. "Although I was expecting it to be at least twenty-five mil. I mean, Malachi's bidding started at five hundred million."

James chuckled. "I was expecting quite a bit more, too. But Judy told me Leo's bottom line was three and a third. She was watching him on another feed in a different room, and while it's hard for her to mindread through a video link she can manage it if it's live. And Leo, bless his orc hide, was alive. And thinking of his payday a lot."

"But —"

"I offered him seventy-five per cent of what he wanted, and he took it. I bought you at a discount! Never pay full retail, Pet."

"Oh, Jamie, you're such a fucking cliche." She kissed him, long and hard, and he discovered she wasn't wearing anything under this dressing gown either.

———————————————————

Lester

Change was coming to the wider world despite his best efforts. If Lester wasn't too late already, eventually the world would go back to the balance of Before Times, and that meant marginalising Lester.

Now NATO was changing, and a new body, the Elf Nation, was moving in. NATO, with its vast technological superiority over Russia, was bad enough, but lords – that was another level. Lords were in power, and Lester remembered what power lords had if they put their minds to it. These new lords were scary.

Change made people think. It stirred ambitions. It created uncertainty.

Humans in the Russian government saw the US leaving NATO as an opening. They thought about the implications. They started to have ambitions. What would happen if Russia tried to regain Crimea? Kaliningrad?

They pointed out that the orcs migrating in vast numbers to Russia could make a tough, semi-magical army of super soldiers. Russia didn't have the technology of the West, but quantity has its own quality, a quote misattributed to Stalin but embraced by the Russian military elite. In other words, the West might have fancy kit, but Russia had a lot of bodies to throw at a war, and the bodies were mostly orcs.

Lester didn't want a war with the West. He certainly didn't want a war with lords and elves, and if Russia attacked Ukraine, Lester knew Kyrylo would fight back on his native country's behalf, and he'd be nasty about it.

But Lester had to keep his own elite happy if he wanted to stay as Tsar, and his elite wanted power, fame, vacations in Italy, and second homes in London. They thought it was time to demonstrate that Russia was a great power and saw no inconsistency with asking to be let back into civilised western life and threatening to invade a peaceful country. They thought that if the West was afraid of Russia, they would get what they wanted. And to make the Western nations afraid, they should invade somewhere to show the power of the new Russian Army.

NATO losing its richest and most well-armed member was the opening they were waiting for.

In Russia, generals studied lines on maps and made plans.

Wendell and LeeAnne

The young couple drove up to the Sandman Signature Lethbridge Lodge in a Rapid Red Mustang convertible.

When the car rental customer service rep handed over the keys, he'd called the Mustang "Cop Bait Red," and he wasn't kidding. They were stopped four times in their drive across Canada, and Wendell was only speeding a little. Yes, he was puttering along over 152 kph when the speed limit was 110, but he had to see what the thing would do at least once, right? As he said to LeeAnne, with all seriousness, you had to know your ride just in case something happened, like orcs chasing them or something. And it was such a nice, empty, straight stretch of highway.

After Wendell was pulled over and endured the cop's lecture and LeeAnne's I-told-you-so glares, he didn't speed again. Not much, anyway. Just enough to get stopped and given warnings. Three times.

It was a lovely car.

The job that took them to Lethbridge wasn't really a job. It was a busman's holiday – an easy and entertaining assignment that was also a reward for having so many not-so-easy assignments that took him away from Lowestoft and LeeAnne. He and LeeAnne had been dating for a couple of years now, and between her uni schedule and his frequent forays to gods-know-where, it was hard to find time to just go away together. So this particular project was a treat.

And it was easy! The easiest assignment he had ever had as a Ranger. All he had to do was drive across southern Canada and play tourist. He and LeeAnne were well-heeled uni students having a little cross-continent adventure drive, ending up in Vancouver, where they'd fly back home. All they had to do was stop off at about five different small towns, stay a couple of days in each, and look for orcs. They were taking an orc census of sorts. That was it.

Admittedly, driving through Saskatchewan in July wasn't the same as lolling on the beaches of Bali, but it wasn't Turkmenistan, either, and Wendell had worked in both. They were having fun just being together, and they spent some nights in dude ranches and luxury lodges and Indian reservations, and the entire trip made LeeAnne happy, so Wendell was happy.

And a happy LeeAnne was very happy between the sheets, which made Wendell even happier.

LeeAnne was pretty good at recognising orcs now. Her training as a physiotherapist made spotting the distinctive rolling gait a snap, and now she didn't even have to look in their eyes or get close to one. Wendell had been trained by elves, so he was very good at it, but by the time they left Toronto, she was better.

Lethbridge was the last of the census towns. They checked into the motel and immediately went for a jog at a nearby Indian Battle Park. The names the locals had given to their landmarks were so plain and to the point that they made LeeAnne giggle. "Old Man River," "Indian Battle Park," "Whoop-Up Drive". Lethbridge was what it said on the tin in direct and unvarnished language.

After the jog in the park, they dressed and drove around the small downtown looking for restaurants, but mostly just looking.

What they discovered about Lethbridge was that it was nice. An unpretentious, honest, working town that locals probably didn't appreciate as much as visitors. They didn't spot a single orc. Not one, which was unusual.

They spent two more days just looking around, then Wendell sent off his report, and they drove on to Vancouver where Wendell, with much heartache, said goodbye to the beautiful Mustang.

Three weeks later, a mysterious consortium started buying up land in Lethbridge between Highway 4 and the airport. A lot of land.

Ivana

Ivana was upset. She ran to the open door, but Yana wouldn't let her out; she had to play in her room. So she plopped down on her diapered and well-padded butt and wailed for Mummy as if her little heart was breaking. When that didn't work she picked up Spoon and ran to the door again, yelling for Mummy, sure she could make an end run around the elf. Yana was only a foot taller than the baby, but she was a lot more agile. Having known how to walk and run for 3,700 years longer than Ivana, she blocked the toddler like a rugby player dancing a haka. Ivana couldn't get past her.

So Ivana fell back on her butt and yelled again with much more success. Daddy came to the door and wanted to know what the matter was, and of course, Daddy would pick her up when no one else would.

"Spoo!" she yelled. Ivana always found yelling was easier than talking. She wasn't screaming; she was just being assertive. Sometimes, amazingly, grown-ups didn't do what she wanted them to do. It was a constant battle to train them, and she found yelling helped.

Kyrylo nodded. "Spoon," he replied. And indeed it was Spoon, even if he looked uncharacteristically tatty. Spoon desperately needed a new bow tie.

"Uh-ohhhh," she said and looked comically sad, her baby lower lip pouting out. And then she theatrically dropped Spoon and leaned over to see what would happen.

Kyrylo looked down and waited for Spoon to bounce up and back into Ivana's chubby fingers. Spoon didn't bounce up. He just lay there. Like a spoon.

Ivana peered down from the great height of her daddy's arms. "Spoo b-bye. Uh-ohhh."

Kyrylo squatted down and picked up Spoon. He frowned and turned Spoon over. It was just a wooden spoon. It wasn't Spoon. Had he gotten tired and moved to a newer version? Ivana was pretty hard on him sometimes. Personally, Kyrylo wouldn't want any toddler to use him as a drumstick, and that's what Ivana usually did when she played with Spoon. She would pound the living daylights out of the poor kitchen utensil.

"Let's go find your Mum," murmured Daddy, which of course was what Ivana had wanted all along.

"Caddy! Have you seen Spoon?"

Now, in a normal household that would be an odd thing to ask one's wife, but this was the Melnyk residence, and such a question was perfectly normal. No, Caddy had not seen Spoon. Not since yesterday.

Kyrylo offered the ex-Spoon back to Ivana, and the baby, with all the drama of a panto dame, pushed it away and cried. She didn't want *that* spoon. She wanted Spoon!

"B-bye, uh-Ohhh," she said again. Caddy frowned. Something wasn't right, so she called for Brenda and asked her to have all of the elves look for Spoon and make sure he/she/it was okay.

An hour later, no one had seen Spoon. All of the utensil drawers were checked, every closet was looked into, and Ivana's (excessive) toy chest was emptied and searched. No Spoon.

Spoon was gone.

Caddy and Kyrylo stood for a minute, listened, and both realised it at the same time.

So was House.

Adem

The Safe Haven that covered House was pretty extensive. It wasn't as large as the elves' Safe Haven, of course, which covered hundreds of acres and was the size of a large town, but it was pretty big. When Caddy first pushed her bike down the path to the settlement, the outhouse that Adem lived in was part of a derelict farming complex of five houses, barns, sheds, and so forth covering about five acres. Over time, the elves had cleaned up and landscaped around Caddy's house, but kept the sheltering woods and buildings as they were to provide a bit of cover and to blend in with the surrounding Ukrainian countryside.

When the elves couldn't find Spoon in the house and sensed that House wasn't inside either, they started looking further out and quickly found something odd.

Caddy and Kyrylo walked through the overgrown brambles and scrub to the settlement with Bram, Brenda, and the elf who had discovered the anomaly.

What he'd found was a squat, metal grain silo, not a huge one that soared into the sky, but a smaller, shorter one used to store grain for the farm's livestock. The top of it had long rusted out, pierced by artillery from a forgotten battle in the Russian War, and it was open to the weather. The elves had cut two holes in the bottom so no one could be trapped in it but otherwise had left it alone.

Now the holes were stopped up. Caddy could see faint wisps of steam rising from the top and floating into the cold Ukrainian sky. When Kyrylo touched the sides of the silo it was warm. Then the wind changed, and they could smell it. The faint whiff of vanilla custard.

It was a cauldron.

"That's a hell of a big cauldron," Kyrylo said to no one in particular.

Caddy nodded. "Do you think we need to get Mandy here?" She looked to Bram, but he was already gone. The lord was sure Mandy would be there in a few minutes. It was the edge of her range, but not so far that she couldn't come.

"It's a House-sized cauldron." Brenda looked up at Caddy, worried. "Do you think he's in there?"

"I've always thought – actually, I knew in my heart – that House was a lord who was trapped in a piece of wood. I think he's decided it's time to do something about it," Caddy said, and she looked at the silo and wondered what would come out. It was very large. Would they get a giant lord?

Kyrylo agreed that House could be in there and told Brenda to get someone to build a temporary shelter in front of the silo so they could sit their vigil. By the evening, Caddy was sitting in a cosy shelter, talking to the silo, and keeping House anchored to this world.

Mandy popped in right away, and Kyrylo stood on a stepstool and lifted her to the top of the rusty silo so she could look in. She took a sample of the yellow goo to analyse back in her office, but what she said when she was back on the ground surprised no one. What they found was a cauldron, a fekkin' big one, and all they could do was pray it worked. She sighed and looked back up, shook her head, and popped out without another word.

Caddy cancelled the next two weeks of her appointments diary and prepared to sit for the long haul. She and Kyrylo sat and talked to House all the first day, but when the word got out, she was far from alone. Alizah insisted on staying with them, leaving Jack alone to take care of the new lords at Aelfeham House, something she had never done before. She relieved Caddy for hours on end, and she never, ever shut up. It seemed that every single person, lord, human, or elf, who had ever stayed or walked through House wanted to come and spend some time talking. And there were a *lot*.

Kyrylo didn't take any time off at all. There were worries about the Russians and unexpected military exercises on the other side of the border, so there was no expectation by anyone that he would sit and talk all day, but he still managed to put in his hour every evening, sitting in the shelter, talking to House, and simultaneously playing with Ivana. Kyrylo was efficient with his time and could multitask.

He and Ivana even came up with a song. It went like this: "Spoon, Spoon, *Spoon,* Spoon, Spoon, Spoon, Spoon, SPOON!" And Ivana danced and danced to it.

James and Sarah

When James and Sarah (finally) spent the night together, she was nervous and he was quick. Very nervous and very quick.

James was a bit abashed and not a little surprised. After all of the heavy make-out sessions with Sarah, he hadn't thought he would be that eager, but he was. He'd been married for fifteen years to a woman he'd loved and who'd loved him, and in his mind, you don't get three kids without having a healthy sex life. While Sarah could vigorously dispute that idea, he didn't think either side of his former marital bed had any complaints.

Sarah was nervous, and it didn't take a scientist to see that she was relieved when the first time was over. But by the second and third encounter, she was relaxing and on her way to enjoying herself – and James thought if he could give her enough time to warm up, she would.

He tried to give himself a break. He hadn't had sex for over four years, not since Lauren's first futile bout of chemotherapy. After that poison entered her system it was just snuggles and kisses, and that was all either of them felt like doing.

Then Sarah came along, and she was certainly healthy and gorgeous, maybe too much so. All she had to do was give him that look, and her eyes started to glow, and he was as hard as a rock. The minute she moved a bit under him he was gone, just like a fifteen-year-old boy with his first girlfriend. It was embarrassing.

But she never complained, never looked disappointed, not even surprised. If anything, when he came, she was delighted, just over the moon that he was having a good time, and would kiss him and snuggle up, practically purring. It made him feel really bad.

She never talked about Leo. Ever. She never spoke of whatever abuse she had suffered, but there were hints. There were certain things he couldn't do that triggered her, and he found out the hard way.

He couldn't hold her head. The first time he put both hands on the side of her head to give her a kiss, she stiffened up, and her eyes went wide. He thought she was going to have a panic attack, but he dropped one hand to her side, and she didn't pull away, but that was the end of that kiss. She was edgy for an hour.

The other thing he couldn't do was sneak up behind her. The first, only, and last time he did that, just to give her a playful goose on her delectable butt, he found himself flat on his back with her knee in his stomach and a knife to his neck, and he had no idea how he got there. Sarah was absolutely distraught and tearfully apologised for almost two days, but James took that as his fault; he should have known better than to sneak up on a Warrior Lord with PTSD, and he promised never to do that again. Lesson learnt.

One evening when Sarah was gone on one of her mysterious assignments, James sat on the couch doing a bit of background work for Rashid. He was looking through personnel files to find people skills that would work on a particular job and stumbled across a locked, confidential folder simply titled "Lords". Being a nosy sort – because that was what he did for a living – being nosy – he clicked to open it, and to his surprise, his eye scan worked. He was, it seemed, "cleared for weird" in RumLot world.

And there it was. As Conary had said, RumLot had a background file of every lord. James didn't know it but when Caddy had first run off to Ukraine using her American passport that no one knew she had, Rashid had made sure that there were no hidden bits of a lord's history that could get in the way of finding them if they disappeared. Every little bit of intel about each of them was there. James looked over his own file, and it was very, very thorough, and from a professional perspective, he had to admire the work. His file had the flippin' present-day address of his first girlfriend, and he could barely remember her name. It also had the time when he was a nineteen-year-old holidaying in Greece and was thrown in jail overnight for public drunkenness. He didn't think *anyone* knew about that.

Sarah had a file, too. James learnt that she had a two-year Associate's Degree in office management. Other than that, there wasn't much to see in her early life. One family, one home address her entire life, no holidays, no boyfriends, nothing official in her life other than a driver's licence. No accidents or tickets. A marriage licence to Leo.

Then a sickening list of calls – by neighbours, by friends, by rabbis – to hotlines reporting spousal abuse. Two or three times a year, someone would call the cops on Leo. Whipping, punches, bruises, multiple reports of where people were sure she had been raped, but then the report would state in very dry, legal language that in the State of Florida there was no such thing as marital rape, so it was not chargeable. Legally, Leo could do what he liked with her as long as he claimed it was marital sex. And if it got a little rough, that was between him and her.

And nothing was done. Nothing. The police would show up at the door, interview Sarah, interview Leo, and even take pictures of Sarah's injuries. And they would leave, and nothing would happen.

James could hear the street cops' frustration in the reports. They knew he was beating her, but she wouldn't press charges. "Mrs Ochs declines to press charges." "Mrs Ochs is worried about who will take care of the kids and declines to press charges." "Mrs Ochs claims the cut was accidental." "Mrs Ochs claims she tripped down the stairs."

Then, in 2018, something changed. After over a decade of marriage, Leo ran afoul of the law. In 2018, marital rape became illegal in Florida; it was a felony conviction, and the victim didn't have to press charges; the state could.

There was one call out in 2018, and Leo was charged with domestic battery. Sarah had been married to an orc for twelve years. The police, who were absolutely sick of the man by then, took a lot of photos of Sarah, and one would always haunt James. The side view showed little points on her ears. She had the shaven head of a married Hasidim, and on the side of her head were little bruises, like fingerprints.

The front view showed an utterly defeated, painfully thin woman. Swollen black eyes. Bruises down the side of her face. At forty-two, she looked like she was seventy years old. But it was the despair in her eyes. He wished he had never seen it, and now it could never be unseen. It was the same dead despair that dulled the eyes of Jews in photos of Dachau.

After 2018, there were no more police reports. Leo was hauled in, sentenced, and given no jail time if he went to court-ordered counselling for his first offence, which he did. There were no more public records of her until she applied for a passport the year before her son graduated from uni. James wondered how long she had been planning on leaving Leo.

When she came back from her assignment and walked into his flat it was hard to believe she was the same person in that photo. Sarah was beautiful, healthy, and one could even say sleek. But most of all she looked happy. She walked up to James and just beamed; she was so delighted to see him.

And he was desperately happy to see her. He just wished he could make her as happy as she deserved. He would work on it.

Adem

The egg didn't rise when Mandy expected, and every day it didn't rise, she would come and personally check the cauldron and leave with a grim expression on her face. On day fifteen, she told Caddy that the only reason she wasn't declaring that House was dead was because of two things. The first was that everyone felt his soul was still in this world, and the second was that the goo didn't smell bad. If it wasn't going to work it would be fetid by now and smell of rotten eggs. So they would just have to wait until that point came.

"It's a huge cauldron. Do you think the egg is slow developing because it's huge, too?"

Dr Mandy shrugged. She had no idea. She had never seen a lord make up his own cauldron before, and in the elf medical literature, there was no record of it ever happening. And in all the literature, there was no record of such huge cauldrons. Even the cauldrons that held centaurs weren't that big.

Caddy didn't say it, but she was thinking what everyone was thinking. This lord was going to be a giant, and as someone who came out of the cauldron not as a normal man, he could have other issues, too. Brain damage, disabilities, chimaera – it could be anything.

She told Kyrylo that night that the unknown was weighing on her, and she couldn't sleep for the worry. If House came out damaged the elves would look to her to tell them what to do with the poor man. What if he was so badly damaged or in agony that she had to have House put down? Her bond-man gave her a hug and said what he always said in such dire times. "We will deal with whatever the stars throw at us together." That was all he could do.

Three days later, the egg rose to the surface, but no one saw it. The cauldron was so tall that it took a special ladder to get to the top, and they'd never bothered to hook up a camera. Later on, Dr Mandy would ask herself why she hadn't ordered one installed, but even the best of healers overlook things, and that was her one mistake.

For the next three days, the egg rose and sank like all the eggs did, but every time it did no one was around to see it.

Dr Mandy did put a temperature probe in the goo, and when the temperature started to rise, she rushed to the cauldron, but it didn't boil over when she expected. It was so big that it took a lot longer to reach its froth point. For three hours, elf nurses stood around the silo with huge nets and a crane, ready to take the giant to a specially prepared barn they had turned into a bedroom.

So imagine their surprise when Adem emerged looking perfectly normal. Actually, for a man, he was rather short.

He'd had to build a huge cauldron that was big enough to hold and cover his huge, fungal bulk when he first slipped under the water, not because the end result was going to be equally huge.

Instead of going to the barn Adem was taken to the spare bedroom in the house, which was no longer named House because House had ceased to exist. Everyone was hugely relieved they weren't dealing with a brain-damaged giant and not a little curious as to what House/Spoon looked like and what he would be like. It was as if they were meeting a long-lost relative. No one even knew his real name.

When he was cleaned up and asleep in bed, Caddy and Kyrylo went to visit him. He was lying in bed flat on his back with his arms to the side as all the newly re-born people were. Caddy saw a short man, about 5'5" or maybe a shade taller, well-proportioned if rather stocky, with round cheeks, a round nose and smiling lips, and, of course, huge ears. A rather jolly Santa Claus face, even with the puffiness that newly born people have. Just looking at him made her smile.

"Welcome back, stranger," she whispered. "We've missed you."

He didn't wake up, but he smiled.

Alizah

Alizah was the first to feed Adem and the first to learn his real name. Adem was the same as everyone else after being reborn, disoriented and woozy. People just out of the cauldron were always a bit unfocused as their brains, nerves, and guts broke in their new pathways, but that didn't stop Alizah from talking to him anyway. She just burbled away, and Adem's bright blue eyes followed her around the room, occasionally whispering some nonsense back, which didn't matter to Alizah either.

But here and there, some sense was made and conversations attempted. Both loved to talk, so he wasn't shy about practising, and she was not the least bit shy about asking him all sorts of strange and impertinent questions.

Through Alizah, Caddy discovered Adem's name, his vast age, and that he had never bonded. In Before Times, he wasn't considered a useful lord, and he didn't have elves to take care of him, even though he was an Elemental. In other words, he was an Elemental with no utility to *elves*, and being gay, he wasn't going to have a woman around to make Scent.

Then, during her last dinner with Caddy and Kyrylo before she left to return to Suffolk and her Jack, Alizah dropped a bombshell. "Did you know what I found out today? I found out that Adem created the Safe Havens. That's his ability, to create bubbles outside of space and time. He made the elves' Safe Haven! That's why this house is a Safe Haven, too."

Kyrylo stopped eating. This was very interesting. He looked at Caddy, but he didn't think she completely understood the importance of what Alizah had just said.

"Zaychik, I would like to know more about this bubble/Safe Haven thing."

Caddy raised an eyebrow. And?

Kyrylo leaned back. "If Adem creates these bubbles outside of space/time that the elves can port to, why can't we port to them, too? We live in one here, and it's perfectly comfortable to us, probably because he created this one on solid land and not out in the ether somewhere. Sarah ported to the elves' Safe Haven and survived. It was where she ported to afterwards that wiped her out, not being in Safe Haven." He leaned forward, running with the idea.

"Can we use a bubble as a way station? Can we have elves port us to a *lord* Safe Haven and then on to anywhere else the way elves can move goods through their Safe Haven? We just need one elf to get us to the way station and another from the other end to pick us up. If we could do that, we wouldn't need port chains across Europe and helicopters over the North Sea. We could even port to Canada!"

He was getting excited, and his eye glowed. "We've never asked an English elf to port directly here, to this Safe Haven. It's never crossed anyone's mind. I wonder if they could."

Caddy cut up a bit of chicken for Ivana and put it on her highchair tray, where she promptly threw it on the floor. "Uh – Oooh," she said and peered down at it, obviously waiting for it to float back up to her. It didn't.

"Enough for you, then!" And Caddy turned to Kyrylo. "We can talk to Adem about all of the subtleties when he's fully back to health and thinking straight. The last thing I want right now is to do any experiments with the elves' Safe Haven. That would upset the clans. But it would be a brilliant thing if that worked out.

She wiped Ivana's protesting face, thinking, "I don't want to barge in on the elves' Safe Haven. It's a private, human-free lord-free space for them, and that has value right there. But if Adem created one for us to use as a way station – well, we'll have to talk to him. We don't know what it will cost him to do that. I don't want him to get hurt either."

Kyrylo nodded. All good points, and they could be patient. Besides, Marylin was bringing in dessert, and he was partial to apple *yabluchnyk*.

Jamie

Jamie the Younger was showing Sarah how to play a video racing game and was winning handily, which was extremely satisfying. He knew she was trying, but she was a very cautious driver, probably because she actually knew how to drive and crashing made her wince every time it happened.

Tactical fighting games like *Call of Duty: Ultimate Black Ops 8,* which were pretty old but still fun didn't do much for her. Being a Warrior Lord herself, they were just too slow, and she argued with the computer all the time. *Orc Invasion 4* was a bit better, but she played it like it was *Tetris* and just sat there killing one orc after another – bam, bam, bam.

Ded was sitting on the sofa watching them play, but mostly doing something for work on his tablet. Chloe was off doing Chloe things with a newly arrived seventeen-year-old lord called Imogene, who hailed from Liberia. Richie had disappeared, and Jamie hadn't seen his brother since their last family dinner. He didn't hang around much any more, and when he did, it wasn't long enough to get a good game in, which was a bummer. He seemed to be busy all the time with his Ranger lessons. Someone said he had a girlfriend. Jamie didn't know if he really did, and certainly couldn't understand why a girl would be taking up all of his brother's time. It was a mystery. He missed his big brother.

Now, Sarah was different. Jamie understood why Sarah took up his Ded's time; who else was he going to hang out with? Sarah was cool, and when the kids were around, she let the family get on with being a family. She didn't push, but when Jamie offered to teach her how to play video games, she didn't say no either. Sarah didn't try to do mothery things or have long, prying conversations; she didn't even ask how he was doing in school. She just listened to Jamie's instructions and played. Sarah was just good enough to make the games fun, but unlike the elves, not *too* good.

When the game was over and Sarah lost again, she turned to Jamie and grinned.

"I have a surprise for you. Chloe said your birthday was coming up next week, and I brought you a card." And she handed him an envelope.

Jamie took the card and politely thanked her. A birthday card was just the sort of old-person gift he would expect from Sarah, but it was nice of her to remember him. James sat up, curious. Frankly, he had forgotten that next week was Jamie's birthday.

The card was a typical, lame, now-you-are-twelve boy's card with a race car on the front towing cartoon balloons. He opened it up. Inside was a brochure and three tickets to a two-hour session for Formula 1 karting. He would go go-kart racing on a real racetrack, and the extra tickets were for his mates so he could have fun with them, too.

Jamie could hardly breathe; he was so excited. He had seen the racing karts on the telly, but that was something other, normal, *human* kids did, not lords. And now Sarah had arranged a day out, even with bodyguards and the whole bit, so Ded wouldn't worry about orcs. For her reward, Sarah got a huge hug that brought tears to her eyes, and he immediately dumped her to run off to the school dormitory wing and show Karol and Mick his tickets.

James hugged her, too and gave her a big kiss as well. "Well, Pet, that was a winner! Well done to you for thinking that up! I don't think he'll ever forget his thirteenth birthday!"

"Thirteen! I thought it was his twelfth."

"No, he's twelve now."

Sarah frowned. "Then when is his Bar Mitzvah? That should be coming up, too."

Uh-oh. Warning! Landmines ahead.

James looked at his tablet. When is Jamie's Bar Mitzvah, indeed? "Ah dinnae ken –"

The lord's eyes glowed, but it wasn't a happy glow. It was a "I'm not going to interfere with how you are raising your kids, but what the hell are you thinking James?" glow.

"And the other two? No Bar and Bat Mitzvah for them, either?"

James sighed. "No, Lauren's parents –"

"You have parents, too, Jamie, who you say are observant. Who I have never met, by the way." Then she stood up and slipped on her shoes to leave. "The kids are lords. They have a natural affinity for languages and only have to read a line from the Torah. Your parents would probably love to see that." Sarah bent down and kissed him. On the cheek. And then went off to her own flat.

James sighed. She was right, of course. After a minute, he logged out of the RumLot stuff and went back into public mode and looked up what exactly a kid needed to do at a Bar Mitzvah. It had been over thirty years since the one and only Bar Mitzvah he had ever been to, his own, and he had no clue what was involved.

Adem

The next time Caddy and Kyrylo rotated to Lowestoft, they not only brought along Ivana but Adem as well.

From almost the first day Caddy had walked into the outhouse, Adem had heard about Lowestoft, and as the Elf Nation grew, visitors from Suffolk were regular guests in Ukraine. They talked about this and that at Aelfeham House until Adem felt he knew the place as well as anyone. But that was an illusion, of course. It was all just pictures in his head, and he knew it.

Adem had travelled around constantly in his old life, a peripatetic bachelor with no fixed abode, always searching for a family or community that would welcome him and he could call his own. During the chaos after Gaia died he literally went to ground and hid from the orcs and humans. Becoming a fungus saved his life, but fungi don't have legs, and he was stuck in one place. Now, as a man again, he could move around in this new world, but his only desire was to move to places where his fellow lords were – and that meant Aelfeham House.

Aelfeham House was now an important hub for the lord tribe. It was their hometown, a private village where they lived, played, ate, learned, mourned, loved, bonded, and worked. Adem in Ukraine was on the outside, could only look in, like a kid with his nose pressed against the candy store window. For a very social person like Adem, to live in a lord-dominated apartment complex didn't mean a lack of privacy; it meant companionship and belonging.

He was, of course, assigned his very own room. No couch surfing for Adem, not ever again! He would have his own lovely, personal space. He was also expected to go through the entire lord training gamut and H2H self-defence training. Until he found a working role, he would wear the redcoat of the junior lords.

Adem was absolutely thrilled with it all. It didn't mean he couldn't live with his beloved Melnyks for as long as he wanted, but Caddy and Kyrylo privately agreed that his visits would probably end up being shorter and shorter. The Melnyks' home wasn't House any longer, and Aelfeham House would provide a constant new stream of entertaining and interesting people that would be much more to Adem's taste. Aelfeham House was the honey to Adem's social butterfly personality.

Jack and Alizah gave him a tour and mentored Adem just like they did any other new lord. Even though he was familiar with most of the lords in residence, he didn't know all of them, not even close.

There were many redcoats who never left the grounds – Chi, for instance.

Chi previously had been the oldest of the Old Farts, but now Adem was the oldest of the five Before Times lords. Only Neptune, who lived in the sea with his merfolk, was older. Adem was also the only redcoat who was an Elemental, although no one understood what exactly he did, much less how he did it.

The elves, though, certainly found utility in Adem now! After rediscovering he was the one who had made the Safe Haven and then made the in-between place deep underground that gave them a place to hibernate indefinitely, there was quite a bit of attention paid to the lord in this modern world. If any single lord could be said to have saved the elves from extinction, it was Adem. They had a debt to repay.

House had come home.

After Adem settled into Aelfeham House, Kyrylo asked him to dinner at their home in Lowestoft. He was right up front about it; he and Caddy wanted to learn more about Adem's "bubbles" in space and if they could be used by lords and elves.

Adem was flattered that Caddy and Kyrylo were curious about his ability, and he was happy to chat about himself. So few people were interested in his ability that it was a bit of an ego boost whenever anyone was. Most of the time, though, once he started to explain that he could diffuse himself into the in-between spaces of something and that he could make in-between bubbles in existing space and time, but it wasn't something they could see, their eyes glazed over (if they were polite) or rolled (if they were rude). The man who was claiming to be an Elemental could make a bubble that no one could see or touch, and didn't move or affect anything.

An elf ported Adem right into the Melnyks' kitchen, and Ivana was the first to welcome him.

"SPOON!" she yelled, and no matter what anyone said or how many times she was corrected, Adem was Spoon, and she called him Spoon forever, long after everyone had forgotten why she called him that. Adem was and always would be Spoon to her, and he was always greeted with a kiss and a hug.

He picked her up, and she gave him sloppy baby kisses and tried to feed him some of the cookie she was working hard to turn into crumbs, and that was the beginning of a happy, noisy dinner with Caddy and Kyrylo, where he was welcomed and loved.

Everything was explained. Adem spent the evening telling his two best friends everything he hadn't been able to articulate when he was a fungus.

He told them details about his early life that no one else knew, not even Alizah, and to Caddy, it was rather sad. Not torturously bad, but sad and lonely. Adem wasn't appreciated because no one could figure out what he did as a lord, so he was just not taken seriously. In a tribe where one's ability conferred class and status, Adem had neither. He didn't have any particular artistic talent. He was clever and well-read and had a lovely singing voice, and said he could play instruments, but so did most lords. He wasn't ugly, but not particularly good-looking either. He was just Adem – a nice guy to chat and hang out with if no one better was around.

Even his birth family didn't pay much attention to him. He was the middle child of two very important lords with flashy abilities that people admired. On top of that, his brothers and sisters were all beautiful, artistically talented, and popular people. The little twinkling star that was Adem just faded into the background compared with the supernovas that made up his family. No one hated him, no one treated him badly, but he was often simply forgotten. When he started roaming, no one missed him.

Caddy could hear the old hurt in his voice, which was quickly covered by a joke, but it was there. All he had ever wanted was a family, and his family didn't want him.

He told them how he would go "in between" and sleep for decades at a time, and that he had slept through Gaia's implosion only to wake up in a world where elves were being slaughtered and most of the lords were gone. His family and friends had all been killed, either in Gaia's explosion or one by one in the slaughter afterwards. In Adem's retelling, the lords who had died with Gaia were the lucky ones.

He didn't have any self-defence skills at all. What lord needed them? Between the Elementals on the Council, the Warrior Lords, and Gaia, no orc or human would dream of hurting, much less killing a lord, so lords didn't bother with anything like learning to box or swordplay unless they were trained Warrior Lords, and there weren't many of them. The Warrior Lords punished anyone who badgered or hurt elves or each other, and not many were needed to enforce the peace and keep balance in the world. The stupid orc who hurt an elf or a weak lord and escaped the range of the elve's clan warriors could expect a visit from a Warrior Lord sooner or later, and that would be the end of their head's close relationship with their body.

Adem exercised his ability regularly, mostly to keep up his strength because he wasn't fed much, and that's how he was able to create his safe spaces when the elves needed them. There were bubbles all over the place where he'd made and abandoned them, so many that he couldn't remember where they all were.

He didn't see any reason why a lord, human, or orc couldn't be ported into one and back out because the spaces weren't made for a specific tribe. Tribe had nothing to do with them.

"So could you make a bubble for us to use? One that we could use as a transfer station that an elf could port a lord to, and then another elf could port a lord back out to someplace else?"

Adem chewed his roast beef thoughtfully. He hadn't tasted anything for over 3,500 years, and eating was a rediscovered pleasure. "Sure. When do you want me to do it?"

Kyrylo was a bit taken aback. Was this going to be as easy as that? "Tomorrow? At Aelfeham House?"

"Sure. You just tell me where and how big you want it to be. Making one the size of the house and grounds in Ukraine will wipe me out for a couple of days, but I'm okay with that. I'll miss a couple of Lord Classes, though. The one on European Political Systems sounded interesting."

Caddy was fine with Adem missing some classes. He could make them up. He had all the time in the world.

Adem

Kyrylo, Conary, and Rashid looked over their map of the Aelfeham House estate and chose a place off the main driveway for Adem to use as his bubble space. If they wanted to port something big, like a lorry, they wanted easy access to the bubble from the road.

Adem walked down the long drive and met them, the only redcoat in the bunch, and Kyrylo told him where he wanted the bubble and how big it should be.

Then they stood back and watched.

The lord stood in the field with his hands on his hips and frowned. Suddenly, his eyes flashed as bright as lasers, and his entire body glowed. Like Caddy when she played her violin to call up elves, he glowed so bright his body was enveloped in an orb of light.

Then, as fast as he'd flared up, the glow went away. Adem was wringing wet with sweat, and he swayed a bit but seemed fine. He turned to Kyrylo and grinned. "Well, that wasn't too bad." And then he turned to walk away. "Now I'm hungry!"

"Wait!" Kyrylo looked at the field. Nothing had changed. "Adem, where's the bubble?"

Adem turned, surprised. He pointed. "There, where you asked me to put it. It's a bit bigger than what you asked for, but that's okay, isn't it? I lost my edges for a minute. Out of practise, I guess."

Conary scratched his head. "Adem, we don't see anything."

"Of course, not; it's invisible. It's not in this space."

Kyrylo could immediately understand why no one in Before Times thought Adem had any talent at all. Whatever it was he did was invisible. "How did the first elf figure out how to use the big Safe Haven when you made it? We can't see a thing. How do we get into it?"

"You just walk into it." Adem looked irritated. He was really hungry now, but instead of going to the Breakfast Room, he trotted to the middle of the bubble and put his hat on the ground.

"Here's the middle of it. It's a circle, a sphere, really, and goes to about – here –" And he trotted back towards the guys and stopped at the edge and looked a bit lost as to what to do. But Conary gave him his hat, and he used it to mark the outer edge.

"Now you need to tell an elf that's outside of this clan, maybe a London or Ukrainian elf, to port here. The first elf to the Safe Haven followed me, but once one goes, he tells the others how to get there. They have some sort of system to pinpoint the location; don't ask me what it is. He won't be able to leave the sphere without getting sick, but he can come in here and go back to his home, wherever it is. I guess you're going to have to build a fence or something so people know the boundaries." The men looked at Adem blankly, and the little man sighed. He guessed he needed to be clearer. "Kyrylo, come here and stand next to me."

Kyrylo walked to Adem, and then they both walked to the centre. Suddenly, he could see the sides of the bubble. It was like being in a huge raindrop. He could see the men standing on the driveway, but they were wavy and distorted like he was looking through old glass or water.

He grinned and gave Adem a huge Kyrylo hug. "You're bloody brilliant, you are! Conary! Rashid! Come here!"

They ran up, and once inside, they both could see it, so it wasn't just a lord thing, but humans could see the edges, too. Once they could see it, they could believe it.

By lunchtime, Conary had convinced a brave elf in London to port into the bubble, and once that happened and he told his friends it was just like porting to the Safe Haven, it opened the floodgates. Elves from all over Europe ported in just to see the front facade of Aelfeham House and say they did it. The space was overcrowded quickly, and when one poor woman was accidentally shoved outside and immediately got sick, Kyrylo shooed them all back home and said only authorised elves could use the transfer node until further notice.

While in theory every single elf in the world could pass through this one central place to move lords around, that made for a very crowded transfer point, especially if they wanted to move lorries or tanks or stuff like that. So Kyrylo decided to have Adem make more bubbles in strategic places just to spread the logistical traffic.

Kyrylo's brain went into overdrive as he thought about the possibilities of this new transport system. The port chain from Calais to the Ukrainian RumLot security HQ required over three hundred elves – or about three hundred steps. If only one elf was distracted by something going on in his house and missed his port, that meant the Lord or goods passing through had to wait until the issue was solved, along with every single elf on the rest of the chain. When you had ten or fifteen people running back and forth, the elves got testy. Porting took energy and a good chunk of their day. But a system with Adem's bubbles only took one elf. One! A lord could go in the bubble and wait for an elf from wherever to port in and then take him to his home, and once in the area, the lord could simply walk, catch a bus, or port locally.

It made Kyrylo all dreamy and warm just thinking about it.

As he told James and the others under his command, if they had transfer stations set up, then a human soldier in France, for instance, could immediately be ported to The Wall in Ukraine if he was needed there, all without disturbing hundreds of elves in between. If you're talking about moving armies, you need a lot of space and nodes. And then there was Canada and Vietnam. Anywhere they could raise elves, they could port to in just two steps. One step to get to the node, the next step to get to the destination. In far-off or dangerous locations, they didn't even have to raise elves locally if the lord or human didn't need a local transfer port.

It only took a few days for the elves of the Aelfeham House clan to erect a building to define the edges of the sphere and make sure no elf was accidentally knocked out of bounds. It looked like a very large circus tent, complete with multicoloured stripes and flags which added a bit of an exotic flavour to the very English front entrance of Aelfeham House. Kyrylo thought "circus" was very appropriate.

Adem slept for two days, just like he said. When he woke up, he had a bluecoat uniform hanging in his closet with epaulettes that had a quarter moon embroidered on them. It took him a long time to wrap his head around the meaning behind that bluecoat. His special ability was valued and would be used to make everyone's life better. He had utility. He wasn't a waste of space.

While Kyrylo dreamt big with the bubbles, logistically it wasn't as easy to send Adem out to make one as it first seemed. For one thing, a place had to be found that RumLot Security or the Elf Nation owned.

Humans had the concept of owning land, and you couldn't plop down a busy transport node just anywhere that looked convenient. The land had to be accessible to a street where trucks could pick up any goods transported. For the comfort and security of the elves and lords using it, it needed to have waiting rooms, ventilation, toilets – all the bits and pieces any modern train station had.

Adem started with small, room-sized bubbles in the embassies and RumLot offices, and that's all they did for a while. The next time Mordecai and Malachi went to Canada to wake up elves, it was decided that Adem would travel with them to create bubbles in Ottawa and at the new RumLot base being built near Calgary.

In the meantime, he took his lord and self-defence classes and relaxed at Aelfeham House playing cards with Judy when she was around or chess with Vrt. One day, Vrt asked him to help her with a tour group at the Embassy, and Adem found another thing he could do that he was good at. It turned out he was very good at hosting delegations. He was endlessly patient with the silly questions ("Yes, these are my real ears." "No, I can't kill people by looking at them."), endlessly cheerful, and a lot more clever and discreet than people gave him credit for being. You don't couch surf for three thousand years without developing some diplomatic skills so you don't piss off your hosts.

While they both lived at Aelfeham House, it was at the Embassy where Adem bumped into Malachai more and more often. For one thing, Malachi was good friends with Conary and Vrt, so he'd stop in and have lunch with them or chat now and then if they were in between meetings. But he also stopped in regularly to see Trevor.

When Alizah told Adem that Malachi was dating Trevor, a human, it didn't shock Adem as much as it had the other Old Farts. Back in Before Times, dating humans was very, very much frowned upon, but for a queer guy or gal, the lord dating options were very limited, and humans were the next best thing. When you were part of a very small tribe like lords and you were a small minority in that tribe, over time, most of the people in your tiny minority ended up being bonded, and that didn't leave very many unbonded gay people to have a relationship with. And, of course, even if you ran into someone wired the same way you were, it didn't mean you liked each other or had anything in common at all.

For all of his vast age, Adem had only had three relationships in his life with another lord, and none of them had resulted in bonding. One was a pretty long-term thing that lasted for almost forty years, but one day he and Charush went to a party and Charush ran into a guy who just reeked of sexy scent and had a really useful ability and a place in society, and, well, he didn't come back home with Adem. Forty years of what Adem thought was a close relationship, and he was dumped in forty minutes. That took a long time to get over.

Malachi talked with Adem when he ran into him, and he was always friendly and polite. But Adem could see that the lord wasn't at all interested in him, and he could also see why. Trevor was very, very good-looking and very, very personable. Adem was very, very average.

Trevor was fun, he was clever, and he was pretty. Seeing Malachi and Trevor together made Adem a bit wistful sometimes. His new life was great, but it would be better to share it with someone who looked at you the way Trevor looked at Malachi. Now that Malachi was at full health and a confident Warrior Lord, he was pretty hunky, too, and Adem could also see why Trevor was attracted to the man. They made a very cute couple.

Going out with a human was simply not a possibility for Adem. He couldn't deal with living, loving, and then losing someone, which would inevitably happen with a lord/human relationship. It would break his heart, and he'd rather be alone than suffer through another crushing loss like he had when Charush left him. It was just too hard.

So Adem put Malachi out of his mind as a romantic prospect and filed the Warrior Lord under a heading marked "casual friend" and left it at that. Adem was over five thousand years old, and one thing he'd learnt in that vast time was that there was absolutely no point in mooning over anyone who didn't have the least bit of interest in you. His life was pretty much perfect now, and if he didn't have any romance, that was not the end of the world. He was used to sleeping alone.

Patricia and Ian

When Patricia and Ian posted Jamie, Jr, another old-fashioned birthday card, but this one came with a fiver folded inside a piece of kitchen foil, Jamie wrote back an old-fashioned, hand-written thank-you note the next day, just like he had been taught by his mother. The foil always made the kids laugh. Grandmother was sure that the foil prevented postal thieves from learning there was cash in the envelope.

And just like Lauren had insisted, the thank-you note wasn't just a "Thanks, Grandmother for the money," but a proper letter with a bit of news in it. If someone took the time to post you a gift, you could take fifteen minutes and properly thank them for it.

The news Jamie passed on was that he and his friends were going to the go-kart track for the day, and he even included a copy of the flyer Sarah had given him because there was no guarantee that Grandmother and Grandfather even knew what a go-kart was.

Patricia wondered why they weren't invited; surely they should attend their grandchild's birthday party! And Ian saw that the track was only two hours away, so they decided to surprise Jamie with a visit. Patricia was sure he'd be delighted to see his grandparents, and Ian didn't see the harm in it. It would be a nice day out, and they could put up with James for an hour or two.

When the day finally came, it wasn't just James and Sarah with Jamie, Karol, and Micky. Chloe, Tiki, Imogene, and Richie wanted to come, so Sarah just told the track to get a couple more karts ready and make sure there was enough food for everyone. For security reasons, she had rented the entire track for the afternoon, and it was closed to everyone but their party.

It turned out that the girl Richie was dating was Imogene, so that was an interesting bit of information to learn.

On the day, the excited kids were booted, suited, and standing in a circle around the track workers getting their safety briefing when a manager tapped Sarah on the elbow and informed her that two visitors were at the entrance claiming to be the birthday boy's grandparents, and could they please come in?

Surprised, Sarah looked at James, and while he smiled, the smile didn't go to his eyes. He was pissed. It was just like Patricia and Ian to pull a stunt like this! If they had simply asked to come along, they would have been welcomed, but to come uninvited was a power play on their part. That made sure James' parents wouldn't also be asked to balance out the grandparent quota, and if there weren't enough seats or food, well, everyone else would simply have to adjust, wouldn't they?

But he certainly wasn't going to make a fuss or be anything other than welcoming and gracious, not in front of the kids and certainly not do anything to spoil Jamie's birthday fun. Of course, Patricia knew that, and Ian didn't care.

Patricia and Ian could tolerate James and did so out of a desire not to alienate their grandchildren. They just didn't like him, and after twenty years, time hadn't mellowed their basic antipathy to the man. The feeling was mutual.

Their only child, the beautiful and talented Lauren, had married a non-commissioned officer, a sergeant, in the Royal Army, who she met when he was taking night courses at a local uni and she was teaching Modern Literature. He was her student! Yes, he was working on his degree in preparation for applying for a commission and becoming an officer, but he wasn't there yet. And he was doing it the hard way, coming up through the ranks and not properly by going to Sandhurst or some other elite military school. He had no money, no family that counted, and he was

Jewish. And if that weren't bad enough, he was Scottish. It was like she was actively trying to find the most inappropriate husband she could manage.

Lauren could have married that nice Baronet's son she was dating, who worked at a bank in London. But no, it was James or no one. Patricia and Ian even refused to pay for the wedding, which Patricia was certain would squash any idea of marriage, but just to spite them, Lauren cheerfully converted to Judaism and had a tiny, stingy, Jewish wedding. Sure, when she was growing up, they hadn't gone to church, but their families were generations of respectable Church of England parishioners, and Lauren just shrugged that all off. After their daughter's marriage to the Jew, Patricia and Ian started going back to church and making a big fuss at Christmas and Easter, if only to show Lauren what she was missing.

They had dreamed of so much more for their lovely daughter, and all they could do was hope for a quick divorce before the lawyer found a new girlfriend.

After Richard was born, there was an uneasy truce. The Cowens didn't make a big fuss about being Jewish; they had a Christmas tree for the kids, and every single time they visited Patricia and Ian for the holidays, the Cowen family ate the ham they were served. Lauren once told James she had never eaten ham growing up; her mother said it was too salty and made her bloat.

Then Lauren died. Patricia and Ian's grief was deep and sincere, and every single thing that they had argued over with Lauren was simply forgotten. She was the perfect daughter, and they had the perfect grandchildren. James took wonderful care of both Lauren and the kids, and while Patricia and Ian appreciated the effort, it was only what Lauren was due; they still didn't like James. He didn't seem so Jewish any more, and he had moved up the ranks to a respectable colonel, but he was still Scottish. The accent he had when he visited them was simply terrible and always seemed to get worse the more they were around him.

When James and his in-laws rounded the corner and walked up to the fence ringing the track, the first thing Patricia and Ian saw were the kids. Ian, of course, yelled, and everyone had to stop the safety briefing, and the grandkids ran over to give their grandparents hugs and make a big fuss over them.

After that obligation was over and the kids ran back to what they were there for – go-kart racing – James steered the grandparents over to Sarah. As he introduced her, he had the profound pleasure of watching the once-in-laws come to terms with meeting a full lord, flaring ears, glowing eyes and all.

Sarah noticed he didn't say, "Sarah, these are my in-laws," and their names. Instead, he said, "Lord Sarah, let me introduce Patricia and Ian – Jamie,

Chloe, and Richie's grandparents." It was a subtle but telling difference.

Not "my in-laws" but "my kid's grandparents", as if they were adopted. James wasn't claiming Patricia and Ian, not at all.

Sarah warmly smiled and bowed, but didn't offer her hand. She wasn't sure if Patricia would even take it. The woman seemed stunned.

As far as the purpose of the day, entertaining the young people with the go-karts, the day went brilliantly. The adults chatted stiffly and politely. James endured Patricia and Ian, and Patricia and Ian endured both James and Lord Sarah. Sarah didn't give a crap. If James didn't like them, he must have his reasons, and all she had to do was make sure he and the kids were happy with her behaviour. So she smiled and made nice, and when Ian asked what she did for a living, Sarah just laughed and said, "I'm a lord. I don't have a real job." James made a point of saying that Sarah was in the senior hierarchy of the Elf Nation, number four to be precise, which made Patricia's eyes widen. At least, Sarah whispered to James during dinner, they didn't ask if these were my real ears.

The shit didn't hit the fan until the next day when James received an email from Ian.

"Dear James,

Please tell Jamie, Chloe, and Richie how much we enjoyed visiting with them yesterday. During our conversation, Jamie mentioned that he is taking bar mitzvah lessons, and when we inquired, it turned out that all three of our grandchildren are taking the Jew classes.

I have to be blunt. This is very difficult for Patricia and me to come to terms with, and we feel it's a repudiation of their heritage and ours. Then we find out that you are consorting with a lord, a person who's not a human being, and to add to that, we find out that the children say they are becoming lords, too!

It's quite extraordinary that Lauren's children are not only moving away from their COE heritage but that you are allowing them to become non-human lords. We strongly object, and our disappointment in you, James, is profound.

We will always love our grandchildren, and if they realise as they mature that they have walked down the wrong path, we will welcome them back with open arms. But until then, we feel that to uphold our values, we must step back from our relationship with you and the children until such time as you come to your senses.

With deep regret,

Ian and Patricia."

When James read that, he didn't know whether to laugh or get really, really fucking angry.

So he showed it to Sarah, who couldn't roll her eyes any further back without looking at her own ass. There was so much wrong to unpack that she didn't know where to start. But she felt she had to say something, so she looked at her bond-man and said, "At least they didn't accuse you of turning the kids into Scots. That would have been a step too far. This relationship is still salvageable."

So James had to laugh, and when he laughed, she laughed, and they laughed all evening over the email. James told the kids that their grandparents had had a nice time but were having real problems with the bar mitzvahs and not to expect any more foil money from Grandmother Patricia. They were fine with that and wouldn't miss the five pounds.

The next morning, James replied to the sender. "Stepping back is not a problem. Lord James"

Malachi and Adem

Kyrylo was eager to get transport bubbles set up in Canada, so a hastily arranged road trip was thrown together. Mordecai, Malachi, Adem, and lords-to-be-named-later were to go to Ottawa first, where on the day they landed, Adem would set up a bubble inside the EN embassy. Then he'd make another big one out in an industrial park inside a massive warehouse the EN had purchased. Then a day of rest and they'd fly to the new base being set up in Lethbridge, and the next day Adem would set up a bubble in the morning. If everything worked the way it should, he'd port back home and be at Aelfeham House in time for lunch.

Mordecai, Malachi, and the other lords and RumLot employees would stay in Lethbridge long enough to wake a few elves on the base (if there were any there to waken) and get a local clan started, then port back home when they were done.

It all seemed rather complicated, but the logistics people were used to arranging complicated things, and all Adem had to do was be there long enough to make his bubbles.

The day came for the mob to fly to Canada. Because Malachi insisted on taking his horses, the huge RumLot jumbo jet flew into Stansted Intl Airport and loaded up two platoons of RumLot soldiers, grooms, redcoats Rita, Tiki, and Gary, and bluecoats Malachi, Mordecai, Adem, and assorted aides, managers, handlers, flunkies, and bottle-washers.

For Adem, the trip to Canada was a flying party. It was Adam's first flight anywhere, and every aspect was fascinating. He and Rita ran around watching the horses being loaded into their special section, visiting the captain and flight crew, and looking at the gazillion dials, levers, and buttons they worked with. When Adem asked if he could come back during the flight and look out the window, the captain laughed.

"Of course, you can!" she said. "You own the plane!"

The lord's enthusiasm for the entire process and his vocal admiration for the crew's professionalism and knowledge were flattering, and when he left, the crew felt proud and pleased to be part of the RumLot team, which had been Adem's goal.

While the other lords watched him running around, chuckling at jokes, admiring the employee's work, paying attention to the lowliest crewmembers, and wondering why on Earth he was doing it, Adem was making sure the humans who were a part of the RumLot team felt important and valued. It was a soft people-management skill Adem did naturally, and one which Caddy and Conary understood and valued when other people didn't. Both of them talked to Adem many times about managing humans and keeping them on the EN side, and it was an important part of Adem's new job. For him, there was no downtime away from it.

Adem, as much as any lord alive, understood the mistake the lords had made in Before Times of not developing close human contacts. Humans were fickle. If they weren't constantly ego-stroked and maintained, they would naturally gravitate to whoever paid the most attention to them, and that usually meant orcs.

Elves didn't need mankind for anything other than to trade with, and in the past, they'd had minimal contact with the humans who lived around their villages. Lords didn't need humans for anything at all, so they simply ignored them except for an occasional screw. Even down to the present day, every culture has "fairy stories" of immortal demigods who wandered into a human village and took a woman or man for a night's pleasure and then abandoned them. The occasional boon that a lord gave the rare human they bothered to talk to didn't make up for the many, many times there was an encounter that left the human feeling used or worse off. There aren't many fairy tales with the fairies as the good guys.

When Gaia died, some humans didn't join the orcs in their killing frenzy, but that didn't mean they stopped the orcs, either. Most of humankind just stayed out of the orcs' nasty business and let them do what they wanted with the leftover lords and the disorganised elves. While a few brave men and women, out of compassion, did aid the lords and elves, they were few and far between. In the end, their weak efforts weren't enough to hold back the tsunami of hate that exterminated the elves and lords who lived among humankind.

In this new world of reborn elves and lords, Caddy wanted to ensure that humans were on the elf and lord side, and that meant relentless marketing and public relations campaigns and creating an army of humans who loved both elves and lords and actively wanted to protect them. Adem, from his old vantage point of being an ignored and disrespected lord, could understand why humans resented the arrogant, disparaging lords, and he had a lot of sympathy for them. Caddy, in Adem's mind, could do no wrong, and it was just another aspect of her brilliance that she recognised the "human problem" and what to do about it.

So Adem learned every RumLot human's name, shook hands and asked questions, and let them talk to a friendly Elemental bluecoat lord. He then repeated the process with every single one of the RumLot soldiers during the course of the flight. He didn't walk down a reception line and make them feel like they were part of a formal meet-and-greet, but simply flitted in and out, chatting and paying attention to them. By the time the flight was over, he was by far the most popular of the lords, and every human on board had a little story to tell their families when they went home of personally meeting a senior bluecoat and how lovely he was.

Malachi watched all this cheerful hyperactivity with amusement. Adem was charming; he had to admit it, but it was exhausting just to watch him. It was an hour after takeoff before he even returned to VIP country from the soldiers' section of the jet, and by that time, Malachi was already bored with the flight. The other lords had settled into their seats and were occupying themselves or napping, so when Adem trotted by (again), Malachi asked him if he wanted to play a game of chess to help pass the time.

Adem gave him a lovely smile and threw himself in the chair opposite and sighed, grateful to have a reason to sit down. They didn't talk much; Adem was pretty talked out by then, and Malachi never said much anyway, so he made the opening move, and they began the game.

Almost immediately, one of the stewards came up and asked Adem (not Malachi) if he wanted anything to drink, and that bit of attention was repeated every fifteen minutes on the dot. Malachi glanced up, took a good look at the stew's face, and twigged what was going on – that the man was hitting on Adem! Fifteen minutes later, the stew returned with more snacks, and by then Malachi was sure of it. Adem was polite, cheerful, and charming, but he didn't flirt back. The steward, however, while not making a pest of himself, didn't give up. After watching this a few times, Malachi couldn't help himself; he had to say something after the steward left again.

"I see you've made a friend."

Adem looked down at the board and smiled. "He's been very nice."

"Nice! He's been all over you! He's not topping up *my* coffee." Malachi snorted and then studied the board; his rook was in danger. "I think he forgot I was even here the last time he came by!" He looked up at Adem. "If you looked at him cross-eyed, he'd give you his phone number."

"He already has, in case I need anything in Ottawa. He says he knows the town."

Malachi looked up, startled. He really didn't think – Adem leaned back in his seat and smiled at Malachi, his eyes twinkling. He was amused, and for the first time, Malachi thought, this man is really attractive. And then an image of Adem and the stew together –

He looked down at the board again. That thought was disorienting. He didn't know why, but it was. The idea of Adem having sex with the steward was, for Malachi, uncomfortable. Jealous? Nonsense. What was there to be jealous about? He pushed the thought out of his head. No, it wasn't jealousy; it was concern for Adem. He didn't want his friend to be hurt.

"Be careful." He moved his rook.

Adem shook his head, whether at the move or the comment, Malachi didn't know. "I don't play with humans. Even very attractive ones. I know some lords do." And he gave a sideways glance to Malachi. "But I've learned from my friends' experiences that it always ends in tears."

Malachi shrugged. "Some are fine."

"I'm sure they are, but it's not for me. I don't do casual. I get very emotionally attached, so it's better for me to stick with lords."

"But you've never bonded. So the lord thing hasn't worked out for you."

"Not yet!" Adem chuckled. "But I'm an optimist! I've had lovers who haven't worked out, but that's life, isn't it? If they had worked out, they'd still be with me a thousand years later. But a human? Fifty years and they're gone. I can't face that."

Malachi nodded. So in the past, Adem had had lord lovers. Until this chess game, he had never once thought about Adem's sex life, but now it was a topic of conversation.

"Checkmate!" Adem grinned, and Malachi looked at the board, surprised. How did he do that? "I'm going to my bunk and take a nap. That was a good game!" And he left, leaving Malachi to think about Trevor, Adem, Adem's lovers, and stewards with phone numbers.

The jet landed in Ottawa, and like it had the last time, it taxied into the huge hangar to offload; however, this time, no buses were waiting for the passengers. Instead, ten elves were waiting for the passengers, and they ported the entire lot directly to the embassy lobby. The soldiers were billeted in a nearby hotel and simply walked over, but the lords stayed on the top floor of the embassy, which had been turned into a private hotel complete with a restaurant and meeting rooms.

The first thing Adem did when he got there, not a half hour from landing, was to go to a special room in the embassy and create a bubble in it. Then he went to his room and took a nap to kill time and take the opportunity to clean up before an official reception planned with Canadian officials. He really didn't need to rest because the bubble wasn't that big, but he desperately wanted to shower. He had been running around all over the jet, and on the sixteen-hour flight from Stansted, he'd only had one turn at the onboard shower and one change of clothes. The last thing he wanted was to be whiffy around Malachi.

The Embassy bubble was just for porting humans and lords, not cargo. An hour later, the first elf from London ported in with Conary and Vrt, and now the lords and elves had their first trans-Atlantic connection. Althea was next to port over, and then Kyrylo and Caddy.

Kyrylo was beside himself with joy over the success of Adem's mini Safe Haven bubbles. Even Caddy was a bit surprised at his glee over the bubbles; to her, it certainly made moving easier and safer, but he was ecstatic over the military possibilities.

The EN reception for the Canadian government officials was packed. Curiosity is a huge draw, and this was the first time the local bureaucrats and parliamentarians had had a chance to see the Embassy since it was finished. Before the elves arrived, the place was an empty shell, but after Mordecai woke up a couple of clans between Ottawa and Montreal, the Ottawa clan finished up the Embassy and started work on the big hub that was going up in the industrial park warehouse. Other than seeing elves around the Embassy, most Canadians didn't notice them at all, except at farmers' markets where the elves sold jam and jelly. The quince jelly was very popular.

The reception was crowded, noisy, and (for the crowd, given that they were government officials on duty) raucous. Adem slipped in unnoticed and was immediately given his preferred watered-down wine, which allowed him to look convivial without the risk of actually getting drunk. With that prop in hand, he stood in a quiet corner and scanned the room for any Canadian guests who looked a bit lost or out of place.

Huddled in one corner, he spotted a small group that turned out to be from New Brunswick. None had ever talked to a lord before, and after some initial shyness, they discovered that Adem wasn't stuffy or took himself too seriously, and they peppered him with questions. When one grandmotherly lady asked him if she could touch his ears, Adem just chuckled and shook his head.

"I'm afraid not, ma'am. Ears on a lord or elf are pretty personal. They can be looked at but not touched, kinda like a woman's decolletage." That got a blush from the woman and a laugh from the rest of the group.

Then Vrt and Malachi wandered by. "I heard that! See, the ears aren't just for looks!" She wiggled hers, which earned a giggle.

Adem introduced them. "Two of our Warrior Lords – Lord Vrt and Lord Malachi. Now I have someone to defend my honour, or at least my ears' honour. The rest of me will have to make do."

"Can't you defend yourself? Aren't you a Warrior Lord, too?" This came from one of the men who was swimming in a very baggy suit. The poor guy had either lost a lot of weight or had no idea how to buy a suit.

Adem threw up his hands in fake horror. "Me? Defend myself? The best I can do is hide in the nearest potted plant. These guys," and he waved and smiled at Vrt and Malachi, "are truly scary people."

Vrt smiled back, "No, my dear friend. You are the truly scary one. An Elemental will always have the last laugh, even over a Warrior Lord." Adem smiled and blushed. It was rude to compare abilities directly, and now the conversation was edging into that.

Malachi looked at Vrt, startled. Vrt was from Before Times and knew so much more about different abilities and lords than probably anyone but Adem and Neptune, and she was saying that Adem – *This Adem?* – was more powerful than a Warrior Lord? She wasn't joking either. Malachi recognised when Vrt was joking. And Vrt was bonded to an Elemental lord.

"But I will defend your honour whenever you need it. I don't think you need me now, so I think I'll attack the buffet instead." She turned to Malachi. "C'mon, Kai, let's go see if they put out the good stuff yet. All they had on earlier were sausage rolls for Lord Cadence."

When they were out of earshot, Malachi asked her directly. "Do you think Adem could take either of us on? I mean, damn, Vrt. He couldn't hurt a fly –"

"Adem doesn't want to hurt anyone, ever. He'd much rather run away –" Vrt looked over the buffet. Surely there must be something on there that didn't rely on dairy products. You'd think the

Canadians were English or something. "But if push came to shove, he'd just look at someone and they would find themselves in their own Void, outside of space and time, quickly going mad."

She looked at Malachi, now entirely serious.

"He and Sarah are Elementals who have never stretched their powers to their breaking point because if they did, gods only know what would happen. Deep down, they're both afraid of themselves, much more than they're afraid of anything else. Adem told me once in passing that people who think Sarah is just a strong elf who can port have no idea of what she can do."

Vrt found some shrimp skewers and piled them on a plate.

"Caddy controls waves, mostly sound, some light. Kyrylo controls energy, another type of wave. Conary controls light waves. Neptune water. But Sarah – she rides on time itself. That's how porting works; she physically moves herself from one point in time to another point in time. And Adem controls space *and* time. Together, they control the forces that make up a black hole, and black holes swallow stars. Galaxies. Think of that next time you have a kickboxing session with Sarah or watch Adem take a tour of school kids around the Embassy. Adem is a destroyer of worlds – if he wanted to. Instead, he chooses to save them like he did with the elves."

Malachi just couldn't wrap his head around Adem being a galactic-level power; that was just crazy.

"So why did Sarah become a Warrior Lord? If she's so powerful, what's the point of it?"

Vrt smiled slyly. She knew because she was the same as Sarah.

"Sarah enjoys beating the crap out of orcs. Zapping them away just isn't as satisfying. And she likes the fact that other people think she's badass. Look at Adem; no one can see his power, and everyone thinks he's a wimp. But he's not interested in being a Warrior Lord, and he *never* shows off. Unlike Sarah and me, he doesn't hate orcs, not the way we do." She turned and gave a sideways glance at Malachi.

"Just like you, Kai. You're just like Sarah and me; you like being badass, too. You like people being a little bit afraid of you when you walk into a room. You like being in control. It turns you on."

Malachi thought about Vrt saying he liked being a badass, and then shrugged. She was right about that.

James

When James told his mum and dad he was leaving the Royal Army and going to work for RumLot Security, they were surprised, but they trusted that their son had thought everything through and was doing the right thing. They didn't even know he was looking for a new job! In the end, all his mother wanted to know was if he was still going to get his military pension, and once she was assured he would, she was fine.

They were very surprised that he sold the house, but if his new job was in Lowestoft he couldn't very well stay in Catterick. It was five hours away! His dad thought he should've just rented it out; it could have been a nice little money earner.

He didn't tell them about Sarah. Or the lord thing. Or about the kids being lords, too.

James was busy, life got in the way, and you just don't tell your parents that you're not human on the phone. It seemed disrespectful. So he kept putting it off until he had time to go to see them in person. But for a person who would live forever, he never had the time.

Then one day, as they were leaving the Breakfast Room after lunch, Sarah asked him when he wanted to schedule the kids' bar and bat mitzvah. They could do all the kids on one day since they were all past thirteen and there was no need to wait for birthdays.

James gave her a blank look.

"They're almost done with their lessons." She spoke softly, which was scary. "Your parents need some time to plan the trip down here." She paused. Even worse. "There should be a family dinner afterwards; a nice restaurant would be a treat –"

She looked at James, who stared at her with that "deer in the headlights" look.

"You haven't told them, have you?"

James slowly shook his head.

"Have you told them anything?"

He shook his head. No.

Sarah gave him a long look. Her eyes glowed, and it wasn't because she was feeling sexy.

"Well, let me know when you do." She kissed him on the cheek and, without another word, turned and went back to work.

Vrt was right behind them, heard everything, and as she walked past, she turned and gave James her own long, long "you've really fucked up" look and gave a tiny shake of her head.

And he had. And to fix it, all he could do was go to his office and call his Mum and see if she and Ded were okay with him coming home tomorrow for a quick visit. Just dropping in because he was going to be in the area anyway. No, nothing was wrong. Kids were all fine. Yes, he could stay for dinner.

"And if you want to bring your young lady with you, that would be fine, too. You know we can always squeeze another place at the table."

James was stunned. How did she know about Sarah? Did Sarah already talk to his parents?

"Jamie? Are you still there?"

And then he could hear his dad in the background laughing, just howling, and his mum telling him to shut up, but she was laughing, too.

"Mum – I –"

"Listen, Mr. SpyGuy – we live out in the middle-of-nowhere Strathglass, but we still have this thing called the World Wide Web. When you told us you were changing jobs to RumLot Securit, didn't you think we'd look that up? We know that's the Elf Nation people. Didn't you think we'd put an alert on our computer for your name, Elf Nation, and RumLot? How do you think we'd find out anything? If we waited for you to write to us, we'd still be reading stone tablets."

Mum couldn't stop laughing. They must have been waiting for this moment for months.

"When you went to that fancy ball in Kyiv, there were photos all over the web. Why didn't you tell us you were going? But no, your mother is always the last to know. And you were with this Lord Sarah. She's very pretty." And his mother's voice choked a bit. "And you looked very happy."

Then Ded yelled from the back. "And we DO talk to our grandkids! *They* send us emails! When's the damn bar mitzvahs?"

All James could do was say he didn't know; that's why he was coming up to see what days were free for them and to talk about things. Although at that point, he didn't know why he was bothering; they seemed to know everything already. And after his mother mentioned her again, he promised to see if Sarah could come, too.

When he put down the phone, all he could do was smile and shake his head. He had fucked up, but they'd had their revenge. He'd hear about it the rest of his life, and he was going to live a very long time.

Becca

Becca peeked out of the window even as James Sr told her to stop being such a nosy curtain-twitcher. Jamie and Sarah were standing out on the road, but how they got there, she hadn't a clue. There wasn't a car in sight. They must have taken a taxi.

Jamie was wearing civvies, not the dark green RumLot Security uniform she had seen on the internet. Becca wished he had; she would have taken a picture even if he always came out a bit blurry, and she was sure he looked handsome in it. He always did in uniform.

His girl Sarah was in a trench coat and a skirt. Even as far away as they were from the house, Becca could see her ears, tall ones just like in the drawings she saw on the internet of the ball in Kyiv.

She just stood there, looking at her feet and holding Jamie's hand, and he leaned over to say something in one of those huge ears. The body language could be read a mile away. The poor dear was scared to death. Becca abruptly stepped back, and James Sr knew that expression on her face. He'd seen it before. Becca was on a rescue mission.

"Get your coat on. We're going out to them. If she's good enough for Jamie, she's more than good enough for us."

"They'll be up here in two seco– " She shot him a look, and without another word, he fetched both of their coats.

For a woman with a gimp knee and a cane, she could move remarkably fast, and by the time James Sr had his own coat on and closed the door behind them, she was halfway down the driveway, yelling, "Jamie! Sarah!" When he caught up, she was hugging Sarah and telling her how happy she was to *finally* meet her. That left the two Jamies to do their own father/son hugs and slaps on the back.

Back in the house, Becca fussed and bustled and generally made a lot of noise getting everyone tea and settled comfortably in the lounge. Ded, don't stand there like a lump; take their coats! Sugar? Cream? Biscuits? No, you two sit on the sofa, I have my own chair here. No, dear, I don't need any help; you just sit down and relax. I'm sure you're both tired. Jamie, when did you grow a beard? What's next, pe'ot? Sarah, that's a lovely jumper; I've always loved a Fair Isle. Do you knit? Naomi, Colin, and their kids are coming for dinner, too, but won't be here until after school. And on and on until everyone was seated, had a cuppa in hand, and she stopped, took a deep breath, and just beamed at the couple.

"Well, what do you two have to say for yourselves?"

"Not a lot, Mum. Can't get a word in edgewise."

Ded laughed and shot a glance at Sarah. She seemed a bit stunned, but she was smiling. Relieved, he was sure. Becca could be a bit overwhelming, and sometimes that put people off, but today the full-on Becca welcome worked a treat.

He nodded to Becca but addressed Sarah. "We've never met a lord before. We're seeing elves at the market but no lords. So don't mind us if we stare a bit; we'll calm down in a few minutes."

Sarah smiled shyly. "Oh, I understand. I'm a bit odd looking –"

"Not odd! Not odd at all." Becca was appalled. "You're lovely! We've just never seen elf ears on a human before. It's different – but beautiful."

James cleared his throat.

"Mum, Sarah's not a human or an elf; she's a lord. And there are a few things I want to let you know, but I wanted to tell you in person, not on the phone. I'm really sorry this has taken so long –"

And that's when Becca and James learned that their son and their grandchildren weren't human, either.

Malachi and Adem

The next morning dawned bright and clear, and right after breakfast, Malachi and Adem were ported to the RumLot warehouse on the industrial estate on Ottawa's east side. Adem was there to create a huge bubble, and Malachi was there as a guard while Adem was vulnerable, just the way he guarded Mordecai when he was in full flame.

Kyrylo and Jameson waited for them. Standing in the vast, empty space and off to the side were about ten warehouse workers waiting for instructions. Adem scanned the area and hesitated. He could bubble the entire space, but it would wipe him out for days, maybe a week, and they still had Lethbridge to do.

Pointing to the far end, he explained the problem. "Kyrylo, do you want this entire space? I can make a very big bubble, but this is the size of a stadium, and it will take me a lot of recovery time."

"Oh, no! We don't need it all. The rest will be used for storing the stuff we bring in. The active area is marked with this blue chalk." And he showed Adem the area. Relieved, Adem nodded. He could do this.

So he walked into the centre and thought about it. The women and men waiting by the walls saw Adem glow, and unlike Caddy and Mordecai, there was no gradual buildup to full flame; Adem exploded into a blue, white-hot fire. And then it was over. Still glowing white hot, he waved to the three men, and they walked over. Once inside, they could see the edges of the bubble. Jameson immediately called the helpers. He and Malachi guided them to the edges, and they marked the perimeter with spray paint.

Kyrylo was very happy. "I'd shake your hand, Adem, but you're too fucking hot, even for me. But thanks so much. This is great. Huge!"

Adem was cooling down now and sweating so much that he was dripping on the floor. Then he looked over and saw Malachi walking towards him and Kyrylo.

"Thanks, Kyrylo. No problem. Gotta go." And with that, he yelled, "Elf port!" and his elf ported him back to his room at the Embassy.

Kyrylo was a bit startled at the abruptness of Adem's departure, but the man was probably really hungry. That was a huge amount of energy flaming through him. He turned to Malachi, but he was lost in thought, staring at the place where Adem had last stood.

Kyrylo shrugged and let the lord have his reverie. Instead, he went off to see Jameson. "Jameson! I think we can get a couple of tanks in here! What do you think?"

Malachi wasn't lost in thought. He was lost in lust.

He had inhaled a full, 100% blast of Adem, and *oh my stars*, it was glorious. He had never smelled anything like that in his life. Then he remembered that he had tasted the scent once before – the first time he walked into Caddy and Kyrylo's home, when it was House, which turned out to be Adem.

But it hadn't been as strong as this. That was a whisper of a heady cologne, the faint echo of sex, a faded memory of Adem – this blast had been a full-on drenching in the most exotic, wonderful –

– he had to get away.

Involuntarily, as soon as he thought of leaving, he gasped again, and deep into his sinuses and lungs he inhaled more of Adem's pheromones; they were so strong he could almost see the vapours riding on the wind.

Holding his breath, Malachi spun around and ran to the men's toilet where he slammed into a booth and leaned onto the cold metal door, heaving fresh air into his congested lungs and trying desperately to control himself. To control the fucking hard-on. To control the wild thoughts. To control everything that was out of control.

He was bonding. Malachi knew it. Everything he had learned in Lord Classes, everything anyone had ever said about their experience, every snicker, eyeroll and joking reference, everything told him he was bonding.

He was *not* going to let that happen. It wasn't possible, and he was not going to permit it. He was *not* going to be in thrall to Adem.

In his heart, he knew Adem didn't want him, either. Looking back, he could see the times Adem had abruptly left him, knowing that they were getting physically too close. Even today, he had ported out so fast that he was rude to Kyrylo. He knew.

Adem knew because he was five thousand years old and had lived with lords in Before Times. To him, bonding wasn't an exotic theory; it was something he had seen every day as he grew up. Keeping clean wasn't a hygienic chore; it was a responsibility to not play with the emotional lives of others.

The Old Farts were much more meticulous with keeping their personal odours wiped clean, while the new lords, the ones who were brought up with humans, were often careless. Malachi took his showers, but frankly, he didn't care if he missed one of the three times a day, especially if he wasn't working up a sweat. Who was he going to bother? Certainly not any female lord or any heterosexual lord; they couldn't smell him at all.

But what about another gay lord? Delicate, little Adem? If he bonded to Malachi, that was his problem. And any closeted male lord or a new queer one coming to Aelfeham House – he'd just have to learn to manage.

Malachi didn't care because he was fully in control of himself; any other gay lord who got a noseful of his scent would just have to take care of themselves. It never occurred to him that he would be the one caught in the trap.

He'd been careless; an arrogant fool who didn't pay attention to his own biology because he didn't give a fuck about other people's. He was too strong, too in control, too fuckin' macho to be in any danger of succumbing to wimpy Adem's effete, frail hormones.

He leaned back against the stall door and heaved, forcing fresh air into his lungs. It was too late. Slowly, his legs gave out, and he slumped to the floor, his eyes wide open but unseeing. All that raced through his brain was how much he had fucked up. A forever, fatal, fuck up, and it was all his own damn fault.

Adem

While Malachi had his bonding breakdown, Adem ported back to the Embassy, where he ate like a pig and then went to sleep for a day and a half. As he slept, life went on around him, and it wasn't until the entire circus was two hours away from flying out to Lethbridge that a housekeeper elf woke him up, giving him just enough time to shower and eat another huge breakfast.

He was ported directly onto the jet, where he went straight to his bunk and slept all the way to the taxiway in Lethbridge when another elf poked him in the arm. This one was wearing cowboy boots and jeans, which made Adem smile. A miniature Malachi and Mordecai! He was ported directly to the transport point that had been built on the new RumLot Security outpost, where he made another huge bubble.

This time, Malachi wasn't there to guard him; Mordecai was. Adem didn't question the change in personnel, figuring rightly that Malachi needed a break from him. He had no idea that Malachi had succumbed so deeply to his scent that he'd bonded. Adem assumed that the lord was just being cautious, as he should be. It was only polite.

Within fifteen minutes of Adem creating the bubble, an elf ported from Aelfeham House to

Lethbridge and ported Adem back home, where he happily had lunch brought to his room. Then he slept for two solid days. He was exhausted.

Malachi and Trevor

Naked, Malachi lay on the bed staring at the ceiling and watching a dusty thread of an ancient spider web sway to an unfelt breeze.

Trevor was not lying next to him as he normally would be, head propped up on an elbow, smiling and playing with Malachi's body as he liked to do after coupling.

There had been no sex because Malachi couldn't do it. Instead of lying exhausted and sated, Trevor was out in the kitchen putting together a tray of pastries and coffee to bring back to the bedroom. He wasn't angry or sad, just accepting, and he'd made all the right noises. "No worries, Malachi; you're stressed and tired from travelling, I know – happens to all of us."

Malachi couldn't tell him. He couldn't tell sweet, sexy, gorgeous Trevor that he was no longer turned on by his boyfriend. That sex with him felt just exactly like when he'd had sex with his wives back in Utah. Only worse, because this time, even friction didn't work. This time, Malachi wasn't trying to overcome a neutral, dutiful, have-to-get-on-with-it feeling, but actual revulsion. Kissing Trevor turned his stomach.

Oh, he tried. He fought it, that feeling of nausea that came with knowing he was doing something he shouldn't. Malachi ported into Trevor's sitting room and practically attacked the man, sure that once his mouth crushed against Trevor's and he felt his wonderful body, he would be back in control and everything would return to normal.

If he could just spend one hour with Trevor, Malachi was sure he'd forget all about Adem. So wordlessly, without even a greeting, he'd grabbed Trevor like a drowning man grabs a lifesaver and kissed him as if a wave of energy and frustrated lust could overwhelm any other feeling. Trevor, who was as excited as a man could be and madly in love with Malachi, didn't notice anything wrong until they landed in bed, and Trevor reached down, and Malachi's rock-hard body wasn't rock-hard everywhere it should have been.

He wasn't even halfway there.

Nothing.

And nothing Trevor did made any difference at all.

When Trevor returned to the bedroom holding the laden tray, he stopped at the door. Malachi was sitting on the edge of the bed, fully dressed, his head in his hands.

"Malachi?"

He looked up, and in his eyes, Trevor didn't see the blue glow of a lord's desire. He saw tears.

And then he knew.

Carefully, he put down the tray and sat on the bed next to the lord. Trevor didn't touch him.

"Malachi, have you bonded?"

Malachi didn't say anything. And saying nothing meant yes.

Trevor gave out a long, shuddering sigh. He had been warned. He'd known this day could come, but oh Jesus, it still hurt.

"I'll always love you, Malachi. Always." Trevor looked at his own hands. They trembled. "I hope he loves you as much as I do. You deserve it."

Malachi said nothing. He couldn't say "I love you" to Trevor. He had never said that to him, but he'd felt it. He couldn't throw Trevor a crumb because he wasn't in control of his own voice. If he spoke those words, he'd break down crying. But he had to say something; he owed it to Trevor.

"Trevor, if I could choose –" Malachi's voice broke. "But I can't. I can't undo this. He doesn't even know – I don't think he even likes me."

Trevor stood up and looked at the lord. This was a man of magic, of great power, who would live forever, and yet faced with his biology, totally powerless. Every bonded couple he saw walk through the embassy just doted on each other. An elf told him once that they bonded because they were meant to be, that they had found someone who fit them perfectly, because otherwise, how could they live together forever?

Malachi had found someone who fit him perfectly, and it wasn't reciprocated.

But Trevor loved Malachi, so he put his hand on his ex-lover's head and stroked the curly hair, careful not to touch his ears because he couldn't do that any more.

"Then you're going to have to make him love you. You won't be happy until he does." He sighed. It was getting hard to hold back the tears, and he didn't want to make this worse. "I think it's time for you to go, Malachi."

And he walked out of his bedroom and back to the kitchen. A few minutes later, he heard the snap of an elf porting out. Trevor's never-ending three days had come to a close.

Malachi and Vrt

Vrt was in the Breakfast Room, hoping to find something like an omelette to nosh on after H2H training with Sarah. Instead, she settled for scrambled eggs because asking an elf to make her a Denver omelette when there were perfectly good eggs on the buffet that needed to be eaten up seemed a bit diva-y.

As she picked through the eggs, Malachi walked in, even more morose and quiet than usual, heading straight to the buffet, and he piled up a plate with bacon and pancakes. Something was bothering him – Vrt knew it – and had been for a couple of days.

"S'up? You don't seem to be your usual bubbly self, Kai."

He grunted, which was a full sentence in Malachi-speak. Patiently, Vrt waited; it would come out. Her friend had made a noise.

"Trevor and I have broken up." He poured half a jug of maple syrup on the pancakes.

"Oh."

"It was time. He was getting too attached anyway."

"I saw him at the Embassy yesterday. He did seem a bit down."

Malachi nodded, but he didn't say anything.

Vrt tried to remember if she had ever broken up with anyone; it would have had to have been before she met Prana. Unbonding and freeing Prana didn't count; it wasn't as if they were tired of each other; that was an act of love on both sides. He had to be free to die, and she had to unbond to live. Nope, she had never been dumped. When she dated, she had been a dump-er, not a dump-ee. She gave Malachi a sideways glance. Had he dumped Trevor or vice versa?

"Humans are fickle; it's their nature. But a bust-up is still sad. How are you doing?"

"I'm fine. I'm over it. He will be, too. No big deal."

Vrt nodded; so it must have been bad then.

"Best if you stick with lords in the future. I know that gay lords aren't falling out of apple trees, but you have a long time ahead of you. They'll show up." Vrt then went in for the kill. "Adem is still single –"

"Adem! Not my type, not pretty enough for me." Malachi looked down at his pancakes and shook his head. "Adem in my bed? Hell no."

Vrt looked up, startled at the vehemence in Malachi's voice. That wasn't like him at all; he was definitely overcompensating. And then she saw Chi standing in the doorway. He had heard everything, and anything that passed through Chi's ears fell out of his mouth sooner or later.

Oh. Shit.

Malachi and Adem

With the success of the Canadian transport bubbles, Kyrylo asked Adem if he would set up smaller nodes in embassies and other locations just to move people around, and larger bulk transport bubbles like the ones set up in warehouses as they were completed. If he did two a week, he would have a couple of days between efforts to rest and feed.

Adem, of course, said yes, but he did ask that if he needed a lord as a guard, could he have Vrt, Sarah, Conary, or Kyrylo? Anyone but Malachi.

Kyrylo paused, a bit surprised, and then thought that maybe the two men were getting too much face time and Adem was being his usual, thoughtful self. Besides, Malachi had plenty to do with Mordecai waking up elves. The request was a no-brainer, really, and so Malachi was quietly taken off that duty, and Adem always had some other person standing guard just in case an emergency happened.

Between the two men's schedules that took them across Europe and Canada, they didn't cross paths that much. If Mordecai woke up elves in a far-flung location, then Adem would follow a week or two later and set up a personnel bubble. When Malachi and Mordecai were resting, Adem was working and vice versa.

When they did cross paths, usually in the Breakfast room or when lords got together to play cards, Adem was always, always cheerful, polite, and never, ever sat next to Malachi.

Malachi didn't get lovesick over Adem because his bonding was full-on complete, and he knew it the way Sam, who knew he was bonded, didn't get lovesick over Grace. Adem, though, was much more aware of the dangers of bonding than Grace had been, so he didn't have the incomplete experience that left him half in/half out. He was as unbonded as he'd ever been.

Neither man had a reason to go see Dr Mandy because Adem was fine with his status, and Malachi was resigned to his.

Malachi, though, was getting less resigned and more – it was hard for him to pinpoint what it was he felt. He wasn't exactly the most introspective of men, and while he might not have been happy with his circumstances as he went through his two hundred years as an Angel of the Faithful, he was usually pretty happy with himself and didn't see the need to change much.

He had a brother who accepted him for what he was; the Faithful women were ordered to accept him for what he was; Trevor enthusiastically accepted him for what he was; and his friends in the EN all accepted him for what he was. What he was was fine.

So he didn't see why Adem shouldn't be fine with him, too.

He bumped into Adem a couple of times at the Embassy, and now and then their paths would cross at Aelfeham House, and he seemed fine talking to Malachi. He didn't hang around long, though, never more than ten minutes, and then he'd suddenly find something important to do.

And then Malachi noticed that when he *did* talk to Adem, it was always under an air conditioning vent blowing away from him. Or in a big open area. Or right after he showered from warrior training and was eating in the Breakfast Room. Adem wasn't going to get caught, not like Malachi had been.

That was very clever of Adem, and Malachi had to admire how natural he made those brief, stage-managed encounters seem. It never felt like he was being steered into a downwind airstream, but steered he was. Then once he began to pay attention, he started noticing other clever things about Adem. Like how his chattering flattered and charmed but revealed almost nothing about himself. People walked away thinking they'd had a real heart-to-heart with the lord when, in fact, almost all of the conversation had been about themselves, and in the meantime, Adem learned their secrets.

The charm, Malachi suddenly understood, was a wall, and when Malachi realised that Adem wasn't all surface glitter, he became even more intrigued. Having found something to capture his interest, Malachi watched Adem more and listened a bit closer to what the man said.

Adem was a genuinely kind and humble person. He liked people and was patient and generous with them, even the idiots. That was the real kicker; if you were nice, it was easy for people to think you were soft and weak, and that's where Malachi had made his first big mistake with Adem, and it took him a while to understand that.

But Adem wasn't soft. There was a bite in there, a touch of acid that most people didn't hear, or if they did, they thought they heard wrong. There was a depth, a keen intelligence, that Adem kept well-hidden but that popped out now and then if a person was paying attention. No wonder Caddy and Kyrylo rated him so highly.

And after watching and listening, Malachi started thinking that Adem wasn't as plain as he'd first thought. Other people thought he was cute; that steward on the flight to Canada certainly had. Oh, he wasn't classically handsome the way Trevor was, but then very few people were. But the full Adem portfolio was very attractive.

Malachi started to think he'd been much too hard on Adem, much too dismissive, and had simply undervalued and misread everything about him. There were a lot worse people to be bonded to, and Malachi decided that he should give Adem another chance.

Malachi was bonded, but he wasn't in love. Love was something that grew from a foundation of respect, and without knowing it, with every little thing he learned about Adem, his respect for him grew.

When Malachi had decided to bed Trevor, he'd seduced him; there was just no other way to describe it. But seducing Trevor was pushing against an unlocked door. It was the easiest thing ever because Trevor wanted Malachi as much as Malachi wanted him. Adem, on the other hand, needed a bit more effort.

A lot more effort. The man didn't show any sexual interest in Malachi at all. No flirting, no accidental touching, no effort made to be in the same county as Malachi, much less in the same room. He was friendly, even collegial, but not anything more than that. It was obvious that Malachi was not considered an available prospect.

It was clear that Adem had no idea Malachi and Trevor weren't a couple any more. Maybe if he casually had lunch one day with him when he was back from one of his little tours of the embassy, he could work it in the conversation and see how Adem took that. He smiled to himself; he could imagine Adem's face; it would light up into one of his lovely smiles, and Malachi could see his eyes twinkling.

It didn't take long for an opportunity to present itself. Malachi kept his eyes open, and he saw Adem port into Aelfeham House about two in the afternoon and head to the Breakfast Room. No one else would be in there at this time of day. Perfect.

Chloe would have admired Malachi's accidentally-on-purpose technique of casually wandering into the Breakfast room and companionably taking a seat across from Adem and asking how his day had gone.

Adem looked up, and just as Malachi expected, gave him a beaming smile and began to chat about the last tour, a group of environmentalists from Sweden who were lobbying for support for increasing whale populations. Of course, elves were land-based, and the Swedes really needed to talk to Neptune, but that didn't stop them from coming anyway.

That led to Adem asking what was new in Malachi's life, which was the perfect opening. Malachi leaned back and gave Adem a sweet, sexy smile that made Adem's heart flip.

"Oh, not much. Mordecai is now scheduled to work with waking elves in Spain, which will be interesting. I've never been to Spain." He looked at Adem, keeping eye contact, and he let his eyes glow a bit, keeping his voice low and silky. "But I was wondering if you and I could do something before I go. Maybe go out for dinner. I don't know if you know, but Trevor and I aren't seeing each other any more. I have some free time to fill, and I know you don't have much going on either, just embassy tours."

Adem's jaw dropped and then closed with a snap. Malachi waited for the excited twittering that was a happy Adem – but nothing. The man just looked at him. There was no returning cheeky smile, no twinkle to his blue eyes. Instead, for the first time, Malachi saw a steely, cold Adem that he had no idea was in there.

But he was polite. "Thank you for the invitation, Malachi, but I'm pretty booked up now. Maybe some other time." And he looked at his plate, paused, and then pushed it away.

Without a word, he rose to leave, and all Malachi could do was stutter, "Sure, well, I understand – If you change your mind –"

Adem stood stock still, then turned to Malachi and pulled himself up to his full five feet six inches. His face was bright red, and he was furious.

"I will not be changing my mind. I'm sorry that you are now at loose ends, but that's something you'll have to deal with yourself." His voice trembled. "I am an Elemental lord. I have a purpose in life that you might not feel *is much going on*, but others feel is pretty fucking important.

"You had a human lover, and now that it's not working out you have the gall to come in to say you have some free time to fill, and now I'm good enough for you to pay attention to? Don't you think I know I'm not your cup of tea? You haven't been shy about telling other people you don't find me attractive. You would barely talk to me when you had your human boy toy. Now it's a bit late to suddenly realise I exist and you have some time to fill, and the second string will have to do."

Stunned, Malachi watched him stalk out of the room. Then Adem turned at the door, his eyes as bright as sunbeams. "I'm a nice guy, Malachi. I deserve better than being treated as yesterday's leftovers." And he left.

For the first time in his life, Malachi had been rejected. He didn't like it. Oh, he always knew he could be turned down by Adem, but deep in his heart, he hadn't really expected it. Not one of his wives had ever denied him. Trevor had given him everything he wanted.

After the initial shock of being turned down and then told off, his anger boiled up. How dare Adem speak to him like that? Who the fuck did he think he was? It was a simple invitation to dinner, and if he couldn't handle that, then fuck'm.

The more he thought about it, the more furious he became at Adem for being such a stupid prick. No wonder the guy was five thousand years old and still single! The man was crazy!

Malachi almost ran to the stables; he needed to get out and do something to clear his mind, but then he realised that in his foul mood, he shouldn't ride Gangster Jack or any other horse. So he leapt up and started flying as far and fast as he could. He flew until he was exhausted.

Fuck'm.

James and Sarah

They were snuggled up on the sofa watching a spy movie on cable. Sarah had a glass of that cheap, sweet wine she liked, there was Chinese food on the coffee table, and James was nursing his second beer.

With no kids around, that made for a perfect old-git Saturday night date.

The spy movie featured an over-muscled leading man who did a lot of fighting in tuxedos.

"I wonder if that's his special ability, to never split his trousers when he's fighting. The ability to make instant haberdashery repairs," Sarah mused.

"Maybe. And her special ability is to do hand-to-hand in court shoes and not ladder her tights." James looked over at Sarah. "Can you fight in court shoes?"

Sarah sat up and reached for an eggroll. "I don't know. I've never tried. Vrt can." She grinned at James. "Maybe that should be my next lesson. I don't know if I can, and you don't know what you don't know. I might have a hidden talent. Hand-to-hand combat while inappropriately dressed."

The actors stopped fighting bad guys and immediately ran to a hotel where they started fucking instead, never mind the aches and pains of having the stuffing knocked out of you. It didn't bother them a bit. Since it was a late-night movie, it was pretty explicit, and the actors' intimacy coach had the female lead climaxing in about thirty seconds flat. James glanced over at Sarah. The movie was putting ideas in his head. She looked bored.

Then the camera focused on the male star, or his stand-in, and there was a full frontal, which got Sarah interested and made James laugh.

"What's so funny?"

"Bad editing. Circumcised in one cut and not circumcised in the next. The guy has a regenerating dick."

Sarah howled. "I didn't notice! I've never seen an uncircumcised man in real life. But compared to this guy, yours is nicer."

"Pet, I thank you, and my little soldier thanks you. In my case, your ignorance is my bliss. Let's keep it that way." Sarah grinned at him, winked, and rolled the eggroll around her tongue, which put more ideas in Jame's head.

You don't know what you don't know. Sarah had only seen two naked men in her life.

Then it hit James so hard he had to turn and look at his bond-wife.

The only two men in her life she'd ever had in bed were a sadistic, wife-beating orc and James. She was a nice, observant Jewish girl, a virgin when she married, and one not comfortable with her body. James would bet good money she had never had an orgasm in her life. She didn't know what she didn't know.

Fekkin' hell – she never complained or looked disappointed or frustrated or any of those things because to her, James was the best lover she'd ever had. *You don't know what you don't know.*

Maybe, he thought, I've been approaching her all wrong. He had assumed she would climax if he were a bit better at it, and they would both peak at pretty much the same time. But she always ended up paying a lot of attention to his needs as she tried to make him happy, and she did make him very happy, very fast. Maybe they both needed to be a lot less James-oriented and a lot more Sarah-oriented.

Sarah was watching the spy crawling up the outside of an office building using suction cups, wondering why he just didn't use the elevator, when James leaned over and kissed her neck. She giggled and kissed him back. Five minutes later, neither of them was paying any attention to the movie at all.

Forty-five minutes later, Sarah had her first orgasm and James had his first experience with a climaxing lord and the glowing light show she gave him. When he finally entered her, it was magic.

Berke

Berke was the son of the great Batu Khan and his last concubine, Nokai. His mother would laugh when she talked about the Khan. He was very old (for a Mongolian at the time) and pretty beat up when she was given to him by her tribe as tribute and a symbol of their fealty to him, and she only bedded with him once, but it was enough. She fell pregnant. She gave him her virginity and ten minutes of her time, and he gave her a fine son for life – a good trade in the end.

It was, she would laugh, the world's most forgettable fuck.

Three months later, Batu Khan was dead, and after a period of turmoil, his brother Berke inherited the Golden Horde, and the new Khan wasn't interested in leftover concubines from extremely obscure clans, especially newly pregnant ones. Nokai was unceremoniously sent back to her tribe to see what would be born. If it were a boy, then Berke Khan's men would kill it because he had enough of his own sons and didn't need any upstarts with ideas to grow like weeds in the hinterlands. If it were a girl, he might use her to placate a minor official if he remembered she existed. Or not.

Nokai was quite happy to go back home. She had stories to tell of the grand Khan's court, a very un-traumatic encounter with a great man to impress any new suitor's family with, and enough nice jewellery as trophies to make her an attractive prospect for a real marriage. She waited for the baby to be born with the full expectation that after the birth, she'd heal up and a few months later she'd marry a husband from a neighbouring clan who didn't mind a slightly used wife who was a minor celebrity. She was very beautiful, too, otherwise she wouldn't have been sent to the Khan, so that helped a lot.

The birth happened, and it was as totally normal and as un-traumatic as the conception. It was a boy, and when Nokai held the baby and looked into his blue, blue eyes, she fell in love and swore to herself that this boy was not going to die by the sword of one of Berke Khan's soldiers. She named him Berke, too, just in case. The Khan wouldn't kill his own namesake, would he?

After Nokai healed up, her father was approached by a matchmaker who had three suitors, all of whom, to him, were perfectly acceptable. So in a fit of generosity, he allowed Nokai to have her pick. One was a rich merchant's son, one was a wealthy Mongol farmer with a very large herd of sheep, and one was a nomadic camel breeder and transporter of goods. The only one who came to visit Nokai before she was married off was the nomad. He wanted to see the goods before he bought them, like any wise negotiator.

Everyone expected her to choose the rich merchant's son and live an easy life in town, but she didn't. She chose the quiet camel breeder and the hard, nomadic life in the desert.

His name was Altan, and he was quite taken with Nokai's beauty, easy good humour, and cleverness. The baby was fine; he had no problem with keeping it, and Nokai knew he'd take good care of her. As a camel breeder and transporter of goods for merchants, he would always be moving around in the vast deserts. She had her private reasons for wanting that. She didn't want to be found and noticed by the Khan's soldiers. She didn't want little Berke's parentage to be remembered. She wanted to disappear into the untracked and eternal sand.

Altan was a good father. He treated Berke as a true son, exactly like his other boys who soon came along and he taught them all how to breed camels and how to manage and train the silly, temperamental beasts. Berke, however, was the best at it, and that was to be expected. Because, as Nokai knew from the day he was born, Berke was a wizard.

Berke grew up a wanderer, a nomad, in a very happy, loving, noisy, nomadic family. His father and mother loved him and taught their odd son, who could talk to camels like they were human, everything they knew about the desert, camels, and the grand court of the khans. As the Mongol hordes fought, slaughtered, and conquered, flowering into a great power, the nomads kept to themselves, paid tribute when they had to, and melted into the desert when the civilised world became too uncivilised to tolerate.

The only time Altan's small clan, who numbered about twenty-five, met with other clans and tribes was during the trading season when they would attend huge festivals where they would contract for jobs with the merchants, trade breeding stock of camels and sheep, buy whatever the woman needed to make their family's lives happy and comfortable, and to learn what was new in the world.

It was at a festival like that when disaster happened. Berke was about twenty then and one evening he sat with his brothers and the young men of the clan around a campfire singing and trying to impress the girls in a nearby clan with their voices, when a demon in the form of a drunken Han soldier screamed and rushed at Berke, running over the fire as if it didn't exist, his slashing sword ready for murder. If he had been more stealthy, he would have certainly made it to Berke in time to kill the unarmed and surprised young man, but being a demon and stupid, he gave plenty of warning and out of the dark Altan sprang in low and stabbed the demon in the gut with his knife, giving everyone just enough time to react. The demon wasn't bothered by the stab wound, but it slowed him down. His maniacal fury took all the clan's men to overcome and kill him but not without Altan getting a bad cut across his cheek that left a forever scar.

Nokai was beside herself. She knew that one day an attack like this was going to happen and had to admit that as the years flew by she'd been lulled into a false sense of security. The entire reason for marrying Altan (at the time) had been to protect Berke from the Khan's (or anyone's) soldiers. And now a soldier demon exploded out of nowhere and attacked her family, and her husband could have been killed. What would happen to the clan if Altan were killed? What would happen to her and the children?

She threw a big, stinking fit, and from then on Berke had to stay back with the women whenever they went to meet outsiders. Altan argued, but he doted on his Nokai and he rolled his eyes, and gave in. Berke argued, but his mother was a force of nature unto herself, and he couldn't push against her. She was right about the dangers, of course, like women usually were, but Altan knew that it wasn't a good solution to keep a young man hiding in the women's tent and told Berke to be patient; he would take care of everything, which he did.

A few months later, after Nokai had calmed down, Altan found an old warrior of some renown, a member of the Emperor Duanzong's guard who'd lost his leg and been sent away to go begging on the streets. In return for teaching Berke and all the young men of the clan how to fight and defend themselves, he allowed the old man to join his clan and live out his life with them. Most of the young men and a couple of the women became warriors.

Years passed, Berke's parents grew very old, and after Nokai died, Altan lost his heart and didn't stay in this world much longer. Berke grew up, and as a warrior, as the leader's eldest son, and as a wizard, he fell naturally into the role of clan leader, and that's where he stayed for over seven hundred and forty years.

As a wizard, Berke could do several things that served his clan. He could talk to animals, of course, and as a camel breeder and trainer that talent was certainly handy. He could hear things – people and machines – from very far away. Thousands of miles if he concentrated, but at that distance the noises blurred, and it was hard to sort out exactly what he was hearing, so he didn't do it very often. There was no point in it. But at closer distances, the ability to hear them meant no bandits, raiding parties, or armies could sneak up on his people, and during times of danger, which happened a lot with the Chinese to the east and the Rus to the west, they could simply avoid anyone who was a threat.

But what he could do that was most useful for a desert-dwelling family was that he could conjure up water out of thin air. He could pull the clouds out of the sky and wring them like an old woman doing her laundry and fill up a depression with precious water. He could pull up water from the ground where it hid in pockets between the rocks. His people and his animals never went thirsty, and so his clan didn't depend on the oases and springs. If they had to hide in the desert to stay away from marauding armies, that was fine; thirst never betrayed them.

Because he was safe with his clan wandering the Gobi desert, and because he had no reason to hide his talent since it served his people, he never grew old. Berke used his abilities every day, and in doing so, he stayed healthy. His hair grew white, and his ears grew to fantastic heights like a corsac fox, but he still managed to hide who he was when it suited him. It helped that the traditional Mongolian shapka was huge and furry. It was brilliant at hiding overgrown ears.

When Berke was about thirty he married a pretty girl from another tribe and had his first real love. With her, he found great joy and learned of the profound sadness that comes when beloved humans grow old and die. They didn't have any children. After Tani passed on he was just too weird-looking, too scary, and too bereft to think about attracting another woman, and he wouldn't negotiate for one.

After Tani had long been gone and Berke was well into his second century, his clan made their yearly visit to Bulgan Soum for the camel festival. Like the night he was attacked by the demon, Berke was sitting around a fire watching the young men dance and sing, and he was laughing and a little bit drunk when he heard a scream of pain. No one else heard it but him, and he jumped up and ran to the sound. Maybe if he hadn't been drunk he wouldn't have been so impulsive, but he was always glad that he had been because that was when he found Köke.

Köke was being jumped by two demons, and if Berke hadn't arrived to save him, he surely would have died. The thin, frail boy was only fifteen and a beggar, working the fringes of the festival. He had been thrown out of his family just months earlier and was starving and weak when the demons found him.

Later, Köke would tell the story of being jumped and how the demons held him down to rape him when the one starting to mount him just exploded, and the next minute, Köke was covered in blood and bits of meat; the demon had disintegrated. The other one screamed and ran away, and then he exploded, too.

Terrified, Köke cowered, and when he looked up, all he could see was a big man bundled up against the frigid March night air, his body and his eyes glowing with a bright blue light. They shone like blue fire.

"Stand up. You're safe now." Berke reached down to the boy, and when their eyes met his shock was almost as great as the boy's. Only he wasn't terrified; he was in wonder. The boy had glowing blue eyes, just like his.

That's when Berke learned he was not alone in the world.

He took the boy home and adopted him into his clan. The humans in his clan were fine with getting another wizard. By that time, they'd had over four generations of living with one, and they'd had nothing but good out of Berke. So as far as they were concerned, adding another one to the clan was a bonus, and Köke was welcomed as Berke's son.

Like his father before him, Berke made sure Köke learned to defend himself by becoming a great warrior, and he and the other men of the clan taught him everything they knew about camels, sheep, and living in the desert.

With the discovery of Köke, Berke started to wonder if there were other wizards about. Maybe even a woman wizard. A woman wizard who wouldn't die in fifty or sixty years, but could be an equal partner for a lonely wizard like his mother and father were partners as well as lovers. And so he started to listen and look. When Köke was old enough to lead the clan and take care of them by himself, Berke began to go a-roaming.

At first, they were short trips to trading posts and the isolated towns of the steppes and desert, but then the trips became longer and further afield. He even ventured into China and past the Wall. Some journeys were high to the north, to the taiga, and others were down to the great mountains of the south. Berke learned about all of the different people in his world. He sat in temples and was taught how to read by the monks. He learned how to survive outside of the desert and in really inhospitable places, like jungles. He walked the great markets on the Silk Road and talked with the pink people from the far side of the Don who came to trade.

But the whole point of the roaming, while fun and interesting, was to find others like him. To listen to the hum of life and find more wizards.

And he did. Every fifty years or so, he'd find one. Always an adult, usually just as they turned from childhood to being a man or woman, and their scent changed from the neutrality of childhood to the pungent odour of a man or woman looking for a mate.

Berke completely understood the process because the animals had told him all about it. It was the most normal thing in life to identify his own kind by their smell and look for a mate. Couldn't he smell the stink of the demons, the wolves asked? Not that he wanted to mate with a demon, but he got the point.

When he found a wizard, he offered them community and a safe place to live, and almost always the offer was gratefully accepted. Berke would take them back to the desert, and he and the clan would welcome them, train them, and give them a purpose in life and a home.

The first time he brought home a female wizard, he was so hopeful. She was in such poor shape he didn't bed her; his kind didn't do well by themselves in the city, but when she walked into the clan's yurt, she smelled Köke and fainted dead away, and that was the end of Berke's hopes. They bonded like two jackals for life and forever. Köke felt a bit guilty over it, but Berke didn't mind – much. He was happy for Köke, and if one was out there, there must be others. So he kept looking.

Over the years, Berke found more wizards, and every time he found one, he'd spend time at home with the clan to get them well-integrated and to make sure everyone was happy. But once he was confident they could manage without him, he'd go a-roaming again and find one or two more and then repeat the cycle. Every time he brought back a woman, she would immediately bond with one of the men, and their scent would fade. They wouldn't be interested in anyone else, including the wizard who had found them.

It became a running joke that Berke could find them but couldn't keep them.

Years passed. The wizards grew into a solitary, mysterious clan that lived in the middle of the Gobi. Over time, the humans in the clan simply died away, much loved and mourned, but not replaced.

The wizards had no reason to hide their powers when they were alone in the desert, and so they generally kept healthy if they had enough to eat, which was their only problem. The bonded couples even had children, and that brought joy to everyone. One pair's child was everyone's child.

By the start of the nineteenth century, they numbered about twenty, and they were so reclusive that they faded into rumour if not myth. They had long ago abandoned their ancient trade of moving goods along the Silk Road, for merchants, when that caused more problems than the money was worth. Multiple wizards with different talents and centuries of practice at their craft didn't need much from the rest of the world, and they became entirely self-sufficient for their daily life. If they needed anything, it was traded for during the festivals they visited.

When they did go to the occasional festival to buy and sell breeding camels and trade for things like iron pots, they pretended to be a clan of inbred, albino outback dwellers, although if anyone looked at them closely, they would see that there was no family resemblance other than the white hair and beards. Some had dark brown skin, like the people from the south side of the great mountains, while others were pale, like those who lived in the far northwest, and some were average. Whatever their skin colour or facial features, all of them had red in their hair until it turned white. And all of the men had blue eyes, and all the women's eyes were green.

Berke would still go a-roaming when he felt the clan was safe and happy, and he'd bring back books and newspapers along with the occasional new wizard. A camel can carry a lot of books, and they had a couple of good, dry caves to store them in. The reading material was always eagerly welcomed as a diversion by the rest of the wizards, most of whom had no desire to ever see another human again, but the information did keep them abreast of the rest of the world.

The twentieth century brought new risks. The humans and demons that surrounded them had cars and trucks and aeroplanes, and the vast Gobi became a little less vast. The Communists in both Russia and China were a real problem. Travelling either east or west (the wizards didn't pay much attention to borders) was more dangerous now, especially as the new bureaucracies demanded travel documents and passports and other ways they used to control their own people and keep them from moving freely. If he were alone, Berke could easily slip in and out of countries and avoid the pesky border posts, but moving a twenty-five-member clan with over two hundred camels – well, that parade was not easy to hide on China National Highway 207.

But they kept their heads down and hid in the shadows, as silent and ephemeral as ghosts.

Then one March, in the year the rest of the world called 2011, the clan went to their first camel festival in twenty years, and Köke saw people talking into little boxes, and the clan learned about mobile phones. A few of the wizards traded two top camels for three smartphones and some SIM cards, a little solar-powered battery pack, and poof! They were hooked up to the internet. The next year, they returned, and the first thing they did was buy new phones and gear for everyone. Talking to clan members miles away from their base camp was very handy.

By the time Judy was imprisoned in China, the wizards had been combing for adult wizards in their eastern Russia/western China range for centuries. Berke couldn't hear child wizards, and most were killed by demons and terrified humans before they could make a noise, but if they survived to young adulthood, he could get a sense of them if they were within a thousand miles or so, and most would come home with him when he approached them.

Some didn't for their own reasons.

He had once met Gang, the old man in prison with Judy, but Gang never admitted to himself that he was a wizard and was too afraid to leave and go to the Gobi to learn more. The night Judy made her break-out, she made a tremendous psychic uproar that Berke heard, but by the time he made his way across the vast distances to find her, she was long gone.

The Chinese authorities wondered where the older lords were. Berke knew. When Judy escaped her prison, the Berke clan numbered thirty-seven, the largest it had ever been. There were twenty-two discovered wizards that Berke had found from roaming for seven hundred years, and they came from Finland, Russia, China, Tibet, Kazakhstan, and the north of the Himalayas. A couple were very dark-skinned and had been brought to the Silk Road as slave children and didn't know where their homeland was, but they all assumed it was Africa. The rest were the children the bonded couples made, most of whom were grown adults themselves.

No wizard ever died under Berke's leadership.

The only difference between what Caddy was doing and what Berke did was that Caddy woke up elves. Berke had never seen or heard of an elf until they were mentioned on the internet.

Elves. Now that was an interesting development. All the wizards were fascinated by the elves, although not a one had ever seen the tribe. Like humans, the wizards thought the tribe was just a myth.

Berke called a council one night, and all the adults, thirty-two of them, sat down around the fire and had a talk. They had two things to talk about; one was an immediate worry.

The Russians were massing on the border. Usually, the clan simply melted away to the interior of the desert when the humans and demons had one of their many wars, but now things were different. They all knew about aeroplanes and nuclear bombs and chemicals, and they could see the devastation that modern wars caused. As powerful as they were, they knew they couldn't survive a well-placed missile. They all worried about the children.

Even the warriors – especially the warriors – were worried about the masses of demons the Rus commanded. They could kill demons all day and night and not make a dent in the numbers they saw gathering, and sooner or later, the strongest warriors of the clan would tire and be overwhelmed. The wizards were not too proud to admit that. When you live in a desert, you respect your limits.

The second item to discuss was this new group of magicians who had emerged at the farthest point away from them to the west in England. They called themselves lords, but it seemed to everyone that they were exactly the same thing as the wizards. On the one hand, it was wonderful that they existed! To have more brothers and sisters suddenly pop up and live in the human world and succeed on their own terms – the wizards really respected that. The old, rescued ones knew how hard that was. But these new wizard/lords also had elves, which was another miracle. Deep in the wizards' DNA something drew them to elves, and to a man and woman, they wanted to see them, to smell them, to be with them.

Berke listened to his people talk, and he knew what he was going to say was going to be hard to hear. The old ones would moan, but it had to be said. They would all do what he told them was the best course, and he wasn't afraid of anyone rebelling, but he hated it when they were afraid and unhappy. But that was life.

"We've lived in the desert for many years. I've been here since 1275, longer than any of you. We could live here in the unchanging desert forever, but it's not unchanging, is it? For hundreds of years – for forever – only a person with a camel could cross it and come to hunt us down, and we could easily deal with that. Even the great Khans couldn't hunt us down. But now the demons have humans with modern machinery. In the last one hundred years, we've watched them develop so much, so fast. They can hunt us down like a lion hunts a gazelle if they smell us. Our hidden corner of the world isn't as safe as it used to be."

The wizards were very quiet. Some were physically sick as they thought of their bonded mates being in danger.

"So I think we need to reach out to these British lords and make friends with them. We need a place to send the children if the worst happens. It'd be good for our unmated brothers and sisters to meet new prospects. We could meet these elves, and maybe some would like to join our clan. Who knows? But most of all, we need allies if the worst happens. We've been alone and hidden for a long time. They probably have, too, but they've decided to make the world dance to their tune now, and I'm sure it's for the same reasons we need to change. I'm sure they're afraid of the demons, too. We've seen on the internet where some have been hurt by demons, and we've seen a couple, their leaders, defend themselves."

Berke looked at the scared, sad faces of his small clan, and they broke his heart, but making hard choices was the dark side of the leadership coin.

"I've decided to contact the Elf Nation and let them know I exist. I'm not going to say anything about the rest of the clan, not yet. I want to visit them and see how they live and hear what they say, and then I'll be back to talk to you. Then we'll decide to either go live with them or take a stand here and do the best we can. Is everyone happy with that? Well, maybe not happy, but you know what I mean. What do you think?"

There wasn't a choice to make. The clan voted to send Berke a-roaming. He would be going further than he ever had in his seven hundred and fifty years, and he wouldn't be bringing back any lords; this was a one-way trip.

That evening, sitting in his yurt deep in the Gobi desert, Berke sent an email from his phone.

Ellen

"Why," asked Ellen, "do all of the weird emails come to me?"

She looked down at her tablet as she sat on the sofa with Rashid while he watched a cricket game. The email had URGENT!! And a red flag. And a couple more exclamation points. And question marks. All that was missing was the puzzled face emoji.

"Because you make the big money?" He looked over at her tablet, curious. She showed him the email.

"Dear Lord Cadence Aeldor, President of the Elf Nation,

Salutations and best wishes for your continued health and prosperity!

My skill in your English language is very poor, but I cannot expect you to know my Mongolian, so I will attempt to write this in English. I beg forgiveness for my errors, and please know my heart is respectful.

It is with great humility that I, Berke, a wizard in my language and a lord in yours, ask for your indulgence of ten minutes of your time to parley with you.

I am presently at my home in the Gobi Desert and will be leaving tomorrow morning on a journey to your magnificent palace in London, England. If all goes well, I will be in Calais, France, in forty-five days. I beg your kind help and advice in transporting my camels across the German Sea. I don't know how I can do that

*since when I searched the internet, nothing
came up. I will have five camels with me.*

*My deep and humble regards to you and your
family and your subject lords and elves.*

Berke"

Rashid looked up and laughed. "Well, you do
get the weird ones, don't you! A Mongol from the
Gobi Desert! Coming here on his camel! We're being
invaded by the Golden Horde!"

Ellen rolled her eyes. The elves wouldn't have
passed this on if they didn't feel it was true, but
goodness! The man who says he is a lord was
informing Caddy he was riding his camel caravan
across Russia and the 'stans and then through Europe
to Calais with the hope of having a cup of tea with her.
Was he planning on a light raping and pillaging on the
way? Selfies as he ransacked Paris?

She thought for a minute and then typed a bit
and hit *reply to sender*.

"Dear Lord Berke,

*Thank you for your kind inquiry. While we look
forward to your visit, at this time, I cannot
promise a visit with Lord Cadence.*

*I'm also concerned that you are taking such a long
and hazardous journey by camel. This is most*

unusual. Wouldn't a flight from Ulaanbaatar be better? I'm happy to send a representative to meet you at Heathrow in London.

Please let me know if this will be a better option for you.

Kind regards, etc."

Almost immediately, she got a reply. He must have been waiting.

"Dear Ms Hadid,

Thank you for your reply and kind questions. It is with profound humiliation and embarrassment that I must undertake this journey by camel. I do not have a passport, and from what I have read on the internet, one must have a current passport to board an aeroplane to fly to London. When I inquired about a passport with the Mongolian government, they replied that my birth year of 1275 was not true, but it is. Then they refused to talk to me. I've investigated other methods of modern transportation, and all will, at some point or other, need a passport to cross present-day borders. With a camel, I will simply ride around such impediments.

Kind regards, etc."

Ellen frowned and wondered if they had another Ratna situation here. It sure looked like it. After some inquiries with Norma, they found that RumLot jets wouldn't be able to land in Mongolia. Neither Russia nor China would allow them fly-over privileges.

"Dear Lord Berke,

Can you get to Tashkent?

Best, Ellen."

Berke read the email. The woman seemed to be trying to be helpful, and Tashkent was much, much closer. And he had been to Tashkent several times, the last time fairly recently in 1853. So he replied,

"Dear Ms Hadid,

> *Yes, Tashkent is much better. I will be there in fourteen days. I will send you an email each day of my journey so that you know my progress. Or you can track me by Find My Phone."*

> *Kind regards, etc."*

Ellen looked at the email and back at Rashid. "This guy says he'll let me track him by his phone!"

"Seems pretty tech savvy for a guy born in 1275. Let's see where he is now."

And just as he said, when Ellen set up the Find My Phone app, Berke's phone pinged out of western Mongolia.

"I get all the weird ones."

Tuân, Ratna and Berke

Tuân and Ratna sat in a van with three RumLot Security agents on the outskirts of Tashkent, watching a large tablet and following the slow but steady progress of the pin labelled Berke.

Then, right on time, over the crest of a hill, a man on a camel appeared with a train of four camels behind him, all carrying bundles. Tuân looked at Ratna and grinned. It was just like watching *Lawrence of Arabia*.

Tuân walked out and waited, directly in the path of the camels. The man, who could only be Berke, stopped about thirty feet in front of the lord, and the two men looked at each other, and then Berke grinned and waved. This young man, who had pointed ears but still had his youth hair, was a lord, and his eyes glowed like Berke's wizard nomads. And he wasn't hiding any of it.

For his part, Tuân saw a man of average height, a handsome Mongolian who could have been cast in any film on Genghis Khan, dressed in an elaborately embroidered nomadic coat that fell mid-calf. He wore a long sword, and tucked in his belt were a couple of knives. On his feet, he wore tall boots and the toes curled up at the tips, and on his head was a huge, fur-trimmed hat that hid his ears. His long, white moustache reached down to his chin, and his hair was plaited into a long, white queue that fell down to the middle of his back. And his eyes glowed bright blue. There was no doubt he was a lord. An Elemental? Tuân thought he was but couldn't tell for sure; he bet Ratna would know.

Tuân bowed. "Welcome, Lord Berke! We've been waiting!"

After a few minutes of hello-hope-you-had-a-good-journey, Ratna walked out and stood next to Tuân, and Berke looked at her with frank admiration. Then, before she could say anything, his grin widened. She was taken; he could smell it. Or rather, he couldn't smell it. Pity. This bright-eyed woman wizard was very beautiful and very healthy. Too late again!

And so it went as anyone would expect; Berke was taken by the van to the Tashkent airport and put on the RumLot jet (his first time flying), and the lord's human employees took care of the baggage and the camels, telling Berke they couldn't bring the beasts along. Berke had a pang about the camels; he hadn't ridden his best just in case this happened. But they were still good ones.

He just shrugged it off. If he'd needed to buy a ticket, the camels would have been sold for the cash anyway. So he sat back and enjoyed the eight-hour flight to Heathrow and the company of the two lords who were sent to meet him.

The only odd thing was when Tuân, with obvious embarrassment, asked Berke to take a shower and change his clothes to the RumLot ones provided.

"So do I smell like a camel?" Berke was joking, and his eyes twinkled, but the rest of his face was serious. He was sure he did; he hadn't had a bath since the last stream he'd crossed, and that had been days ago. Ratna and Tuân looked at each other, and Ratna just came out and said it. "No, Lord Berke, you smell like an unbonded lord. In our world, we try to keep our personal scents under control, and at this moment, your scent is going to be disturbing to the unbonded women you meet."

Poor things. They were almost squirming with embarrassment at telling a guest he needed to wash the sex stink off, and Berke let them suffer for a minute, and then he burst out laughing; he couldn't help it. Naturally, he knew that. Hadn't he lived with wizards for hundreds of years?

"Of course. If Tuân can come and show me how to use your shower, that would be most helpful. I've seen them on the internet, but never used one. We take baths in the yurt." And he could see the relief on both their faces. It was really funny.

So Tuân stood in the shower room and demonstrated every little knob, including the toilet and sink, and stood and chatted while Berke showered. A half hour later, he was clean enough to meet a virgin. With new clothes from the skin out, including some very uncomfortable boots, when they landed at Heathrow, Berke was ready to be ported directly to the Embassy. Ratna told him his old clothes would be cleaned and returned to him, so that was fine. Berke put on his sword and knife belt, and no one said anything at all.

At the Embassy, he was greeted by more lords, but most amazingly, he saw elves. Ratna was looking at him when he had his first glimpse of elves, and she told Tuân later that she was sure the man was going to cry. His reaction made her tear up, too. "You forget how much they mean to us as a tribe. Berke said he's never seen an elf in his life, but meeting one for the first time, it sings to our soul."

Berke met Lord Cadence, who was very cute, and of course, bonded, but he knew that. Her marriage to Lord Kyrylo was all over the internet. He could feel her authority; she was a woman who was in charge of her world, and he could feel her power. It crackled around her. Inside his clan, Berke was the most powerful lord, no question about it. Here, he wasn't so sure. Lord Cadence was certainly his equal. He could feel it.

He formally asked her if he could stay in her palace for a short time, a week if she was willing, and learn about the English lord clan, and she was very gracious.

"A new lord is always welcome at my table. All I ask is that you follow our rules, which are for you to do three things. One is to take three baths a day, the second is to take our self-defence classes so that you can defend yourself against our enemies, and the third is to take our lord classes. It's all very easy, and learning about us is what you want to do anyway. You can leave at any time, no questions asked, and no insult taken."

Berke was very happy with that. She bowed, he bowed back, and he was dismissed.

When the meeting was over, he met Lord Vrt, a warrior who was surely the most beautiful woman he had ever seen, and again, she was bonded. Berke sincerely hoped there would be a couple of unbonded women around, but now he was beginning to wonder. Too late again.

Lord Vrt introduced him to his guides, Lords Jack and Alizah, and they showed him how to port to Aelfeham House. In a day of firsts, learning to work with elves and port was the most memorable. By the time he was shown his very luxurious room at the lord's palace, Berke was as tired as he had ever been, mentally and physically. He had been riding since dawn, Tashkhent time, flying on the jet for eight hours, and then two hours at the Embassy. And every time he turned around, there was something new and bizarre to experience. It was all mentally exhausting, and when the elf in his room asked him if he'd like a little something to eat in his room and then go to bed, he gratefully accepted.

The next morning, an elf woke Berke up and asked him if he would like to go to PT today or not, and since physical training was one of Lord Cadence's requirements, of course Berke said yes. The elf showed him how to use the shower, which seemed odd before going to exercise, and the shitpot. Then the elf helped him with his PT clothes and ported him to the area. That's when Berke found out why he had to shower first. There were women there. Single, unbonded women.

A head elf named Victor, a stocky man with a foul expression on his face, walked out to assess Berke's fighting skills, and an elf was sent to attack him to see if he could defend himself. Berke easily rebuffed the poor thing and sent him flying. Then he came back, but a bit harder and faster, and Berke did it again. Victor frowned.

A couple of elves, Warriors, strolled up and made a comment in a language Berke could almost understand, and that made the elf who'd attacked Berke pissed. Berke grinned. He could see that this was going to get interesting.

The elf circled, and now Berke could see by the set of his shoulders and the gleam in his eye that he meant business. No holding back for the new guy. The warriors hooted and placed bets, and Berke smiled to himself. He knew what that meant; at least one person was betting on him.

The elf charged, and *shaa,* he was fast! He flipped around at the last minute, but not last-minute enough. Berke caught him by the leg and used the warrior's own momentum to fling him around and hard. The elf almost slammed into a wall but ported out at the last minute.

The warrior elves screamed and moaned depending on how they'd bet, and the losers paid up. Victor shook his head and smiled. This Berke was a Warrior Lord. A bit rough around the edges, but it was all there.

"Tomorrow, your porter will bring you to the Warrior training area. You'll have fun." Victor grinned a little wickedly, and that was the end of the first day's PT.

The elf ported Berke to his room, another shower, and then, dressed in the red uniform of the Elf

Nation, he went to breakfast and met still more lords. There were loads of them! And unbonded women!

They ate and had a good time. Berke answered a lot of questions, and the women seemed interested in him, which was unusual. Back in Mongolia, the unbonded women liked Berke and some even flirted a bit, but not much. They quickly just became friends. It was like they were all too closely related, and every woman he met was his sister.

But here, they were much more interested, and their eyes snapped and glowed with speculation. They were thinking about him.

Lords Jack and Alizah gave him a tour of Aelfeham House, and Berke immediately understood that the place wasn't as it seemed; the elf magic was at work here. He could figure out the layout easily enough while he was inside, but it didn't match the outside at all, and Berke didn't think it was because he was used to yurts and tents.

In the afternoon, he had a private Lord Lesson on the history of elves and lords going back to Before Times, and what he learned was profoundly shocking. From the lesson he learnt that all of the elves he'd met were more than 3,500 years old, he learnt about their hibernation and why they'd escaped into it, and he learnt about the genocide of the lords and elves. He learnt it all. Normally, a Lord lesson was about an hour, and then they had something called Abilities Practise, but Berke's lesson took all afternoon.

The elf told Berke of Lord Cadence's goal of achieving balance, the way it was before the lord leader Gaia committed suicide. When the lesson was over, he went back to his room to rest a bit and shower before he went to the evening meal. He had a few minutes to lie on the too-soft bed and stare at the ceiling, absorbing and thinking about what the elves told him and how that merged with his own experience.

He didn't think Lord Cadence could do it. Berke knew how big the world was even before there was such a thing as the internet. The Gobi Desert might be vast and empty, but the Silk Road had been a crowded superhighway long before there were such things as trains and cars. He'd been hiding from and fighting orcs for over seven hundred years, and wizards such as himself were so rare – they were like blades of grass fighting an encroaching dune.

But if there were people out there, humans and demons, who wanted to stay on top of the heap and were willing to kill to do so, then wizards had no choice but to fight. Berke had no doubt these lords were correct on that score.

He sighed. He'd never lost a wizard; none had died under his leadership. And he had long suspected that wizards were immortal on a human timescale, but they did die; he knew it because some were killed before he could rescue them. There used to be thousands of lords, but now he had no idea how many lords followed Lord Cadence, and he very much doubted that they numbered much more than his tiny clan. And that was a pitifully small number.

However, blades of grass working together won't destroy a sand dune, but they can certainly stabilise one. They had no choice but to work together.

He sent a text to Köke in Mongolian that he was fine, had learned a lot, and told him he would text again tomorrow.

Berke might be pushing eight hundred years old and live in the middle of the Gobi Desert, but he wasn't a technological fool. He'd spent a lot of time studying the technology of humans as each new invention made its way to his part of the world, and the internet just made it easier. He had no doubt his phone was tapped once he hooked into the palace's wi-fi.

Köke, who was even more into human technology than Berke, agreed, and with that knowledge, they had decided that Berke would only talk to Köke. He'd relay everything Berke said to the rest of the clan, and they would never discuss the existence of other members. If these lords and elves listened in, they wouldn't know Köke was a lord-wizard, and they would think he was a human family member or some such person.

The evening meal was a lot of fun. Berke met more lords, and he had lively conversations with several about what they did during the day because, without the chore of looking for water, food, or taking care of a herd, they had to do *something*; otherwise, they'd die of boredom. Berke had learned that a long time ago, after the wizards had become very good at providing the basics and ended up with too much time on their hands. That had just made them unhappy and lazy, so he'd decreed that everyone had to learn warrior skills and a craft that the clan needed. It had helped a lot and drastically cut down on the squabbling.

After only a couple of days, Berke was speaking Elvish fluently. He hadn't realised that he was speaking it all along when he spoke to animals, so it was just a matter of readjusting his wiring a bit. It was certainly better for everyone else since they didn't have to wade through his heavily accented English.

They tried very hard to find out about his day, his family, and most of all, his powers as a wizard, but for some reason, they usually ended up talking about themselves. It became a game, and Berke had seven hundred years of experience in his travels and at a hundred festivals deflecting nosy questions put to him by some very wily interrogators. And he knew better than to lie to wizards and lords. By the end of the evening, even Conary was amused and frustrated by the simple camel herder who roamed the desert looking for water and sleeping under the stars. And he didn't believe a bit of it.

"So, Berke, do you have any kids? A woman? Or is it just you and the camels?" Chi had a way with words, and his way made his fellow lords roll their eyes. But it didn't stop them from looking over at Berke and waiting for an answer. Chi had his uses.

Berke chuckled. "No children, no woman. And the camels don't like me. They're picky beasts."

Rita sighed and looked sympathetic. "It must be a lonely life." Berke smiled back and successfully kept his eyes on her face and not drifting downwards. The woman really needed to put on more clothes.

They tried all during dinner to find out what Berke's ability was, but he just deflected. When Chi asked him directly, Berke shrugged and moved a beer glass a few inches on the table, and his eyes glowed bright as if he was trying as hard as he could. When Chi raised an eyebrow and exclaimed, "Is that *it*?" Berke's comically downcast expression made everyone start talking about something else. Only Vrt noticed the amused glint in the new guy's eyes; it was exactly like Conary's when he was teasing. Or hiding.

But that glint changed when Judy walked in, and Vrt saw that, too. She smiled to herself. At last, a chink in the camel herder's armour.

Judy

There were reports to finish up, so Judy walked in late from work and scanned the ravaged buffet with a resigned expression on her face. She wasn't going to ask the elves to make her anything, but pickings were getting slim, and a little pot of rice would have bulked out her meal nicely and given her the carbs she needed. You can't eat pasta every day. She sighed again and spooned fusilli onto her plate.

Everyone was crowded around the new guy so tightly that she could barely make him out in the scrum, but she had heard gossip about him all day. New lords were always a hot topic, and a lord who rode in on a caravan of camels was going to cause a lot of comment. The Girl Spy Network said he was cute and that he'd beat up the Warrior Elves the first time out, which was impressive. And that to other lords and elves, he felt pretty powerful, probably an Elemental, but no one knew anything about what he could do. Tuân and Ratna liked him.

Rita was drooling, and she'd only seen him once, at breakfast. Judy saw her in the crowd, sitting right in front of him. She was wearing civvies, and if that low-cut blouse and push-up bra weren't an invitation, Judy didn't know what was. Rita was not subtle.

Dinner over, Judy got up to leave, and Vrt called her over to introduce her to the new guy. His name was Berke, and he politely stood up and bowed, and she just as politely waved him back down and welcomed him to Aelfeham House and hoped he'd find a home there. Then Rita knocked over a glass of water, and that was Judy's opening to leave and finally go to her room. She was tired, she needed a shower, and the new guy was everything the GSN said.

A sexy beast indeed.

Berke

Lord Judy was the most beautiful woman Berke had ever seen. Prettier than Lord Vrt and only this morning Lord Vrt had the top spot in Berke's lifetime list of observed beauties, and he'd seen his share in seven hundred years.

She was Northern Han Chinese with huge eyes, a straight nose, and a perfect oval face. And lips – *shaaa*, that mouth –

She was unbonded. How that oversight could happen was a total mystery to Berke, but hey, he wasn't going to argue. She was available. He could smell it, and she smelled as good as she looked.

After a bit of subtle conversational manoeuvring, he started the "how old are you" game, which was no risk for him as they already knew how old he was. He found out that Vrt was 3,500 years old, Chi over 3,000, Rita was 45, Conary not even 80 yet, and Judy was 65. Mature enough not to be a silly child, but still very young. And unbonded! Amazing.

He didn't ask any more about her because the last thing he wanted to do was be too eager and scare her away. And scaring away skittish women happened a lot with him, but tomorrow he'd learn more. A question here from one person, a comment there to someone else, and he'd find out everything he needed to know, like what her wizard talent was and if she was crazy, cruel, or stupid.

In the meantime, this group of curious lords was entertaining. Lord Vrt asked him if he could play chess and what card games he knew, and Lord Rita was pestering him with questions about camels and sheep. Why, he had no idea; maybe she wanted to knit herself a sweater. She certainly looked like she would be cold.

Morning came, and Berke found himself in a different group for self-defence and PT. This time the group was just himself, Lord Vrt, Lord Malachi, and Lord Sarah. He hadn't met Sarah and Malachi, and they were as well-mannered and welcoming as everyone else he'd met. Sarah and Vrt were fast-bonded, and Malachi bedded men, and that meant

Berke didn't have to guard against uncontrolled sweating, and so all of them could practise and fight without having that in the back of their minds.

Fight they did. All three were what they called "Warrior Lords," and that meant a very high level of training. For the first time in a long time, Berke had to think about his fighting and put some muscle into it. At first, he held back against the women, but that was a mistake. By the second round, he was just looking at an opponent, not a pretty face. They certainly didn't hold back for him.

By the end of the session, Berke was sweating like a racing camel, and he had learnt a few moves, which was hugely fun. Victor told him where he'd made mistakes, and while the Warrior Lords made him work, he made them work, too, and everyone left in a good mood.

Vrt (he didn't call them "Lord" any more; that formality was set aside) told Berke that some of them played a game called poker, and she wanted to know if he had ever played it. It was a gambling game, and a group of them played in the Breakfast Room some evenings. She said that Malachi and Judy often played as well as whoever else wanted to sit in. Then she asked him about chess, and that led Malachi to talk about that game, and they talked about chess and its variations all the way back to Aelfeham House.

Back in his room, Berke texted Köke, and they had a short conversation in Mongolian. Berke said he was fine and no surprises. Everything was going okay back home, but Köke was hearing the wolves howl around the flock. Berke reread the text and frowned.

No one was afraid of wolves; if he really had wolves around sniffing at the sheep and goats, Köke would just talk to them. Wolves were their code for the Rus. Köke was saying that the Russians were gathering on the border, and he was worried.

"If you need me, just let me know."

And with that, he ended the conversation.

Rashid and James

Lord Cadence had tasked Rashid and Lord James with finding out the background of this new lord. She said he was hiding something, and her instincts were usually pretty good. He was, she said, just being a little too affable and a little too humble. It didn't ring true.

When Victor said the man was a Warrior Lord, that piqued her interest even more. Why on earth would he have to know more than what was needed for his basic self-defence if all he was doing was guarding camels? Kyrylo pointed out that he didn't have elves around, so maybe he felt he needed a higher level of training just to stay alive, but Caddy wasn't convinced. The man was very, very healthy. He used his ability, whatever it was, all the time. He was a warrior, and according to Victor, not rusty in that area either.

"He must be one hell of a camel herder," she said dryly, and no one could disagree.

Rashid and Lord James read the report of the intercepted text between Lord Berke and the person known as Köke. The only interesting thing about the very short conversation was the comment, "I'm hearing wolves howl around the flock." The elf analyst pointed out that traditionally, Mongolian herders were not worried about wolves since they considered them a spirit animal.

"So who is he worried about?" wondered Lord James. Bandits? Chinese?

James ordered satellite updates near the location of the first Find My Phone ping. Maybe he could spot the nomads' camp or anyone else who looked interesting.

Berke

Between the fight practice and lunch, Berke found a couple of free hours and spent the time on his tablet learning Western-style poker. He occasionally played Chinese poker, but the rules were quite a bit different from Texas Hold'm or Five Card Stud; at least the cards were the same, and in the end, a game is a game. You learn the rules, you study the odds, and the winner is usually the one who's the best bluffer.

Since he was up against regular players and it would take him a while to get comfortable with the game, he wasn't worried about losing. He just wanted to make a reasonable show of it and not embarrass himself. The goal was to learn more about his opponents, not become a poker professional.

Lunch was good, and today the elves added a nice lamb stew to the buffet that Berke enjoyed. There was a different mix of people, and he met Mordecai and Althea, and they spoke about their jobs in the EN, which was fascinating because they both worked with elves. Mordecai woke them up, and Althea was a healer, and their work took up all of their time. Rita, Chi, and Malachi were in the Breakfast Room, but Vrt, Conary, Adem, and Judy were working at the palace in London and ate lunch there.

After lunch, Berke had a class about orcs, which he called demons and learned a few things, but not much. He knew his demons. The only real news he heard in his hour of instruction was about how the demons were now learning about themselves and seemed to be organising. Alarming but not surprising. Berke had seen them clump together in the past and work for different khans and emperors, and they had certainly known they were demons then.

It was during Abilities Practise that things got a bit testy. Gerald, the elf trainer, wasn't at all happy with Berke's efforts to move feathers and lift teaspoons.

"You're holding back. How can I help you get stronger if I don't know your limits? Holding back doesn't do either of us any good."

For the first time, the affable Berke mask slipped, and he looked at the elf with icy irritation. His eyes glowed bright. Very bright.

"I don't think you want to know my limits," he said softly, and the elf went pale. Mordecai, who was shuffling some heavy plates around, stopped and turned to look. Two very young lords who were still at the feather stage stared, their eyes darting between Berke and Gerald.

He couldn't lie to the elf and say he wasn't holding back; of course, he was, and lying was beneath him and wouldn't work anyway. Not against this elf. This one knew. But Berke wasn't going to show him what his limits were either. That was his business.

But Gerald stood his ground.

"Okay, maybe you don't need to move spoons around, but you do need to get out and stretch yourself. Lords need to use their abilities to stay healthy. How long has it been since you did anything? At least a couple of days, even if you did something on your way here."

He looked at the elf, expressionless. This Gerald was correct; he needed to exercise. He was feeling a bit tight. Tense. And that was because he wasn't doing his wizard thing, because no one needed him to find water in England. The place was awash with it.

There were other lords in the room, and they were watching him.

"Gerald, I know you are trying to do your job, but what you are asking is hard for me. You're asking me to overturn seven hundred years of embedded caution. Lords or wizards who show off in public don't live long, do they? I don't do my abilities, as you call them, in front of people. I don't shit in front of people. I don't fuck in front of people. And both are natural acts that are good for me. I don't practise my magic in front of people."

Gerald couldn't say anything to that, so he tried another angle.

"Okay, so when you're back in Mongolia, where do you practise? You must practise every day. Look how healthy you are!"

Berke smiled, but he wasn't going to fall for flattery.

"I live in a desert. I go out in the middle of nowhere, and I do what I want. No one else is around, and I know that. I have good ears."

"This is England. We don't have any deserts here, but I can port you to a place with no people around. Where you can be absolutely alone." He sighed. "In the end, we just want you to be stronger and stay healthy. Maybe one day you'll trust us enough to let us see what you can do, but in the meantime, I can take you someplace today where you can stretch a bit."

"Absolutely alone."

"Yeah." Gerald sighed again. He was telling the truth.

Berke thought about it and agreed. Gerald ported him to a beach in Norfolk and said he'd be back in an hour. And there Berke stood, listening, and just as Gerald had promised, he was as alone as he was going to get in England.

Actually, he thought, this is perfect. He could condense a couple of clouds and throw their water into the sea, leaving no evidence behind. And there were always clouds in the UK. It was like living in a wet sponge.

So he gathered up and threw down clouds into the sea, which felt good after no activity for almost a week. Then he reversed the process and made the sea boil up and make new clouds. When that was done, he made an iceberg, and then he melted it. Moving tons and tons of water from state to state was easy, but it worked up a good glow, and when he was done, Berke still had a half hour to wait for the elf to come and port him back. So he stretched out on a sand dune, took out his pipe, and had a good smoke while he watched the gulls and enjoyed the quiet. He hadn't done that for a week either.

Judy

Judy enjoyed the Breakfast Room poker games and looked forward to the decompression they gave after a busy day of dipping into messy human minds. The lords, and it was *only* lords, played for an hour or two and gossiped and laughed, and it was more of a way to keep their hands busy while they nurtured friendship bonds than a serious poker game. Tonight, Vrt showed up, and she hadn't for a long time. So did the new guy, Berke. So tonight it was Judy, Vrt, Chi, Adem, and Berke.

Berke readily admitted that he didn't know the game and had just looked up the rules that afternoon. But he did know Chinese poker, and at the Breakfast Room level of play, that would probably be enough.

Good gods, this Berke was easy on the eyes. His heady, musky man-scent floated in the air, and for a minute Judy wondered if she should be this close to him. But his scent was faint enough to be controllable; she was across the table, and she could feel a slight breeze from a cracked window at her back. With all of that, she decided to risk the gamble and pushed any concerns out of her head. Instead, she concentrated on her friends and the game.

It was just a friendly game using house chips, but Judy liked to win.

Between Adem and Chi, there was plenty of chatter and giggles. Adem slyly asked Chi how Talia was doing, and the little man blushed bright red, making Vrt hoot.

"Look at you! Can't even mention her name and you get all flustered!" She turned to Berke. "Our little hyper-sexed friend here is being chased, and he doesn't know what to do about it. Chi likes to chase, but *being* chased – that's a different thing."

Chi studied his cards and pretended he hadn't heard anything.

Berke smiled at Chi. "Maybe Chi enjoys the hunt but doesn't like being hunted. In a hunt, the hunter is in control, but no one likes being prey." He looked at his cards and gave a tiny wince to bluff. Truthfully, it was a pretty good hand if having a lot of face cards meant anything. "But on the other side of the coin, being pursued can be very flattering. No one likes being prey, but everyone likes being wanted."

"That's true. There's a big difference between being prey and being wanted." Adem studied his cards, frowning.

Judy quickly glanced around, and the entire table was telegraphing their hands with their tells. If she was in a real casino with real players, she wouldn't even bother to use her abilities and dip into the humans' chaotic minds. Her hand was not great, but workable.

"So, Berke, are you a hunter or are you prey?" Vrt asked.

Berke laughed at that one and had to take a sip of his beer – what she said was so funny. He wasn't even in the hunt.

"I'm neither; I'm just watching from the sidelines. All the gods know that no one is chasing me, and I'm not chasing anyone. I think I'd be like Chi here if I started chasing a woman. Not sure what I'd do with one if I caught her."

"Oh, don't lie to a lord, Berke. You'd know what to do with a woman if you caught her." Chi hooted, then peeked at his cards again and placed a bet.

Berke shrugged and bet, too. A small one. "Maybe so, but that goes back to the first question. Is the pursuit wanted? I won't force myself on anyone. I'm sitting here with the two most beautiful women in England, and I'm sure both of you have had unwanted attention. Being prey didn't make you love the person, did it?"

Vrt smiled and shot Judy a glance. The woman wasn't concentrating on her cards at all, something Vrt was sure hadn't happened in decades. The hunky camel-trader had all of her attention, every bit of it.

It was time to turn the conversation to something less heavy, so Vrt folded and joked about a human woman who was an envoy from Italy who made a total fool of herself chasing after Conary during a reception. She hadn't known that Conary was fast-bonded and not going to do anything with anyone else, human or lord. They laughed and wondered about humans and their fixations and inability to bond.

Berke gave a little of himself to the group and told them he had once had a human wife. He thought humans could bond, but in their own way. It was very sad when they died, and he said it in a quiet way that made the table go quiet.

Adem broke the silence. "Vrt, Chi, and me, we're from Before Times and never took a human to bond with. Ratna did, but she refuses to remember their names because losing them was so hard. Many of the lords who were born later had human partners."

Berke nodded. "I had one, and losing her broke my heart. My Tani died six hundred and nine years ago, but I still think of her often. Not every day, not any more, but enough to remind me not to go through that again. Bonding with a human is a temporary joy, and the pain of losing them is forever."

They were quiet, each lost in their thoughts for a few minutes, and then Chi cracked a silly joke about his diminishing pile of chips, and everyone was happy to return to the game.

Bets were placed, players folded or played, and the game finished up. Berke won the first hand because he was holding all the queens, but by the time the party broke up for the evening, Berke had lost his entire house pot. Judy, as usual, won the evening.

James

The satellite photo of the western Mongolian desert didn't show much, but across the border in Russia – now that was another story. Scattered around highway P-256, the intel analysts saw an alarming number of Russian military units.

When the photos were compared with older images, the difference was startling. There weren't many older images to use because the area wasn't well covered, and frankly, for Western eyes, there wasn't much of interest to warrant covering the area. But there was enough information to see a change in troop levels.

Now it was different, and Lord Berke had reasons to worry about the area. The wolves were indeed out and sniffing around the flock.

James, Kyrylo, Rashid, and Jameson had a meeting and discussed the situation. What were the Russians doing out there? Why gather near the Mongolian border? At first glance, it wasn't a huge force, but then a "special operation" in that part of the world wouldn't need a huge force, just an overwhelming one. There weren't many people out there, and it didn't look like the Mongolians and the Chinese were countering with their buildup. Maybe they didn't know. Maybe they did know and weren't worried.

James ordered more photos of the Russian eastern borders and set the analysts to work. Something was going on; he could feel it in his bones. In the meantime, RumLot Security came up with their own plans just in case they needed to go in and rescue Köke, whoever he or she was.

Tuân and Ratna were sent out to wander the area and see what they could see. The mountains and desert of western Mongolia would be interesting to them, and a bit of roaming was just their cup of tea.

Berke

The days passed, and almost every day Berke practised-fought with whoever of the three Warrior Lords showed up. There was a rhythm with Malachi gone to wake elves up two days a week and Sarah in and out doing whatever it was she did. Berke was never told, and he never asked, knowing he wouldn't be told her business anyway. Vrt was there most days. Between the three of them, there was usually one to practise against, and when they all were gone, Berke fought against the Warrior Elves.

He was learning a lot and refining his skills. Berke was happy with the certainty that when he went back to his clan, he'd have a lot to teach them. About five of them could easily grow to Warrior Lord level because, like him, they just needed to smooth out a few rough edges.

Every third day, he texted Köke. He had moved the herd to the mountains, and while the wolves were still a worry, they had moved further away. The crows were the problem now. They'd peck the eyes out of the lambs, and when the ewes rejected their blind babies, the poor things would die, and the crows would feast. He spent a lot of time shooting crows, he said. And soaring so high they were black dots in the sky, he saw eagles.

This was more disturbing news. In Köke-code, the wolves were Russians, and crows were drones. Eagles were helicopters. The wizards could hide from the drones; that wasn't a problem. They had learned when they bought their smartphones that modern electronics couldn't take a picture of a wizard, but they couldn't hide the tents and the herds. A seemingly deserted camp would, if anything, attract more interest if the Russians came raiding.

Berke started thinking about returning. His part of the desert was divided up by the human boundaries of Russia, Mongolia, China, and Kazakhstan, and there was a fifty-mile area where all the borders met. Köke and the clan were hidden in the Altai Mountains now, but if need be, they could slip over the border into China or Kazakhstan and hope any marauding Russian demons wouldn't follow them. Kazakhstan would be better. Berke didn't trust the Chinese any more than he trusted the Russians.

In the meantime, Köke led the clan well and kept them safe. He would ask for help when he needed it.

Berke was quiet at lunch, so quiet that people noticed his introspective mood. His single bowl of mutton stew was reported up the chain by the housekeeper elves. By Lord Class time, Caddy was told, and in the classic game of Chinese Whispers, Berke's quiet mood had morphed into a major depression. He wasn't talking, and he wasn't eating well. When the news reached Conary, he was informed Berke was on the edge of suicide and had refused all food. Alarmed, Conary told Vrt, and Vrt suggested that Judy be sent to talk to him. If anyone would break down his defences and give anyone a hint of what was wrong, it would be Judy.

No one other than Vrt had a clue that Judy was of special interest to Berke, including Judy herself, but Conary trusted his bond-wife in matters of the heart, and Judy was called in and asked if she would be willing to go have a chat with the Mongolian and find out what, if anything, was bothering him. Maybe they could do something.

Judy thought about it, weighed the odds of her getting too close to Berke, and gambled that she could handle it. Besides, the man was hurting. She couldn't read his mind, but her deep knowledge of psychology might mean that she could get a glimpse of his heart if she could get him to talk about what was bothering him. Judy was confident he'd talk to her. Everyone did – to the point it was annoying. Sometimes she felt like the world's busiest confessional booth.

So she ordered a big bag of Chinese takeaway because she hadn't had any lunch either, and talking over food always loosened people up. An elf ported her to the Aelfeham House transport bubble, and she asked a local elf to port her to wherever Berke was.

She forgot how literal elves could be, and when she found herself absolutely alone in the middle of the god's sandy acre, she was very glad Berke wasn't on the shitter.

Well, the elf ported her where the man was, even if she couldn't see him. Judy stood at the bottom of a large dune, and she could hear the sea on the other side, so she climbed to the top, which wasn't at all easy while gripping a huge bag of Chinese takeaway and wearing a pencil skirt and high heels. It didn't occur to her to kick the heels off – Judy wasn't a country girl – so she tottered to the top of the dune and, yes, there was a beach. She still didn't see Berke, so she called out, and he popped up from behind some nasty, spiny sea bushes.

"What the hell are you doing here?" He yelled back, visibly angry. He was glowing, and his eyes were bright stars, but that didn't faze Judy at all. It wasn't like she'd never seen a lord before.

"I have lunch! The elves working the buffet said you weren't eating!" She took a step forward, lost her balance when her high heel dug in the soft sand, dropped the takeaway, leaned way back, windmilling her arms, and then overcompensated forward and tumbled face-first down the dune. Judy was a klutz, which was of no surprise to anyone except Berke.

She stomach-surfed down the dune to the feet of the gobsmacked lord, spitting sand and wondering if she still had her shoes on. She did not. Before she could sit up, he had his hands looped under her armpits and picked her straight up as if she were nothing until her feet were dangling in mid-air.

"*Shaaaaa* – Judy! Are you alright?"

"I'm fine." Heavens, he smelled good. Too good. It made her grin like the silly goose that she was. "You can put me down now." She had to get rid of him – fast. She couldn't think.

Back on her own two feet, she made a big show of brushing off the sand while moving downwind and asked him to please go fetch the takeaway. She'd had enough of climbing sand dunes for today.

When he returned with the bag, he was frowning again. "Okay, now tell me why you're here. I'm supposed to be alone out here. Gerald promised me."

Judy squatted and began to unpack the bag. She hadn't thought to bring a blanket or anything to sit on, and she sighed. But hey, it wasn't as if she didn't already have a ton of sand in her knickers, so she gave up and plopped on the sand. She felt the slit up the back of the skirt rip.

"I told you. The housekeeping elves said you weren't eating lunch. They were concerned and sent up a report, which went up the chain." She opened the first container. It was mutton stew; she made a face and handed it up to Berke, who took it.

"Then somehow the report got to Conary, who told Vrt, who asked me to bring you some lunch. She wants me to find out if anything is bothering you." Judy smiled brightly at Berke, who was just standing there. "So eat!"

All Berke could do was stare down at the woman. There was Judy, looking like she had been through a sandstorm, hair all over the place and covered in sand and bits of grass and seaweed, smiling up at him, looking perfectly gorgeous. Taking care of him. It might have been at the behest of others, but she could have said no, and they would have sent an elf. But she hadn't said no.

He sat down, and Judy reached in the bag and took out two bottles of water and another container, this one of chicken fried rice made in the American style she liked, and she dug in, too. She was hungry.

"Gerald promised me I'd be alone."

Judy shrugged. "Elves are a very literal tribe. You have to be careful with them. Their ability to parse an order is how they survived with lords who took advantage of them. It depends on how the conversation with Gerald went. Was privacy just for that day? Did it just apply to him? Was it just about humans or other lords? Was it just at certain times?" She pointed her chopsticks towards the dune. "I asked to be brought to you, but my porter didn't do that; he put me over there. You were here. The elf ported me to the other side of the dune, and he then ported away. As far as he was concerned, you still had your privacy, and if I wandered by later, that was my business."

She was talking too much and turned back to her rice. Berke just shook his head and worked on his mutton, and they ate in silence, but it was a good silence. He wasn't angry any more, and when the breeze was going in the right direction, he could smell her perfume.

"So you've been sent to learn what my problem is. What happens if you go back and say I'm fine?"

She looked up, startled. "Then you're fine. I'm not here to spy, I'm here to offer help to a friend. We're a clan. We help each other when it's wanted and stay out of each other's business when it's not."

Berke looked out at the sea. He understood clan. "If I need help, I'll ask."

Judy nodded. That was all she was going to get out of him today, and she knew it. "I'll pass that on."

Berke looked over at Judy; there was a slight scratch on her cheek where a thorn had scraped her during her epic tumble, and he reached out to touch it. "You have a scratch."

Judy froze, but she didn't pull away, and his finger traced down the curve of her cheekbone to the line of her jaw, as light and delicate as a whisper. He could feel her heart beating and her breath quicken. Her eyes were glowing. He leaned forward –

And she jumped up as if she were spring-loaded. "Well, I'm glad we got that all hashed out. I have to get back to work, and before I go, I need a shower. I have sand in my –"

She froze.

Judy blushed bright red, yelled "Port!" and a second later, an elf was there, and she was gone, and all that was left of Judy was a faint glitter of golden sparks that hung in the air for just a second, like her perfume.

Berke leaned back, took out his pipe, and slowly turned to lie in the sand to watch the clouds and think. The beautiful Judy could be his if he played his hand right. Provided he didn't scare her off. She wasn't sure, but Berke was. They just needed more time alone, to talk, to learn about each other.

When the pipe was done, Berke gathered up the take-away and went looking for Judy's shoes. When the elf came to port him back home, he was in a very good mood. The elf took the rubbish away, but Berke kept the shoes. He'd give them back to Judy himself.

Judy

Judy didn't know what to think. She couldn't think. She stood in her two-room flat, shedding sand all over the floor and had a full-blown, flame-out, multi-story panic attack. She hadn't felt this out of control since she'd been autistic and couldn't keep the roar of human noise out of her head.

Her body, her head, her soul – they weren't her own any more. Berke demanded his share of her.

She didn't know this man, not at all, but here she was falling hard for him, and she knew it. She wasn't playing poker; she was playing blackjack, and all the cards were face down, and she had to bet. She didn't know the deck. She didn't know anything, and the bet was her life. Winner takes all.

When he'd touched her, just a little touch, she could have just as easily leaned an inch forward and let him rip her clothes off, and she would have loved it. Oh, gods, she'd wanted to.

For the first time in her life, she'd felt the pull of a bond. She'd had her lord lessons; she understood the lord anatomy, the musth that came with bonding. Bonding had an evolutionary purpose; it wasn't the same as human lust. And, gods knew, during her decades working in the casinos, she'd learnt how humans lusted. She read the hot and slimy minds of men whether she wanted to or not.

Bonding kept the tiny lord population from fighting over mates. It ensured that lords worked as couples to protect their rare and precious babies and not as harems pumping out masses of offspring in the hope some would survive. If a male lord had a harem of female lords, that meant an excess of frustrated single males, and if they had been lions or walruses, those extra frustrated males would simply be shunted to the side into bachelor groups. A frustrated male lord who thought he had a chance with another man's woman had his magic and could cause untold damage to the small community.

Look at Lester, prime example number one. The minute there weren't any Warrior Lords or Elementals to keep him under control, he used his weak powers to eliminate all rivals. He was just too stupid to understand why he had that drive and to stop when he was the alpha and look for a woman.

Now biology and evolution were kicking Judy in the teeth and saying, "Wake up, bitch! I'm still here!"

Berke was born in 12-fucking-75 and had never bonded, probably because he'd never met a female lord. He didn't know the power of bonding, of what he was doing to her and to himself, so Judy didn't blame him for touching her and starting her hormone cascade. She was ripe and ready, and all it took was a feather-light touch.

She didn't know him. She didn't know what his abilities were, his character, his past, his anything.

She couldn't read his mind.

He said he didn't have a woman back in the desert, and she believed him, but he was living with someone. He would go back. Could she follow him back to his nomad life? She couldn't even walk up a sand dune on an English beach.

She was going to make a piss-poor nomad, living on mutton and drinking fermented camel's milk. Judy didn't like mutton. She was lactose intolerant.

Judy told herself she'd felt the pull of the bond, but if she was honest with herself, if she could read her own mind, she'd know that was not true. The city girl had walked across a busy highway, hadn't looked both ways, and had been hit by a truck. There was no "pull" that implied incompleteness; there was no off-ramp she could wiggle onto.

Judy had bonded.

Louis

The porter elf who ported Judy back to her room took one look at her, took a quick sniff, and immediately ported to The Dirty Hen in Safe Haven because they always gave the best odds. He placed a bet on Lord Judy bonding to Lord Berke, and they gave him excellent odds, almost 500-1, because he was the first one to place such a bet, and who paid any attention to Louis anyway? The elf always lost.

But once a bet was posted, elves paid attention and made their wagers.

Judy took her shower, scraped off the sand, put on a new blue suit, and ported back to work.

By the time she was at the embassy reporting to Conary that Berke was fine, the odds at the Dirty Hen were tumbling so fast that the oddsmakers had to put a temporary halt to the wagers.

Louis made a killing.

Berke

After taking a shower and making himself presentable, Berke asked one of the housekeeper elves for a bag to put Judy's shoes in so he could give them back to her the next time he saw her. He didn't want to carry them loose like he was some sort of cross-dressing Genghis Khan. Besides, the other lords would get nosy.

The Georgiana, the housekeeper, brought him a bag, saw the shoes, gave her own delicate little sniff at the lord, and just grinned. He and Judy matched exactly. Of course, the housekeeper didn't say anything, just did her job, then hustled as fast as she could to the Safe Haven. But she was a wee bit late, and the odds were already tumbling, so she made a bet on when they'd complete their dance. She thought it would take a week because it usually did.

Dinner was fine, but he didn't expect to see Judy. He figured she'd avoid him for a couple of days, especially after that blushing display right before she'd ported out. And that was okay. He wasn't going to pester her. When she felt she was back in control, she'd be back, and Berke smiled.

Then he would touch her again.

In the meantime, he'd find out a bit more about her history and what her talent was. It must be something useful for her to work at the palace directly under Grand Vizier Conary and equal to Vrt.

Adem sat next to him, just the person Berke needed to talk to. Adem was an Elemental, a really big deal, and wore the silver moon epaulettes like Sarah.

But even better, he worked at the embassy and was a very chatty fellow. He knew everything.

So he asked Adem how his day went, and they were off to the camel races! Adem burbled on about a really interesting group of Australian defence contractors who wanted to sell the EN a new drone with laser capabilities. Kyrylo, James, and all the military side were going to watch a demo tomorrow, and they'd decide if it was worth buying. The Aussies were going to haggle hard because once the price was set with the EN, they'd have a hard time selling it for much more to other countries. Then there were bespoke options and agreements not to sell to unfriendlies. Defence purchasing was complicated, and the price wasn't set simply on the cost of manufacture.

Berke was quite familiar with haggling. "Do we have an idea of their bottom line? How much does it cost to build one? I bet the elves could figure it out."

Adem waved that away. "Oh, Purchasing knows what it costs, but sometimes it's not just that. Selling to the EN is prestigious; defence departments around the world know we investigate the hell out of everything and don't buy junk, so sometimes they'll sell to us at a rock bottom price just to get the reputation. Besides, we have Judy. She'll know exactly what their bottom line is."

Judy? She was an accountant? Berke frowned. "I'm sure she'll try her best."

Adem shrugged. "She's never wrong, although sometimes in the middle of a negotiation, things change. She just sits there, looking sweet, and reads their mind as they're talking, so she keeps up."

Judy read minds. Berke was nonplussed but didn't blink as he gave Adem all the attention he wanted. That was a very interesting ability. Could she read his mind? Gods, he hoped not. He'd had some very personal thoughts about her that would flash through his brain, and they were hard to control. No wonder she was skittish!

"It must be hard to keep everyone's thoughts apart during a negotiation. It must be like everyone talking at once."

Adem agreed. "That's why she really likes the quiet and why she likes it here. The embassy wears her out. At least here with elves and lords, it's quieter. That's why you don't see human workers in places like the Breakfast Room. Goodness knows what it must be like to always be around humans like she was before she came to us. She told me once that when she was a kid, it was horrible. She was insane, something humans call autistic, but she learned to cope as she got older. Conary makes sure she doesn't work too hard."

Berke nodded and chewed thoughtfully at his steak. Using the fussy Western knives and forks properly helped keep his focus on the food as Adem talked. And the talk of wearing out reminded him not to pry too hard with Adem. He liked Adem, but he was also useful, and Berke didn't want the man to worry that he was talking too much to the outsider.

Talking to Adem was a stroke of luck and gave him a lot to think about.

"So, Australians. They like bar-b-que, don't they? Are you going to take them out to dinner? Get them drunk?"

Adem laughed, and the conversation moved from Judy's special ability to Australian dining habits and the lengths the EN devised to keep visitors happy.

When Adem finished dinner and excused himself from the table, Berke wondered what the little man's real ability was. He would have to find out. You didn't get those epaulettes for knowing which beer Australians were fond of.

After dinner, he spent some time in the TV room and watched a silly movie about space aliens with Rita, Farah, Talia, and Chi. Rita walked in and sat next to Berke on the big sofa. When she turned to talk, she stopped and gave him a puzzled look. Then she finished what she was going to say, something about the movie, and turned to watch the show. That was the last time Rita spoke directly to him that night.

She had lost interest in him, but Berke was fine with that. It happened all the time.

After the movie, Berke went back to his room and spent a couple of hours on the internet studying autism, and when he read about that, he learned about sensory overload. He was fine with Judy needing quiet; so did he. Maybe not to the extent that she did, but she had learned to adapt and was social now. Sometimes he wondered about himself.

The next day, he didn't see her at all. He went through his normal daily routine, and the lecture in Lord Class was about elf and lord trading practices and finance, which was very interesting indeed. He'd wondered where all the money came from! In the afternoon, instead of Abilities Practise, he asked to go wherever they were storing his luggage. All of the bundles removed from his camels contained his camping supplies, a few weapons, some books, a lot of clothes because he hadn't known he would be provided EN uniforms, and he hadn't known the dress codes of the Palace. Hidden deep in the packs, there was one special bundle, and it was that special bundle he wanted to find.

Back in his room, Berke untied the cords and unrolled the bundle on his bed. As the bundle unrolled, it revealed a glittering hoard of gems and precious metals – all of his mother's and Tani's jewellery. When his mother died, he'd split her jewellery (she had a lot) between him and his human brothers, but over the years as they passed on, bits had come back to him. His doting and generous father loved to bring back something pretty from the festivals and surprise his mother. Their long marriage meant a big pile of very nice shiny things, and Berke's own decades with Tani had simply increased the treasure.

Being an optimist and being a nomad used to carrying all of his worldly possessions with him, Berke had carted the women's jewellery across the Gobi, through the mountains, and on to Suffolk.

Lying on his bed was a riot of colour, mostly silver, Nepalese coral, and huge chunks of turquoise. Here was a bundle of intricately worked earrings. There, wrapped in silk, he had massive, elaborately constructed headpieces with three-foot-long, gem-beaded fringes. Gold, pearls, and jade from China were worked into fantastic hairpins. He would eventually give the lot to Judy, but it was the hairpins he wanted tonight.

Berke had seen Lord Cadence wear a large hairpin that had an emerald in it that would choke a horse. When he mentioned it to Vrt, she explained that it was a gift from Kyrylo and was her bonding pin with much the same symbolism as a human wedding ring. Well, if a hairpin was good enough for the EN

Primary, then it was good enough for Judy, and Berke had some stunners to choose from.

He picked a large Chinese-made set of gold, gemstone, jade, and pearl Buyao hair pins shaped like flowers, phoenixes, and five-toed dragons that was over eight hundred years old. The merchant who'd sold it to his dad had claimed it was once owned by the Empress Daoping herself. Probably not, but it was a good story.

After carefully wrapping them up in a piece of brocade, he put the roll next to the plastic bag that held Judy's shoes and spent the rest of the evening putting jewellery away and remembering when he'd seen this or that piece being worn by his mother or Tani.

How could a piece of rock and metal hold memories that make a person so sad and happy at the same time? It was a mystery and its own magic.

The next morning, as he stepped out of the shower, his phone buzzed. There was a text from Köke, and it was very short and very simple. "We need you back here."

His reply was equally short. "I'm on my way."

There was no panic; Berke was too old and experienced at war to panic. It didn't take him long to get ready because he knew exactly what he needed to do.

He went to the wardrobe and there were all of his original nomadic clothes, only a lot cleaner, along with his hat, boots, and all of his weapons. He dressed exactly the same way he had been dressed when he'd first waved to Tuân that life-changing day on the outskirts of Tashkent.

Berke called for an elf, and one popped up immediately. It was amazing how quickly a person got used to them. The elf frowned at the nomad and then looked worried.

"I need you to do two things. First, you must take me to wherever Lord Cadence is. Then, when you're done with me, that bundle on the dresser and the bag – those must go to Lord Judy."

The elf nodded and ported Berke to the transport hub in front of Aelfeham House, and another elf ported him to Ukraine directly in front of the Melnyks' house.

Caddy and Kyrylo

When Berke received his message, it also went to the intel elves tapping his phone and then immediately passed to James and Kyrylo. Intel elves studied satellite photos of the area and intercepted radio and internet transmissions, and from what they could see, not much was happening. But the Gobi

Desert was a long, long way away, and they weren't on the ground.

An elf called Brenda and said that Berke was on his way. Caddy and Kyrylo walked out the front door just as Berke ported in.

Startled, he stood for a second and caught his breath and started his bow, but Kyrylo wasn't having any of it.

"Come, come! It's cold out here, and we have a lot to talk about."

Inside, Berke was hustled into the huge kitchen and told to sit at the table; they were going to talk during breakfast.

No one seemed at all surprised to see him, and that in itself was a bit discombobulating. Actually, it was a lot discombobulating. Berke was planning to formally ask for a jet to take him back to Tashkent, but Caddy and Kyrylo seemed intent on getting coffee cake and scrambled eggs into him.

"I'm sorry, Lord Cadence, but I really need to talk –"

"Yes, yes, all in good time. Would you like some coffee?"

"Lord Kyryl –"

"We're waiting for a couple more people. In the meantime, eat up. It might be your last meal for a while."

Then Ivana roared in and demanded that she try on his hat. Berke put it on her head, and immediately it covered everything down to her shoulders, blinding her, and she ran off screaming into the next room, chased by two elves.

"Oh, you made her happy!" cooed Caddy.

"She can keep the hat. Lord Cad –"

"You can call me Caddy, but only if you tell me who Köke is."

Berke stared at the Primary; he really didn't expect her to just come out and say she was tapping his phone. Her eyes were snapping green.

"Time to come clean, Berke. We can only help you if we know what we are getting into."

Berke looked at his eggs and sighed.

"Köke is my son. He's also my second in command."

Kyrylo cocked his head. "Second-in-command implies people to command."

Berke looked down at his eggs again. His jaw twitched – and then he sighed, a deep sigh from the heart. He'd had seven hundred years of keeping his clan a secret, and now it was all or nothing. He needed their help, and they wouldn't help him unless they knew the risks. It was reasonable.

"Köke is my son. I adopted him when he was a boy." Then he looked at Caddy. "Six hundred years ago."

Her eyes widened. "A lord then! So we need to go rescue a lord!"

"Neither Köke nor I are asking to be rescued. We won't go anywhere without the rest of our clan." Berke's voice was soft. "We also have children, Caddy."

"How many are in your clan? A hundred? A thousand?"

"Thirty-seven, but Delbee is pregnant. Thirty-eight very soon."

Caddy breathed out, obviously relieved. "We can handle that. We were worried that you had a huge clan and worried about the problems with gathering them all up."

Kyrylo looked at Berke. The man was still holding back.

"So you and your son Köke are lords. How long have you been leading this clan?"

"Seven hundred years, give or take."

"And your people don't mind being led by lords? Can they come and go freely? If they come here, you can't hold them."

Offended, Berke put down his coffee cup, and his voice was ice. "Lord Kyrylo, I don't keep slaves. My people choose to stay in our clan just like the lords at Aelfeham House chose to stay. I couldn't hold them if I wanted to."

Caddy jumped in, ready to smooth ruffled feathers. "Yes, Berke, of course, but we have to ask. We won't take anyone unless they come of their own free will. And two lords in a clan wield a lot of power."

"Caddy, they're *all* lords."

Berke had to smile at the expression on her face. It was quite satisfying after just being accused of slaveholding.

"Well then." She peered at him. "*All* of them? All thirty-seven?"

Berke nodded.

Kyrylo looked at Caddy, and then he grinned. "I guess you should put the kettle on. I think we're going to have a full house."

He turned to Berke. "We have a plan –"

Judy

The elf knocked on her door just as Judy was getting ready to go to work. She planned to eat breakfast at the Embassy canteen because she just wasn't ready to see Berke yet.

Every time she thought about him, her stomach flipped, and the overwhelming feeling was a combination of dread and lust. Dread at what she was letting herself get into and lust for the exact same reason.

Wild thoughts would flash through her brain. What if he couldn't bond to her? He was over seven hundred years old and had never bonded. A confirmed bachelor? No, she was very sure he wasn't gay. What if she slept with him, just once, to get him out of her system? She'd never had sex with a man before. What if she found out she didn't like it? That sounded stupid even to her. What? If? How? Could he? Would he? Every crazy, impossible thought flashed through her mind. An internal cacophony of insecurity only she could hear screamed and echoed in her skull.

But now she had an elf at her door.

The elf handed her a bundle and a white shopping bag.

"These are from Lord Berke. He said to give them to you as soon as he was gone."

"GONE! Where has he gone?"

"To see Lord Cadence."

The blood drained out of Judy's face, and for a full minute she felt her world rise and fall like she was on a boat in a storm.

"He's leaving? Is he leaving Aelfeham House?"

The elf considered this. "I don't think so; his stuff is all still in his room. He could have taken it or told us to pack it up, but he didn't do either."

Concerned, the elf looked at the lord; she was obviously upset. "Why don't you call him?"

Because, thought Judy, I don't have his fucking number. But she didn't say that. She just nodded, thanked the elf, and shut the door.

The bag held her shoes. Berke had gone back and looked for her shoes and found them for her. They were ruined, of course, but that wasn't the point. Judy didn't know why, but it seemed a very sweet gesture. He was taking care of her.

The bundle – she opened it up and gasped. Inside were the most beautiful hairpins. There were nine of them, each more beautiful and precious than the last.

Pins you give to your bonded wife.

It took Judy a good hour to stop crying and get herself in a fit state to go to work. Every time she thought she had pulled herself together, she'd look at the pins again and start bawling all over again. But eventually she managed, and when she finally walked out the door, she was wearing one of the pins in her hair.

Berke

Berke found out what Sarah's Elemental ability was. She could bend time and space and port anywhere. He also found out what Adem's Elemental ability was; he could make spaces outside of time and space and had made the transport hubs/Safe Havens.

The English lords had their secrets, too.

The plan was for Sarah to port Berke to his clan's hideout. Porting with him was the only way she could get an exact fix on the place, but it took twice as much energy. She had a long, long way to go, and traversing space meant stopping time. Once he was there, she'd port back and bring Adem. Adem would make a transport hub. Once that happened, the elves would have a place they could port to and take an exhausted Sarah, Adem, Berke, and each of his clan back to Aelfeham House one at a time.

The children, pregnant Delbee, and those who weren't warriors would leave first. Then the warriors, and last to leave would be Berke.

So no, Berke didn't need an eight-hour flight on the jet and another two-week camel ride back to the mountains. It would take about three hours at most. They could leave some cameras to monitor the place, and if they wanted, they could go back later and pick up their stuff.

Berke texted Köke, "Coming in by magic. Put everyone in the library. You'll hear a loud boom, and you'll know I'm there."

Köke texted back. "When?"

Berke looked at Sarah. "Any time you're ready," she said.

He texted, "Now."

Sarah held Berke's hand, and like Dorothy in the *Wizard of Oz,* he thought of home.

Köke

Shit! *Now?* Köke stuck his phone back in his pocket and started to yell at everyone, herding them to the cave where they kept the library. The warriors were used to obeying commands in an instant, but the herders, craftsmen/women, and the kids – not so much.

No, he didn't have time to explain. No, they couldn't go get their stuffed animals. No, don't worry about the bread baking –

MOVE!

The last person had barely made it into the cave (and it *would* have to be Bayalag; she was always slow) when he heard a tremendous boom that vibrated the stone, making the kids scream and Bayalag move faster than Köke thought possible.

Swords drawn, he and a couple of the guys went to the cave's entrance, and there stood Berke, holding hands with a brightly glowing woman. Berke stepped away, then turned and waved to her. She waved back, and BANG, another huge boom, and she was gone.

That was some serious magic, and Köke and the men all whooped their appreciation and mobbed Berke, pounding him on the back like he was a baby choking on a grape. A couple cried; they were so happy to see him.

Berke ran into the cave, and they erupted, too. Laughing and crying, everyone wanted to give him a hug, but he would have none of it. That was for later.

He explained that they were all going to move to England and stay with the wizards there until the Rus came to their senses. The English lords were going to make a doorway, and once the doorway was built, they could come back and forth pretty easily. Demons and humans couldn't use it.

"I know this is very quick, but you have to trust me. You trusted me when you came here, and I kept you safe, and we had a good life. Now that good life isn't over, but it's moving, and you need to trust me once more."

Put that way, what could they do? They were always moving anyway, and Berke never led them to a bad place.

But what about the camels? Their sheep? Could they have a bit of time to pack?

There was another huge boom, and Berke ran out. Standing exactly where she was before, Sarah stood with Adem, holding his hand.

She was swaying, and the wizards could all see that she was on her last legs and needed to recover. But they were all wizards and didn't have any fear of a glowing, exhausted lord, so they pulled her into a tent and began to stuff her with bread, meat, and strong Mongol cheese.

In the meantime, Adem made the bubble. He was also a glowing mass, but the wizards couldn't see what he did. As always, it looked like he put out a lot of effort to no effect.

Berke ran into the bubble and, with a stick, drew a line in the sand that showed its edges. He told his people to put rocks and whatever they had around the perimeter so that they knew where the elves could port.

Minutes later, the first elf ported in. Sarah walked over to him, and he ported her out. The wizards gathered around the circle, mothers with babies on their hips, fathers in front keeping them safe, and everyone watched intently. Then another elf ported in, and Adem left with a wave and a cheery goodbye. "I'll see all of you at Aelfeham House!"

Five warrior elves ported in, ready to move the lord/wizards.

Berke turned to his clan. "The children and their parents are going first. One parent first, so the kids have someone waiting for them, then the kids, then the second parent. Now, who's first?"

No one moved.

Berke sighed. You don't tell a camel to move; you make the camel think moving in that direction was his idea in the first place. Same with a wizard.

"*Someone* here must have balls – We're wizards! Those English lords didn't have any worries about porting. I do it every day."

And of course, *then* he had volunteers.

Two hours later, the camp was abandoned. Fires were put out and cameras and motion detectors were set up, and everyone was gone – almost. Erdene was missing. Berke sent Köke through to Aelfeham House to get the clan settled, and he went to look for Erdene.

There was always one.

Erdene

The first big boom scared the shit out of Chim, and she ran off in a panic down the path to the sheep pen. The second boom just drove her further out.

Chim wasn't good with loud noises; they hurt her ears, but usually she managed to hold her nerve when the herders used their guns, which was almost never. But those booms rattled the mountains and vibrated in your bones, and Erdene was not surprised they were just too much for the big dog.

She knew where Chim always hid, so after the joy of greeting Berke, finding out that the camp was moving and learning what to do with the elves (ELVES!!!), Erdene set off for the camels. Chim would be on the very edge of the camp, pretending to guard the camels, and when Erdene walked up to the silly dog, she'd roll on her back and ask for a belly rub and say she really wasn't scared at all. She just needed to make sure the camels were okay.

The camels were scattered, too, spooked by the booms, but Erdene could see that they were slowly wandering back to the water hole, taking their time and looking for anything to eat as they made their way back home. Unlike other nomads, the clan didn't tether them because all they had to do was tell them not to go far, and usually they didn't. Same with the sheep and goats. The herds had wizards who kept the wolves away, usually with a sharp word or two, and a few of the Bankhar dogs like Chim, but if one of the herd animals was foolish enough to wander away and sacrifice themselves to the leopards and wolves, they were allowed to do that. The wizards had plenty for their own needs, and the hunting animals needed to eat, too.

Erdene spotted a group of four camels well down the mountain, grazing in a clump of the wiry desert grass, and she knew Chim would be there with the furthest and most inconvenient camels. Grumbling to herself, she trotted to the herd.

She didn't see the drone.

"CHIM!"

Erdene listened for a returning bark, but heard nothing. The camels stopped grazing and looked at her, and by the time she reached them, they were back to foraging, so they weren't worried about anything. Where was Chim?

It turned out the four camels weren't the furthest and most inconvenient, just the second most inconvenient. An inconvenient-er pair was a couple of hundred yards away, and Chim was with them. Almost hidden in the grass, panting and watching Erdene run up to her, the embarrassed dog's tail wagged slowly.

"Chim! You silly dog, we need to –"

And the ground exploded around her. The drone Erdene hadn't seen dropped a fragmentation grenade, and it surely would have killed her if a camel hadn't moved at the last minute to pluck at a particularly enticing clump of grass, and the unlucky cow shielded her. Erdene and Chim were peppered with fine shrapnel, and the concussion knocked her down, but the brunt of the explosion was taken by the cow. It shredded her.

"Shit. Shit —" Erdene had had the wind knocked out of her, but the adrenaline spike kept her alert. Everything slowed down. Time slowed down. She tasted copper.

She saw the drone and knew what that meant. They'd been seeing drones now for over a week, and all the wizards talked about them, but none had been this close to the camp. The drones were why Köke called Berke back. The drones — and their Russian masters — were heading in this direction. The warriors thought they had at least a week, and the camp was already getting packed up to move deep into the mountains and on to Kazakhstan.

But here they were, and one had almost killed her. Almost.

Almost on purpose. It had missed her and killed the camel.

Erdene's mind raced. More would be coming if the thing had a camera that could see her unripe form and know she was still alive. But it hadn't dropped the grenade on her; it had missed, and while the Rus were terrible shots, they weren't *that* terrible. This drone wanted her alive and scared, maybe injured just a little.

They would follow her back to the camp.

They would find the camp if Erdene went running back home in terror like any silly girl.

"Chim! Come here!" She looked up. The drone was still there, a tiny speck high in the sky. It was watching her.

Erdene thought fast. Someone would come looking for her. They would find the camel, see the blast debris, and keep looking for her. But she couldn't lead the drones back to the camp.

So she could lead them away.

She'd go to the little spring base camp. If no one came for her, she'd at least have water, and there was a cache there for emergencies. Gods willing, she could escape the drones, maybe out-range them, and disappear into the mountains. If she could stay alive, she'd find her clan sooner or later. They would find her; she knew that in her heart. Her mom and dad would move the world to find her.

She acted like she was stunned and crawled around. Hiding what she was doing from the drone, under her body she quickly scooped rocks and made an arrow, then she ran back to the second most inconvenient camels who were still grazing where she'd left them. She made one kneel down, and she jumped on his back and told him where to go – and MOVE!

Riding a semi-wild Bactrian camel without any kind of saddle or reins wasn't the most comfortable mode of transportation, but Erdene was used to it. She didn't need reins since she just talked to the camel, and once she pointed him in the right direction he just loped along on his own.

She was lucky that she'd picked a good one. He seemed more sensible than most and was willing to work for the young wizard.

Chim couldn't keep up with the camel and soon fell back, but Erdene wasn't worried. She'd told Chim where she was going and told her to meet her at the water hole. Chim had been there many times before, and she could always follow the scent trail of the camel.

Erdene was far more worried about drones. Would they spot her as she raced away across the desert? If they did, would they kill her or follow her?

Well, she would find out.

Berke

Berke went to the sheep first and looked for Erdene there, wondering if she was concerned about the lambs. But no, no Erdene and the sheep hadn't seen her and neither had the dogs. He told the dogs that the wizards were all leaving and they didn't know how long they would be gone, but to take care of themselves as best they could.

They were upset, but what could he do? The old ones stayed with the sheep, but two of the young ones followed the wizard. They were curious. Where was he going that they couldn't come along?

The camels were in their area, some out grazing and some in the rough paddock, which was not there to cage the camels but to keep them from wandering into the camp and getting in the way. They were calm, chewing their cud. None had seen Erdene, although to be fair, all the young wizards looked alike to them.

Berke was getting concerned – and then he saw two camels off in the far distance wandering back, and one was limping.

He trotted out to them, and what they said scared the crap out of him. Yes, they had seen a young wizard. A bird had dropped an egg on them, and it wasn't a normal egg, but a fire egg, and it had killed a cow, and a bit of the egg's shell had cut his leg. The wizard had jumped on a bull and fled.

No, they didn't know which direction because they were running away, too.

Berke didn't hesitate; there were two camels, and one was perfectly fine. He jumped on the healthy cow and told her to take him to where the bird had dropped the egg. She did *not* want to go, but Berke was a powerful wizard, and after a bit of physical persuasion on his part, she decided she much preferred cooperating to being stung on the rump, and she trotted back to the dead cow. She wanted to go there anyway.

The scene was grim, and the vultures and the crows were already flying their lazy circles as they eyed the carcass. There wasn't much left of the dead camel cow, and pieces of meat and bone were scattered in a wide area, but he saw a blank spot, a rain shadow where something had blocked the gore, and in that spot someone had arranged five rocks. An arrow.

He kicked and scattered the rocks and then looked up at the vultures. Were there more drones hiding in them?

Erdene was going to the small spring in the mountains. She thought she was being followed; that was obvious from the arrow. She wouldn't need to set the arrow if she were heading back to the main camp. Berke called back the cow and made her kneel down, and after a lot of persuasion, she did.

She was going to be a handful, but he didn't want to waste time finding another camel. If Erdene was running from something, she would be flying on her bull, and they were already far ahead.

The wizard-girl would be riding fast, possibly with drones following her, and behind both the girl and the drones, Berke could expect soldiers.

Köke had told Berke during the time they were setting up the cameras that a nearby clan of human nomads had been rounded up and sent gods-knew-where. The wolves had told him. The *Rus'* were clearing out the area for their masters in Moscow, just like they had for Stalin. Mongolia was independent, but that wasn't stopping them. A buffer state between the Russian *Urusaar* and China would help Moscow.

Where was the Mongolian army? The Chinese? They were asleep, it seemed. They would wake up soon, but it would be too late for many small nomadic clans who wandered the western edge of Mongolia.

All he could do now was text what was going on to Köke and move forward. He knew the EN would intercept the texts, which wasn't nearly as irritating today as it had been yesterday. Afterwards, he turned off the phone and its FindMyPhone app. He didn't want the Russians tracking his signal, even if they couldn't crack the texts.

Erdene

Erdene was getting tired, but the camel just loped along at an easy but ground-eating pace. Now and then, she stopped and scanned the sky, but if a drone was watching her, it was so high up she couldn't see it.

Ahead, she saw the line of trees that marked a dry wadi. The dry riverbed led up into the mountains where seasonal rains had, over millennia, cut a deep and narrow ravine into the granite. Once she made it into the ravine, the drones would have to come down lower to track her, and it would take some skill to fly them in the gorges, especially since the layers of water-eroded rock often created overhangs. She would still be in danger, but she knew the maze of gorges and ravines like the back of her hand. The drone operator wouldn't.

She might have a chance to shake them if she made it to the ravines.

Berke

Berke followed Erdene's tracks as fast as the balky camel cow would go. The girl was making a straight line to a wadi that they often used as an entrance to the mountain gorges. He knew a better, more hidden route across the desert, but what do you expect from a fourteen-year-old? She was trying her best, and she was risking everything to protect her people. You had to admire that.

Far ahead, he could see a drone, a tiny black pepper-speck in the sky. So far, he hadn't seen any dust clouds that would tell him that dune-buggies or ATVs were chasing her, but he expected them at any time. There was no point in tracking her if they didn't intend to use the information for something.

If he could see the drone, then the drone could surely see him, but it could be concentrating on the girl. If it spun around and scanned for people chasing her, then he would probably end up with his own personal drone. If they thought she was heading home, they would have no reason to think that anyone from her tribe was chasing her.

He stopped and looked and listened again, his huge ears scanning as far as he could. He heard a lot of background noise, but nothing too close. Not yet.

Far in the distance, the mountains loomed, and he could see the white peak of Tsambagarav Uul. As it always was with mountains, they were a lot further away than they seemed at first glance, but Erdene didn't have to make it to the highest peaks; she just had to make it to the ravines and gorges at their base.

He pressed on, but this camel wasn't going to allow him to catch up with her unless Erdene stopped to rest and water her camel. There were a couple of tiny streams they would be passing as they left the desert, but there was no guarantee of water, and although the camels wouldn't need it, by nature, they would insist on stopping for a few minutes to top off. Erdene would need the water long before her camel would.

The Drone

The drone hugged the ground for long stretches and then rose high up in the sky to reestablish the track of the nomad on the camel. Once that was accomplished, it would hide again. The operator knew that the nomad would stop occasionally to look in the sky, so he simply made sure he wasn't visible. The drones flew just as well at ten metres up from the gently rolling, treeless terrain as they did at three hundred, so there was no point in continuously flying high and being spotted.

On the treeless plain, the black dot of the camel was easy to spot even if the nomad himself was just a tiny blur.

They wanted this nomad to go back to his camp, where they would round up an entire clan.

The nomads were a pain. They knew every nook and cranny and gerbil hole of the desert, and they weren't fond of the Russian government or its soldiers, so they ratted on them. Then, if they were really mad, they'd take pot shots at their patrols, always killing a couple and then melting back into the desert. It was very bad for morale.

The goal of HQ was to eliminate or relocate as many as they could without alerting the Chinese or the Mongolian government. This was a clearing operation as a prelude to something serious, and so far it was working. Every nomad who was neutralised one way or the other was one less danger to a Russian soldier. Very few were relocated back into Russia. Most were eliminated. It was an easier and cleaner solution than the expense of moving sullen, independent, pain-in-the-ass barbarians. Except for captured young women and children. The Russians kept them.

Clearing out the nomads was patriotic, and the drone operator was happy doing his job.

A couple of platoons had already been sent out from the highway, almost forty klicks away, but they were on dune buggies, so they could go pretty fast. When the drone operator went on one of his swings skyward to keep the nomad in sight, he looked ahead to see if there were any camps, but he didn't see anything and reported that to his captain. The platoons held back, hidden by a parallel ridge; they didn't want to spook the nomad, and all they had to do was let him pass. He was heading right towards them.

They quietly waited and let the rabbit run.

Erdene

If one were a normal nomad, right ahead of Erdene was a split in the ridge that allowed a camel train to pass right through, giving easy access to the wadis that led to the canyons and gulches of the mountain or back down a wide valley that led to a highway and a few small farming villages. But Erdene didn't come from a normal nomadic clan.

Her clan had survived for at least seven hundred years, maybe longer if you include the time when it was all human, by not following the well-trodden trails. Normal, well-used trails attracted bandits, soldiers, taxmen, raiders, and adventure tourists wanting selfies – all people a nomad found irritating and worth avoiding.

Her clan knew a way to the mountains that didn't go through this obvious mountain pass. With an entrance hidden by brush, it was difficult and very narrow, especially for the most heavily laden camels, but the sheep did fine, and generally, if the weather was decent, everyone managed quite well. Today it was just Erdene, one unladen camel, and clear, blue sky. There would be no problem at all.

Her ruler-straight beeline to the wadi suddenly veered off. She disappeared.

The Drone

The drone operator was angry. He'd lost his rabbit. Where the hell did he go? One minute, the fucking camel-jockey was on a line to go directly in front of the hidden patrols, and the drone sank to its hiding level. Five minutes later, when the drone went back up high, he just wasn't there.

If he lost this guy, they lost the mission, and his captain would not be pleased, not at all. Not when they were so close to capturing the entire tribe.

He went back up high and circled the area where he'd last seen the nomad. He had lost him.

Then he saw a dot off in the distance. Another nomad, following the exact same track, also on a fucking camel.

He told his captain what had happened and about the second nomad. The captain was pleased. Two nomads going to the same place; there must be a camp hidden in the gulches.

The captain told him to hold fast, keep an eye out for number one, but stay aloft this time. Don't lose sight of number two. They'd get both eventually.

So that's what the operator did.

___

Berke

Berke saw the drone almost at the same time the drone saw him. He was also getting a buzz in his ears that was a worry, and he'd stop and listen soon. He had an old Mauser M88 slung across his back, but the drone would have to get very close before he had a chance of shooting it from the sky with a conventional bullet. He'd bought the Mauser in 1910 and he wasn't thinking about drones at the time.

If he used his wizard powers – that would take some energy, and he was saving that up for now. He might need everything he had later on, and taking pot shots at drones was a waste of calories.

The drone moved in a bit closer and then hovered. They knew he was here. He knew they were watching. They'd already spotted him, so let them watch.

If they were watching him now, they either had Erdene already or they had lost her.

He was only a mile from the passage over the ridge when he stopped and listened.

Berke didn't hear anything. No talking, no clanks of machinery, no engines. He didn't hear any yelling or screaming from Erdene. No brays from the camel. He heard nothing but the wind and the distant caw of the crows.

He moved forward, but slowly, so he could keep listening.

The Drone

The drone operator saw the second nomad stop. He wasn't a black dot anymore but a dark man-shaped blob on a camel. Then the nomad urged the camel forward, but at a walk.

He told the captain.

"Something has spooked this guy. He knows something isn't right. "

The captain called the platoon and told them to go pick the nomad up. If they couldn't follow him to his tribe, they would encourage him to tell the Russians where they were.

Berke

Suddenly, there was noise. Dune buggies, from the sound of the engines, were coming through the pass. There were six of them; Berke could hear each individual engine.

Well, he had a choice to make – go forward or go back.

Berke nudged the camel forward.

The Drone

The drone operator and the captain watched the screen. Neither was very excited; it would just be a matter of how long it was going to take the patrol to pick up this guy and if he would put up a fight. They were told to take him alive, so they'd probably shoot the camel first.

The drone flew to the high point of the sloping pass, where it could see down both sides. On one side was the nomad who was still walking the camel, and on the other were the six dune buggies, each holding three fully armed soldiers, and two of the buggies had 50 cals mounted on the roof manned by a standing soldier.

Five minutes before the dune buggies crested the hill, the nomad stopped. The drone operator thought he could probably hear them by now; they made a lot of noise, and the soldiers liked revving the engines. It was cool. They roared up the pass, two by two.

The captain frowned. The nomad didn't turn and run away, which is what anyone with a sane brain cell would expect. He just waited, sitting on the camel.

The first two dune buggies crested the hill.

And blew up.

A second later, the next two crested the hill. They blew up. There was nothing left. Not even the frame of the buggies, which is what you'd expect from a shoulder-fired missile or something like that. Their guys were atomised.

The captain grabbed the com and screamed to abort, but it was too late; the last two crested the hill and were obliterated.

The operator looked at the screen, slack-jawed. They were gone, just gone. All that was left was a black stain on the grass.

The nomad kicked the camel and sedately trotted forward as if it were his turn to go through a green light. He didn't even stop to look at the stains on the ground. The last thing the operator saw was an antique bolt-action rifle swinging around the black blob of the nomad and then pointing at the drone.

The screen went blank.

Erdene

The bushes and scrubby trees hid the entrance to the wadi quite well. A couple of twists and turns, and it appeared for all the world that you hit a dead end and faced a steep thirty-foot drop. But off to the side, if you looked closely, was a flat rock, and that rock was the front door of a narrow, rocky trail that worked its way down to the wadi floor.

Then there was a sliver of a gap, and a gulch opened up, and then the gulch widened into a narrow ravine, and the ravine shot into the heart of the mountains. Not a half mile to the south, there was another well-known and well-travelled ravine, but this one was a private entrance for Erdene's clan.

As she led the camel down to the gulch, she heard explosions. Six of them.

"Boom, Boom, Boom," she whispered to make a lucky number nine, and she told the camel to stay with her as she walked ahead. Once she was in the gulch, no one would find her, not even a drone. She and the camel could walk under the overhanging rock for miles, and as long as there weren't any flash floods, she'd be fine, but she'd smell the rain and feel the vibrations of flood water well before she would get in trouble. Erdene wasn't worried.

She relaxed now, totally alone.

And then she wasn't.

On a big boulder sat a young man in jeans and a t-shirt. He was sitting there looking at his phone exactly like a million young men sitting in a thousand parks across the world, ignoring the beauty around him for the lure of the tiny screen.

He looked up and grinned. His eyes glowed blue.

"Hi, Erdene! I've got your mum and dad on the phone here. Do you want to tell them you're okay?"

Berke

Berke was wiped out, and he still had to find Erdene. Grimly, he turned into the brush, and as he rode in, he saw a couple of newly broken twigs. Erdene had passed by, or at least the camel had.

There was fresh camel dung on the flat rock, and that was heartening, but now he had to walk his camel down the trail, and his legs were shaking. As soon as he found Erdene, he'd have to go to ground and rest.

"Hey, Berke!" He swung around, and there was Ratna! For a wild moment, he wondered if he was still in Suffolk, maybe had fallen asleep in the TV room, and this was all a dream.

"Ratna! I –"

"You look exhausted, Berke. That was very impressive back there. A bit excessive though." She frowned at him. "Really, you could have killed them with a much lower kilo-tonnage of whatever it was you did. Now you're over-tired."

"I have problems holding back. It's a guy thing."

Ratna grinned. "Too much information, Berke; that's between you and your therapist. In the meantime, we have Erdene. She's with Tuân. Let's get under some shelter, get some food in you, and figure out how we're going to get home. I think they're going to send Sarah and Adem back here and do it that way. She can home in on Tuân."

And that's exactly what happened.

Berke didn't know how he got back to Aelfeham House. One minute, he was sitting under a rocky overhang in the ravine, eating protein bars. Then he asked if anyone minded if he took a little nap, but to wake him if anything happened, like orcs or Russians or polar bears invading.

When he woke up, it was midnight, and he was sleeping in his bedroom on his too-soft mattress and desperately needing to piss. He had slept through Sarah's booming entrance with Adem, Adem's newest bubble, and the elves porting in to take them all back to Suffolk.

He didn't know how the elves moved him, but later, when he asked one, the little guy just shrugged. "We're used to moving drunken lords. No difference with a sleeping one. And you were exhausted."

He was still exhausted, but the call of the bladder couldn't be ignored, and so, half asleep, he staggered to the toilet and then stumbled back to bed. He flopped down, turned on his side, and buried his face in a woman's hair.

Now that woke him up.

The hair was attached to a body, a woman's body, and the body shifted a bit in her sleep.

The elves had put him in the wrong room. With thirty-seven new lords suddenly flooding in, someone had gotten mixed up. Shit, what if he was in Rita's room? What would Judy think?

Slowly, very slowly, he sat up and untangled himself from the bedclothes, the hair, and the woman. Buried in the blankets and curled in a tight ball, she snuffled in her sleep, and then her breathing steadied again. Very gently, he slipped out of bed and, as quickly and quietly as he was able, grabbed a pair of jeans and a t-shirt out of the wardrobe and slipped through the door to the hall, silently shutting the door behind him.

Only it wasn't a hall; it was a sitting room. This was a flat. Completely disoriented now, he turned on the light and looked around. His crap was thrown in a corner, still smelling of camel. His sword, the rifle, and his knives were hanging on a peg above them.

It was a very nice flat. There was a sofa, a TV, and a coffee table, and on the coffee table were three trays of cold cuts, bread, cheese, and finger food.

And lying neatly on the brocade, next to a half-eaten bowl of rice and scrambled egg, were the nine hairpins he'd sent to Judy.

He stared at the hairpins for a long time. Then Berke made himself a huge sandwich, ate it, and went back to bed.

He thought, as tired as he was, that once he peed and ate, he'd have no trouble sleeping, but Berke was quite mistaken. All he could do was stare at the dark and listen to the soft breathing next to him. He was fairly sure that he was sleeping next to Judy. Pretty sure. Ninety-two per cent. The woman smelled like her; really, really good.

And he was fairly sure she knew he was in the bed before she got in it. Maybe.

Well, he thought, I have every right to make sure this is Judy and not someone from the clan or another random Aelfeham House woman. If it's not Judy, I'll just wake her up, apologise, and leave. We'll all have a good laugh later.

Turning very, very carefully, he tried to prop himself up enough to lift the blanket so he could see her face, but the too-soft mattress sank and she rolled, turning in her sleep from her right side to her left, and now she was curled up against him, her face in his armpit. She murmured in her sleep and threw her arm around his waist.

He lay back and had to laugh at himself. Here he was trapped by a woman who was probably, maybe ninety-six-per-cent-Judy, who was in so deep a sleep she was practically comatose, and now he had a massive hard-on. If she moved her arm down just a couple of inches –

Berke wasn't going to wake her, especially if it looked like he was demanding sex. Ninety-six-per-cent-Judy was skittish as it was, and he remembered the last sexual encounter he'd had. He would go slow.

Last time was a fucking disaster. More precisely, it was a non-fucking disaster.

Tani had died of extreme old age. Her time on this earth was done, and when she died, they hadn't bedded for almost twenty years. She wouldn't have blamed him if he found relief elsewhere, but it would have hurt her feelings, and he wouldn't do that for the world.

A few years later, he was in Ulaanbaatar doing some trading for the clan, and probably because he was feeling good from a bit too much arkhi (actually, he was pretty drunk), he got a little too friendly with one of the prostitutes at the inn and followed the woman to her little cubicle. She was a professional who didn't want to dally around, and they very quickly got down to business. She was okay with the ears when he took his hat off, but when his eyes started to glow and his skin flashed, she took one look and ran screaming from the room. That was a real buzz-kill, and he simply never tried sex with a human again. Tani had accepted him gladly from the first night, and he had assumed that other women would be okay with a wizard, too. Obviously not.

But Sleeping-Judy was snuggling against him, and he didn't see any harm in slipping his hands under the blanket and stroking her back. He could be patient.

That was a mistake, though, because unlike a woman who was used to living in a sub-zero climate in a tent, she was not wrapped up in thick, warmth-conserving nightclothes. Judy was a city girl who had been brought up in Florida. She wasn't wearing any clothes at all.

She shifted, and Berke looked down and saw two glowing green eyes. Her hands started their own exploration, and he found he didn't have to be patient at all. Not anymore.

Judy

Judy woke up first, a little sore, but whatever aches and pains that came from her first time with a man were more than compensated for by the man and the relief of knowing she enjoyed sex with him very much indeed.

She had been dreading it. She wasn't worried about Berke having a good time; she was worried about herself. For over fifty years, every single hetero or bisexual man she'd had a conversation with had allowed a brief image to flash through his brain of him having sex with Judy. Every damn one. The vast majority of the thoughts were very short and quickly suppressed; some were sad, some were very, very detailed, and a few were really disgusting. The images were the main reason she never took a man to bed; it was simply a turn-off to know exactly what any prospective lover was thinking at the most intimate of moments.

When she found out that she couldn't read another lord's mind, after the first, tearful relief that she could have actual friends who kept their damn thoughts to themselves, she started thinking about sleeping with one. Really, really started thinking about it. A lot.

But the male lords were either bonded or she just wasn't interested in them, and that lack of interest made her wonder if there was something wrong with her. She was well-versed in psychology and knew that everyone had different libidos, and while some couldn't stop thinking about sex, at the other end of the spectrum, others weren't bothered by urges at all. She couldn't figure out which end of the spectrum she occupied.

But she couldn't read Berke's mind, thank the gods, and that meant a few wonderful surprises and the ability to think about her own desires and not be flooded with his.

When the elves, who knew that Judy and Berke were bonded without being told, asked her where he should sleep, she told them to replace her mattress with his and put him in her flat. She was resigned to the inevitable; it was going to happen sooner or later, so it might as well be sooner. All Judy could hope was that he would be okay with her and she could make sure that, at the very least, he was comfortable in her bed. The mattress was horrible, but she would get used to it.

Judy lay on her stomach, propped up on a pillow, watching Berke sleep. She couldn't take her eyes off him. Good heavens, he was gorgeous and, miracle of miracles, he seemed to like her. She wasn't used to that. Men lusted for her, some thought she was useful, some admired her brain, but liking her? No. They were usually intimidated by her. Her cool rejection of their advances made them angry. If she'd heard "frigid bitch" once, she'd heard it a thousand times.

If anything, Berke seemed worried that she wouldn't like him or would be afraid of him. She didn't know; all she could do was guess. Judy couldn't read his mind!

But it was time to get up and move on to the next phase of their lives. If he still needed to sleep, that was fine; she would go to work and let him rest, but she didn't want to leave without letting him know. He might think she was avoiding him, and after her wonderful first encounter, she certainly didn't want him to think that. He might not want to do it again.

She reached over and smoothed out his long moustache, and his eyes flew open.

"I'm going to go take my shower and get dressed, but before I go, what're you going to do today? Do you have plans?"

He grinned at her. "Do? I'm planning to do you!" And he rolled on top of her and started sniffing her neck, making her giggle. Then he started kissing her, and she forgot what she wanted to talk about, and it took quite a long time before she could get back on track. If the housekeepers couldn't gather Scent off these sheets, then they never would.

"I like it when you glow." Berke turned on his back, panting. "It's beautiful."

Judy turned and stared at him. Glow? What was he talking about? It must be her eyes.

"Oh. Thanks." She thought about it. "I'll take your word for it. The only time I've seen a female lord glow was when Caddy wakes elves." Before he could say anything, she turned and propped herself up on her elbows. "She's going to call you in, you know. Soon. And ask what you plan to do."

Berke turned and looked at his bond-wife. The expression on her face told him she was worried. "What do you mean?"

"She does it with everyone; she did it with me. She'll call you in and either ask what you want to do for the EN or give you an offer to work for the EN. Then it will be either work for the EN or go back to Mongolia or wherever. Not be a part of us."

Us. Her people. She was worried he'd leave, and then what would she do? Berke twirled a lock of her hair in his fingers and smiled.

"When I brought my people here, I told them that things were going to change, that we can't be in

Mongolia until the Russians become sane. Judy –" he whispered, " – the Russians never become sane. For the last seven hundred years, it's been either the Rus going insane and invading Mongolia or the Chinese taking their turn. Some of my clan will want to go back, but they'll all end up living in the west, I'm sure of it. The pull of being with other lords and elves is going to be too strong. They came to live with me because they didn't want to be alone. They'll go back for a month, maybe a year, but not as nomads. That time is done."

"So what are you going to do? Caddy is the Queen Bee here. You've been a leader, a King Bee, for a long time. She'll make you an offer because you're a proven warrior, and now half of the lords here are loyal to you. She'll need you to settle them in, to get them to be a part of the EN. But she'll be nervous because you are a risk, too. That's what she told me when I was called. One time offer, go or stay, because she said I was too great a risk to keep at Aelfeham House if I'm not committed."

Berke nodded. He could see that. From Caddy's point of view, he could run off and make his own power base and threaten hers.

"I won't run off and make a kingdom. For one thing, what makes her powerful is that she can call up elves. I can't do that, or I would have done it already. Elves are a draw for my clan, so if I did run off, not all would come. The more I think about it, the more I doubt if most would, not when they've been here a while. What do you think I should do if I stay? You know this place and all of the jobs. I want to keep busy, I want to feel I'm making a difference."

Judy put her chin on her hand and thought of what the other lords did. Berke wasn't a creator like Sam or Mordecai. He didn't have the abilities of Sarah or Adem, but he did have the warrior skills of Vrt and Malachi, but not the same type of military skills as James and Kyrylo. Diplomacy like Conary? Maybe. He was very intelligent, curious, and adaptable; with minimal training he could go anywhere like the Rangers. She could see him in her old world of casinos and hobnobbing with the elite, and then going to a pub and having a beer with a teamster. Berke was a listener. He listened to *her*!

"Tuân and Ratna travel the world working special assignments as they come up. That's why they were looking for you, to be there if you needed them. They rescued me –"

"When were you rescued?"

Judy waved that away. "I'll tell you later when we have time and you're bored. But anyway, they're lord hunters. So, that is one option, to be sent off to do secret, special assignments and to find and rescue lords. One day Tuân will discover his ability, and he might not want to do that anymore. Ratna misses her craftwork, but she won't let Tuân out of her sight, not while he's working as a Ranger and can't defend himself with an ability. The other possibility is to work with Conary like I do. He is very busy with the diplomatic side of the EN and can use the help, I think. So think about those two things. Caddy will ask you or tell you, but it's good to have a counteroffer if you don't like her suggestions. She can't make you do anything you don't want to do." Judy smiled and kissed Berke's hand. "I'll support you and be with you, whatever you decide – you need to know that. I'm bonded tight."

Berke leaned over and kissed her, but when his hand ran down her back, Judy laughed and jumped up. "But not bonded so tight I won't take a shower! We have things to do, and I'm going to go to work while you rest up and think!" Naked, she ran off to the bathroom, giving Berke a brand new view to remember.

Berke lay back and thought about what Judy had said, and by the time her very long shower was over, he had made up his mind. When Caddy called, he would be ready for her.

Judy left the bathroom dressed and ready for the Embassy and whatever it was she did. She looked gorgeous even in the navy-blue uniform, and Berke told her so. Today, though, instead of the knee-length, form-fitting pencil skirt, she was wearing a miniskirt and tights, and it occurred to Berke that none of the other female lords wore skirts to work. Not that he had seen anyway. So he asked her why.

Grinning mischievously, Judy told him. "I wear skirts and heels because they distract the human men. They think I have nice legs and ass, and a distracted man is easy to mind-read. Vrt and Sarah don't wear skirts because they are Warriors ready to fight if they have to. So they wear trousers. I couldn't fight my way out of a retirement home Bingo game. Besides, a sword and a skirt don't work as an outfit."

She put her hands on her hips and gave him a flirty wiggle. "I go, sit in the corner with a steno pad, and they think I'm a bit of fluff in the corner taking minutes. I've never taken a serious minute in my life. There are elves doing that. What I do is listen and then write a report of what I heard and what I think about it, and I tell the Primaries what I think they'll do."

"No wonder Caddy didn't want you to be a loose cannon. You could cause a lot of damage."

"Yep. So now I'm off to cause damage to other people." She leaned over to kiss him. "One last thing before I go. Will you give me your phone number? I think we're close enough to text each other now. It's a commitment, but I'm ready."

"It's tapped. Just letting you know."

"They're all tapped. There is no such thing as privacy inside the EN. We're clan."

And with Berke's phone number in hand, she left. As Judy walked out, Berke saw one of his pins in her hair and smiled.

Then she ducked her head back in the doorway. "Get something to eat! And make sure you shower good. You smell like a camel!"

Berke

Since his bond-wife had given him an order, he had to do it. Berke showered and made ready to go to the Breakfast Room and break his fast. It took him a few minutes to dress because he had to look over the new uniform hanging in the wardrobe. It was navy blue and had epaulettes with quarter moons embroidered in silver.

Someone was pretty sure he was going to stay. Someone said he was an Elemental, equal to the top-tier lords.

He wondered if Judy knew about the new uniform, but he bet she didn't. She would have mentioned it. Berke fingered the epaulettes; he'd never worn rank before. He was a leader of his clan for many reasons, but to outsiders, he had always been just another member.

Judy didn't have a clue as to what his abilities were. She hadn't mentioned that either because it didn't matter to her. As far as she knew, he was a redcoat who was a good fighter. It would, he thought, be a nice surprise.

If he put the uniform on, it told all of the lords, EN and nomad, where he stood and to whom he owed allegiance. It meant something.

Berke put it on, looked in the mirror, and suddenly grinned at his reflection. He looked pretty damn good.

Although it was getting late for the morning meal, the Breakfast Room was crowded. There were some of the old guys there and some of the new nomads, and they all seemed to be getting along okay. They weren't sitting in two groups, and that was a good sign.

Berke greeted his clan with hugs and backslaps and asked them if they were doing okay. He especially asked about their children. There were only two sets of parents in the Breakfast Room, but they both seemed happy.

But in the end, other than troubleshooting if there was a problem, the wizard's lives were now out of his hands. Elves advised and helped the nomad lords, elves fed them and provided housing, and each one had an elf to remind them to go to Lord Class and

PT and port them around. Probably the busiest people were Jack and Alizah, who were looking frazzled, but that would smooth out. It was only the second day, after all.

After two hundred and forty-five *thousand* days, non-stop, Berke was no longer responsible for protecting and guiding his clan. His job was done. He had rescued twenty-five lords from across Asia and Russia. Sixteen had bonded and produced twelve children, and some of those children were adults now, ready to look for their own mates. He had kept them all safe, and on his watch, not a single one had died. They'd lived in one of the most inhospitable places on earth and endured almost constant war – the great Khan's upheavals, the Chinese emperor's oppression, Communists' purges, bandits, and human and demon hate.

In the coming days, as the nomads moved on with their lives and changed from wizards living in isolation to lords with elves as partners living in the wide human world, no one came to thank him, no one acknowledged his extraordinary achievement, and he was fine with that. Berke would have been surprised if anyone had. When chicks grow up and fly the nest, they don't look back. They only looked forward. Berke himself was not looking back at what he had but was looking forward to what he had gained.

Only one person ever sat down and thought about what Berke had done, and that was Caddy. She knew. She told Kyrylo she didn't think she could have done what she had done without elves by her side, not a bit. And especially not for seven hundred years. But Berke had.

His clan didn't know what the bluecoat meant yet, but the old EN lords did, and he got a grin and a handshake from Malachi. Chi asked him who he'd slept with to get the epaulettes, and Talia told him to shut up, so he did.

As breakfast wound down and Berke thought he should go look for Köke, an elf poked him in the arm and said he had an appointment with Lord Cadence and didn't he check his phone? She was at the Embassy, and he had fifteen minutes to get there.

Berke was at her door right on time. The lords of the Elf Nation didn't operate on nomad time and got fussy when people were late, and Berke had learned that early on. The meeting was just as Judy had predicted. Caddy grinned when he walked in wearing the uniform; it was exactly what she wanted to see. She formally asked him what he intended to do. Berke said he wanted to stay and work, and if it was useful, he wanted to be a lord finder and freelance Warrior Lord or Ranger like Ratna and Tuân. At least for a while.

"I think that's a very good choice, and you'll be most useful. And I think you'll enjoy it." Caddy tilted her head and narrowed her eyes, thinking. "Judy will be a good partner, but not in the wilderness bits. I don't think she's much of a camper. And she'll never hike far in those high heels. But in cities she'll be invaluable."

"So you know Judy and I are bonded?" Berke was surprised.

Caddy rolled her eyes. "I know all the gossip. When she came to work wearing that pin, all I had to do was ask an elf who gave it to her. As Kyrylo says, there are no secrets, just delayed communications."

After that, there wasn't much more to say. Caddy told Berke he looked very smart in his new uniform and that he should take Judy out to lunch. With a handshake, he was sent on his way.

The Queen of the Fairies had work to do.

End of Book 6

Book 7

The Glowing of Such Fire

Continue the adventure!

This and all books in

The Return of the Tribes Series

are available for download on

Amazon Kindle
or
The Rum Lot Publishing

www.rumlot.com

E-Publishing, Hardback and Paperback versions of all books are available on amazon.com

Please Donate
to the Excelsior Trust

If you enjoyed this book (and we hope you did!), please consider a small donation to The Excelsior Trust, a registered charity that is dedicated to preserving heritage fishing boats, in particular The Excelsior, LT 472, a wonderful fishing smack that is featured in Book Two.

As part of the trust's mission to preserve Britain's maritime heritage, they also subsidise unique training and sailing experiences for young people.

https://www.theexcelsiortrust.co.uk/

https://www.theexcelsiortrust.co.uk/donate
Registered Charity Number 285899